FORTY NIGHTS IN ARUBA

BEA ANN ARGH

All characters appearing in this work are fictitious. Any resemblance to real persons, living or dead, is purely coincidental.

Copyright © Bea Ann Argh 2024

All rights reserved. No part of this publication may be reproduced, stored in a retrieval system, or transmitted in any form or by any means, mechanical, photocopying, recording, or otherwise, without prior permission in writing of the author.
ISBN: **979-8327896079**

DEDICATION

I would like to dedicate this book to the wonderful people of Aruba. You share your island with open arms to strangers and make us feel at home. We should all learn from you and the harmony you have developed in your country. "Danki pa su bondat. Mi ta desea bo felicidad y prosperidad den bo isla paradisico!"

FORTY NIGHTS IN ARUBA

Eddy Sweeney had just spent the last four years of his young life studying at the University of Akron and finally received his degree in Information Technology. The 1998 college graduate was recently hired by Canton Timken and was so happy to be able to start his career in his Ohio hometown. At twenty-two years old, the sky was the limit for the young computer whiz.

One summer night, Eddy and two of his friends were drinking at Flanagan's Pub when he noticed a very sexy blonde approaching their table. She was alone and introduced herself to the boys as Stacey Johnson. She began flirting with Eddy immediately and made it perfectly clear that she was looking for a good time. After two hours of heavy drinking, the two strangers left the bar and spent a wild night together at Eddy's apartment.

Eddy never saw her again until two months later when Stacey knocked on his door one evening in early November. He was happy to see her until she informed him that she was pregnant with his child. Stacey then bewildered the panic-stricken man by admitting that she was only seventeen years old. She had gotten into the bar on a fake ID and was really a senior at Canton McKinley High School.

Eddy was horrified and tried to process her story. "How can this be possible…. We only did it one time and I don't even remember your name…. You said that you were on the pill…. My life just got started and now it's over!" He questioned her about everything she revealed and demanded a paternity test to prove that he was the real father.

Stacey began to cry and angrily replied, "Do you think that I want this baby? I won't be able to go to my senior prom because I'll be showing and my boyfriend will dump me as soon as he finds out…. All I want from you is money for an abortion."

Eddy was a staunch Catholic by faith and refused that option. "If the baby is truly mine, I'll do whatever is needed, but we must keep the child. I could never sleep peacefully again if I knew you had an abortion." They talked the entire night as he reasoned with her and he reassured Stacey that he would take care of her and the child.

The paternity test proved that Eddy was the father and all their parents demanded that they wed. Against her wishes, Stacey became a wife and then a mother at the age of eighteen. Sara Sweeney came into the world unwanted by her mom, who blamed the newborn for "stealing" her youth. Every cry the infant made was a reminder of the mistake she made with a man she had no romantic feelings toward.

Eddy was climbing up the company ladder and spent very little time with little Sara. He loved his daughter, but her smile and perky blue eyes reminded him of the woman who deceived him at Flanagan's Pub, now over a year ago. His older sister was very supportive of his situation and was always there when Eddy needed a shoulder to cry on.

SARA'S ANGEL

Kathy Sweeney was just twenty-five and teaching at Canton Central High School when Sara came into her life. She adored her niece and played with her at all of the family functions. She was more than a willing babysitter when Stacey would dump her daughter off on her way to a night out with the girls.

Kathy was a very independent woman who was very attractive and outgoing, but never desired a husband. Every time she became close to a lover, she would break it off and move on to the next guy. She was driven to succeed and wanted no man in her way. Kathy always focused on advancing her career and avoiding love until Sara smiled at her for the first time.

As Sara aged into a little girl, she would spend the summers with her aunt when Kathy was on school break. Kathy enjoyed the responsibility that Sara's parents forced upon her as she nurtured her niece. Stacey eventually enrolled in a community college and left her child to be cared for by Kathy and all four grandparents. Sara was raised by the entire village.

When Sara was eight, the marriage that was never meant to be, finally dissolved. Stacey was romantically involved with two men at the same time and was not discreet about it. Sara would hide in her room and cry while Eddy and Stacey fought it out. When the divorce was final, Sara remained with her father as Stacey relinquished all legal rights to her daughter. Stacey was now free to live the life she felt cheated out of nine years ago.

Kathy tried to spend as much time as she could with Sara, comforting the girl from her sad home life. Sara always looked forward to her trips to

Aunt Kathy's house. It was her place of sanctuary and the two were inseparable during the summer months. Kathy would always spend precious time teaching and playing with Sara, giving her a normal home life as a parent would provide for her child. As Sara grew into her teens, Kathy provided information that every young female needed to know and they bonded together as close friends.

Kathy's career blossomed as she became the Superintendent of Stark County Schools and the extra workload prevented her from frequently socializing with her friends. She continued to date, but still distanced herself from any serious relationship with a man.

She always jokingly told Sara, "Men and I have only one thing on our minds so I give it to them and then move on before they get stupid.... Listen to me very carefully, Kiddo. Don't rush into a relationship until you understand what love is and DO NOT act as foolish as I do. I'm thirty-eight years old and still haven't figured out men."

Sara's beauty and bubbly personality made her very popular in high school. Kathy tried to attend as many school activities as she could and encouraged Sara to always work hard toward her future goals. Kathy was very proud of her niece's accomplishments and wished her real parents could appreciate their daughter as she evolved into a woman.

The two would talk on the phone like schoolgirls late into the night and that's when Kathy confessed her passion for travel. "The one thing in my life that I desire is to see all the beautiful places that I've been reading about for years. I've worked my butt off to get where I am in my career and soon, I'm going to experience those places for myself."

Before Sara's sophomore year at high school, Kathy became the youngest president of Malone University in Canton, Ohio. It was a dream come true for the forty year old to finally achieve her ultimate goal. Her accomplishment was so satisfying that Kathy decided to celebrate by booking a future vacation with a guy she recently started to date.

On Christmas Eve, Kathy made a proposal to her niece, "I've decided that Mike is getting too serious with our relationship. Last night he started talking about marriage and that scared the crap out of me…. We were planning on a trip to Aruba this summer, but I'm going to break up with him before it gets too far…. I want you to get your passport and if you get straight A's the rest of the year, you and I are going to Aruba." Sara jumped up and down and exclaimed, "I am so getting all A's and we are going to Aruba!" She hugged Kathy and gleefully asked, "Where's Aruba?"

ARUBA

Late June of 2014, the two excited Americans got their first view of the tropical paradise by air. "My God! Look at the water. It has so many shades of blue." Kathy joyfully replied to her niece, "I wouldn't believe this, if I hadn't seen it with my own two eyes." It was love at first sight for Kathy and Sara. They went through customs, got their luggage, and hailed a taxi to the Costa Linda Resort on Eagle Beach. Kathy had rented a week at the resort from a timeshare owner who she knew from her college.

The taxi ride took them through downtown Oranjestad and Sara was fascinated as she saw the blue water and the colorful buildings that lined the streets. The driver's name was Hyro and he graciously pointed out points of interest to the first-time visitors. Ten minutes later, they arrived at Costa Linda and were greeted by Wilmer, who took their bags as Kathy checked in for their room on the fourth floor. The open-air lobby was full of guests drinking complimentary rum punch and the steelpan drums playing completed the tropical vibe. Sara was so excited and walked through the lobby smiling and talking to everyone along her way.

Once they arrived at the room, the girls were jumping up and down like children, admiring the gorgeous two-bedroom suite. Sara ran to the balcony and suddenly became silent. Kathy anxiously joined her niece and she too, was silently amazed at the spectacular view of Eagle Beach.

Sara embraced her aunt and became emotional, "Thank you, Kathy, for everything you have ever done for me and for sharing your life with me…. I love you so much." Kathy fought back her tears and said, "Come on. Let's get our bikinis on…. That beach is calling our names."

They threw their suitcases on the bed and grabbed their swimsuits, and then made a mad dash to the beach to enjoy the day's remaining sun. Both women looked stunning as they quickly walked past the pool and found an empty palapa on the beach.

Kathy went to get towels while Sara walked on the most perfect sand in the world. Her feet felt like they were being warmly massaged as she strolled into the water and floated in the calm sea. Her mind went blank as the gentle waves moved her back and forth. Kathy joined her and awoke Sara from her state of utopia. "Are we in heaven?" Kathy asked.

The girls spent the next three hours in and out of the water. The Aruban sun instantly warmed and dried their half-naked bodies. As the sun began its quick descent, Kathy looked at Sara and challenged her. "I've always wanted to watch a sunset in the water…. I'll race you!" They ran into the water just in time to see a glorious sunset, complete with the "green flash" and Kathy gushed, "I could die now."

The next couple of days the girls hung out on the beach and socialized with the timeshare owners. Kathy kept a close eye on her niece who was well built for a teenager and looked like an adult. Everyone thought the two girls were sisters because Kathy was a very young looking forty year old woman. When they played pool volleyball the men flocked after the aunt and her niece.

Kathy began to let her hair down after Rosie brought her a few Aruba Arbia cocktails. She met an attractive man who was drinking with his two buddies at the Water's Edge Bar and the flirting began. Sara gave Kathy her blessings and left to walk the beach alone.

Sara walked all the way past Amsterdam Manor and watched the sunset behind the fofoti tree. She was stunned by the tree's beauty and mesmerized by the water crashing up against the volcanic rock. She watched lovers holding hands and enjoying their romantic dinners on the beach at Passions Restaurant. Sara was very stimulated as she watched the guys kissing their girls and fantasized that she would soon find a boyfriend at home.

Suddenly a young handsome man approached her and asked, "Are you staying at La Cabana?" Sara told him that she was staying down the beach at

Costa Linda and she needed to get back soon. He requested with a gleam in his brown eyes, "I'm Todd Powell. Can I walk you back to your resort?" She smiled and answered, "Sure, I'd like that…. I'm Sara, from Ohio."

Todd escorted Sara back and told her about himself. He was nineteen, lived in Albany, New York, and was a freshman at Rutgers University. His family owned a timeshare at La Cabana for the last week of June and he had been coming to Aruba during that same week since he was a small child. "I'm not from New York City. I'm from New York State and there's a big difference between the two." Sara didn't understand so he smirked, "You'll find out the hard way!"

Todd asked her if she ever snorkeled and Sara blissfully replied, "No, but I love being in the water and hope to snorkel before our trip is over." Todd cheerfully suggested, "Well, you're in luck. My family and I are going to Boca Catalina tomorrow to snorkel and we've got room for one more." Sara replied, "I don't know…. I'd love to, but I'd have to ask my aunt for permission…. I'm only fifteen years old and that might not be appropriate. I can ask her and call you once I find out." Todd punched his phone number in her cell phone and said goodnight.

When Sara returned to their suite, she could hear noises at the end of the living room. As she investigated closer, Sara could now clearly hear the moaning of two people having sex in the master bedroom. She was not unsettled by the actions but instead was very curious. Sara didn't want to ruin her aunt's enjoyment, so she quietly listened for a while and then returned to the beach. Sara was happy for her aunt, but realized that she too, was becoming a woman with needs and urges. She found a palapa and fell asleep listening to the hypnotic crashing of the waves.

Sara was awakened at 3 AM by her sobbing aunt, who begged her forgiveness. "Oh my God, I am so sorry Sara.... I was so selfish not to consider your feelings. I was paralyzed with fear when I saw that you weren't in your room...." Sara stopped her while she was apologizing.

"Kathy. Please, don't feel guilty.... I want you to be happy and I started to get turned on just listening to you. I think I'm starting to have urges to be with guys, but I don't want to be stupid like my mom and get pregnant. A lot of my friends have started on birth control and I'd like your permission to begin taking the pill." Kathy agreed and the two had a long talk about the "birds and bees" until the light of day unveiled the beauty of the Caribbean Sea.

Kathy permitted Sara to go snorkeling with Todd in the afternoon and he picked her up in a Jeep rental. She asked where his family members were and he said they were meeting them at Boca Catalina Beach.

This was the first time that Sara had seen the rest of the island and she was amazed by the high-rise hotels on Palm Beach. Todd advised her, "If you want action in Aruba, Palm Beach is where it's at." Soon they pulled into a parking spot overlooking the beautiful water. Todd handed her a mask, snorkel, and fins. "This equipment belongs to my sister…. My family is not going to be here today. It's just going to be me and you."

Sara wasn't fazed, but did remark, "You should have told me that from the start. I would have still wanted to come…. Just don't try anything funny." She looked at the pirate ships and boats surrounding the area and became very enthusiastic. "Please Todd, show me how to snorkel."

Todd gave her a brief training lesson and soon they were in the water. Sara caught on very fast and was immersed in life under the sea. She followed a turtle out to the seagrass and lost Todd. Her fins made Sara move like a fish and she snorkeled for two hours while Todd returned to the shore.

When she got out of the water Todd threw her a towel and laughed, "I thought you were going to snorkel all the way to Mexico." Sara smooched him on his cheek. "Thank you so much, Todd. That was by far the greatest thing I've ever done" and then she kissed him on the lips. Todd enjoyed her enthusiasm and informed his guest, "Get some sun and dry off. We're going for a ride." Sara was so happy and blurted out, "I'll go anywhere with you."

Todd drove her up to the California Lighthouse to get a couple of coconut waters and they appreciated the view from the high ground. There was a lot of construction going on around the lighthouse, so they took off on an offroad trail toward the east coast of the island. The closer they got to the water; the more fascinated Sara became watching the waves crash into the volcanic rock formations. Todd pulled over near a local hut and the two watched the waves until the sun started to lower from the sky.

Sara thanked Todd for the fun afternoon and began to slowly kiss him. As he was running his fingers through her windblown hair, he could feel her hand slowly begin to grope him. He intercepted her hand and gently moved it away. "Sorry, but I don't want to take advantage of you…. You're not ready for that."

Sara pushed him away and said dejectedly. "I want to have sex with you, but I guess I'm not your type." Todd tenderly held her arms and regrettably disagreed. "You are definitely my type, but you are only fifteen years old and I'm guessing you're still a virgin…. You look me up in five years, and we'll finish this, but right now, I'd better get you home."

Sara was quiet as Todd continued up the coast and headed toward Alto Vista Chapel. She became enthusiastic after she got out of the jeep and toured the beautiful church. "My aunt would love this place." She kissed Todd and thanked him for not taking advantage of her. "You're a nice guy and I'm going to take you up on that offer in five years." They drove back through Noord just as it got dark, and she kissed him goodbye one last time.

Kathy was beginning to worry about Sara until she saw her happy face enter the room and Sara began storytelling about her fun day. They walked to the Screaming Eagle for a late dinner and Kathy had a surprise for her niece. "We're going to rent a car next year and see the whole island." Sara curiously asked, "Next year?"

Kathy explained herself. "While you were gone this afternoon, I stopped at the sales office and inquired about buying a week at Costa Linda. JoAnn happened to have a two bedroom on the third floor for this exact week, so I wired my bank and bought it…. We are officially timeshare owners right here in Aruba. You and me, Kiddo."

Sara quickly got out of her chair and ran to embrace her aunt. "Are you serious? Oh My God…. Our own little piece of paradise!" Kathy responded,

"This place feels so right. The locals are friendly, the staff is fantastic, and I feel safe here." Sara serenely insisted, "I don't think one week is enough."

The girls spent their last two days sunning on the beach. Kathy disappeared a couple of times with her new buddy and always came back to the beach smiling. For their last dinner on the island, they walked down the road to Chalet Suisse and were met at the door by Benny.

"Hello my beautiful ladies…. Do you have a reservation tonight?" Kathy sadly said no, but Benny looked around the room and cheerfully accommodated them. "Follow me ladies." It was the perfect way to end their seven days in Aruba. Kathy let Sara order a raspberry cosmopolitan and they ended dinner with chocolate mousse and "hot framboise kisses" for dessert. The girls promised each other that they would end every trip at Chalet Suisse.

Friday was a sad day for all the guests leaving for home. Kathy and Sara got up early and walked the beach to Divi. Kathy revealed to her niece, "You know, Sara, you've always been like a daughter to me. I promise that I will always be there for you, whether it's talking about school or your sex life. You can always depend on me." Sara hugged her aunt and acknowledged, "I would be nothing in this world if it wasn't for your love…. Thank you, Mom!" Kathy slept most of the plane trip home, while Sara lovingly gazed at her hero.

WOMANHOOD

The next four years brought a lot of changes and turmoil in Sara's life. Stacey was still in the loop, but was always too busy with her new job or boyfriends to spend any quality time with her daughter.

Her father remarried to a younger woman named Megan and started a family that he actually wanted. Eddy still cared about his firstborn, but Megan saw her as an invisible outsider. Sara was now an afterthought in both her parents' lives and moved in with Kathy for her senior year of high school. She got a part time job at a clothing store in Belden Village Mall and worked as much as possible.

Sara had grown into a gorgeous woman that every high school guy desired to be with. She was the homecoming queen and valedictorian of her class, but she still treated everyone with kindness and respect. She started dating Danny, who was the popular star quarterback of the football team, and they were "Barbie and Ken" of Canton McKinley High School.

Kathy assumed the parent role and supported Sara financially and emotionally. The high school senior was able to get a full scholarship for the nursing program at Kathy's college, Malone University. Sara always enjoyed helping other people and looked forward to her career in medicine.

Even with everything happening in their lives, Sara and Kathy always circled the last week of June on their calendars. It was their week in paradise together far away from the crazy outside world. As soon as their eyes saw their "second home" from the air, Kathy would squeeze Sara's hand and smile. The girls now knew all the staff at Costa Linda by name and they developed into an island family. The "old schoolers" of the resort traveled in their own social circles, but most of them became friendly when they finally acknowledged Kathy as a fellow timeshare owner at Costa Linda.

Kathy continued her "island affair" with Hank who she met the first year. Hank was ten years older than Kathy, but was youthful in his demeanor. He owned a construction company in Michigan and vacationed in Aruba in the winter with his family. Hank also owned the last week in June and he always came down with his buddies to golf during that week. Kathy knew that he was married, but she was only interested in sharing his company for seven days a year. The less she knew about Hank, the better it was for both lovers.

When Sara turned eighteen, she inherited the same outlook on life as her aunt. She had the body of a woman three years earlier and now her mental demeanor had joined it. She enjoyed wearing her string bikinis and strutting the beach while driving the men, young and old, crazy. Sara had a very conservative attitude back in Ohio but was very outgoing on the island.

Every year she would run past La Cabana and search for Todd on the beach. When she would see him she always playfully reminded Todd how many years were left until his promise was fulfilled. Sara always enjoyed talking to him about Aruba, knowing he was still very interested in their future date. They never talked about their home life or the people they left behind for one special week; Aruba was the only place on their minds.

Her second year at Malone University was a very stressful one for Sara. She concentrated on her schoolwork and her part time job in a local nursing home and had little time for anything else.

Sara and Danny parted ways after graduation and he posted some inappropriate pictures of her on the internet during her freshman year in college. Sara was terribly hurt that Danny violated her trust and soon began to hide herself in a protective bubble, always dressing and acting conservatively on campus.

She stopped dating guys and her fun outgoing personality was replaced by a professional attitude.

In the Spring of 2019, Sara began to fantasize about her afternoon date with Todd when she was fifteen years old. It was now five years of waiting and she was determined to find him on the beach and finish what they started. She hoped his family still owned at La Cabana and he would be staying there this year. "He's so cute and such a gentleman." The thought of her and Todd entangled together naked on the beach gave Sara that mental focus that helped get her through her sophomore year of college. The end of June couldn't come fast enough.

Kathy was also daydreaming of her seven days in paradise after a long and complicated year running the college and its always changing agendas. She had just turned 45 and was longing for more travel adventures. Her goal was to work ten more years and then take Sara on a tour of their "bucket list" destinations. Both women were fluent in several languages and looked forward to learning from the people who lived in all those special places. For entertainment at home, they would sit together for hours on the computer and plot their future trips.

ARUBA 2019

When their plane touched down on the runway of Reina Beatrix Airport, Kathy sighed, "We made it back home." and Sara joyfully smiled and kissed Kathy on the cheek. Hans was waiting with their rental car and they were off to Costa Linda. They checked their luggage with Wilmer who welcomed back his old friends and Lina helped to get them checked into their room quickly. The girls' next stop was the Water's Edge for drinks and they said hello to Luigi along the way. The first day ended like it always did with Kathy and Sara swimming in the ocean and watching the gorgeous sunset.

Sara started Saturday morning with a workout at the gym. She gave Andreas a hug and she was off for a jog on the beach. As Sara approached La Cabana Resort, she was pleasantly surprised to see Todd sitting in a beach chair at a front row palapa. Her heart was pounding as she began to walk toward him and she smiled when he noticed her. "Hey Todd…. The five year wait is officially over."

Todd's reaction was very unexpected. "Do I know you?" A woman sunbathing raised up and asked, "Who's she Todd?" Todd completely ignored Sara and replied, "I don't have a clue who she is?" Now the woman got up and started walking toward Sara. "Well, she knows who you are." She looked at

FORTY NIGHTS IN ARUBA

Sara and revealed, "Hi, I'm Amy.... Todd's fiancée. And you are who?"

Sara quickly blurted out, "I met Todd five years ago when I hung out with his sister one afternoon." Amy smirked, "His sister isn't here, so why don't you take a hike."

Sara was seething inside and was tired of being disrespected by the couple. She walked over to the next palapa and asked the elderly man if he would watch her stuff while she went for a swim. The man happily agreed and watched Sara slowly take off her shorts and tank top to reveal a white sting bikini. She slowly walked into the calm water and floated close to shore. A small crowd was now watching her tanned body shimmer in the sunlight and soon a group of men began to surround her in the water. For thirty minutes Todd and Amy watched the sensual exhibition along with most of the men at La Cabana.

Sara left the water and jogged towards the grateful old man and his now group of friends, who all volunteered their towels. She stood in front of Todd drying her hair as the seawater dripped off her sundrenched body and then she whispered in his ear. "Do you remember me now?"

Todd was speechless, staring closely at her voluptuous breasts and when she left, some of the men watching followed her down the beach. As Sara walked back to her resort, she ardently smiled at every young guy she passed and thought to herself, "I'm going to have some fun this week teasing the boys.... I want them all to remember Sara Sweeney."

She found her aunt reading in their palapa and told her about Todd. "Well, I found out that my Prince Charming is off the market." Kathy looked at Sara and shared in her disappointment. "I guess we're both screwed.... I saw Hank at the pool with his family and he didn't even look at me."

Sara was stunned. "He brought his wife this week.... WOW! That sucks. Hank and Todd are the losers Auntie.... They could be banging two hot chicks from Ohio." Kathy began to laugh and playfully asked, "Do you know what we need badly?" Sara yelled, "Snorkel Trip!"

The two hot chicks from Ohio grabbed their snorkel gear, jumped into the car, and headed for Malmok Beach. The girls always enjoyed snorkeling in the undersea world of the Caribbean. It was so peaceful to be a part of that realm and to experience the many creatures who lived there. They knew from past experiences where the best spots were and stayed away from the tourist boats who overcrowded the waters.

After two hours in the water, they both sunbathed on the rocks until the hot sun chased them to the Holiday Inn parking lot. Kathy and Sara snuck into the resort from the beach and used their pool to rinse off the salt and then walked the Palm Beach Boardwalk.

Palm Beach was always action packed with good looking men. The girls enjoyed fishing for guys by asking them if they would share their palapa with them. If the answer was "YES", it would usually lead to free drinks and sometimes to lunch. Today the girls would have no luck as the females were very protective of their men, but they had fun trying. Sara looked at Kathy and enthusiastically suggested, "Let's Go Tubing" and they were off for another adventure. It was a long, fun filled afternoon.

The girls spent the next three days snorkeling at their favorite spots. They drove southeast to enjoy Baby Beach and had drinks and a refreshing swim at Rum Reef. They were always fascinated with the abandoned homes of the "Colony" and would drive the neighborhood, looking at the new improvements.

The favorite part of their excursion was climbing the rugged cliffs near Seroe Colorado Lighthouse to see the powerful waves up close. Sara would stare in complete silence, mesmerized by the pounding of the saltwater against the cliffs.

After watching the magic of the waves, they would drive past the Red Anchor and continue up the weathered coast to the huge windmills. Sara always enjoyed stopping near Boca Grandi Beach and watching the windsurfers. She wanted desperately to try the sport, but Kathy didn't want any part of that and refused Sara's request.

    After five years, the girls knew the island very well and had fun "getting lost". Their favorite snorkel was Mangel Halto Reef and they enjoyed the friendly locals of the Savaneta area. They always stopped at Zeerovers for fresh seafood and then Kathy would drive down past the Yacht Club on the return trip home. The islanders were so kind to them and most Arubans spoke at least four languages. The girls decided to learn Papiamento to honor their host.

    Every morning, Sara would put on a sexy bikini and jog the beach down past La Cabana to make sure Todd remembered her. Each day the guys would line the beach to watch her run by. On Thursday a new runner joined her workout. "I'm sorry I lied about you, but I'm engaged…. You can understand that, can't you?"

    Sara stopped and told Todd, "I get it and I'm okay with what you did…. I probably would have done the same thing, but I would have at least acknowledged that I knew you…. That was a special day for me five years ago and you were a special guy. Am I that forgettable?"

    Todd looked at her stunning blue eyes, too afraid to admire her body. "You're kidding me, right? I always enjoyed our talks over the last five years…. I used to sneak up to Costa Linda at sunset to watch you and your aunt play in the water.... I remember you, Sara Sweeney, and I've admired you since we first met, but I'm engaged now and you are a regret that I need to bury."

As Todd turned to walk away, Sara grabbed his shoulders and pulled the surprised man into her chest. She kissed him deeply and then whispered in his ear. "Don't ever forget me Todd.... I'll never forget you." She jogged away as he admired the view and thought, "How could I ever forget you, Sara."

Sara went to their suite to tell Kathy about her encounter with Todd, but she was busy entertaining a man in her room. Sara made enough noise in the kitchen for the moaning to stop and soon Kathy came out in a robe with Hank following behind her. Sara was upset with her aunt and asked Hank, "Are your wife and kids in that room too?" Hank ignored her question and kissed Kathy goodbye.

Kathy got into a heated discussion with her niece. "It's none of your business who I screw. Hank is my perk every year I come here. Don't make me feel guilty about that." Sara fired back, "He's married and he didn't even give you the time of day earlier this week. You can do better than him."

Kathy grabbed Sara's hands and sat with her on the couch and confessed. "I don't want to do better than him.... Sara, I'm never going to get married and guys like Hank are an outlet for me to enjoy men without a commitment. I don't want you to grow up to be like me or your mother. You need to be yourself and follow your own destiny. Please, don't judge me for my needs and desires."

Sara realized that she had no right to be critical of her aunt after she just kissed an engaged man. "I'm sorry Aunt Kathy.... I just don't want to see you hurt. You mean the world to me." Kathy embraced her niece and asked, "How did I ever get so lucky to have a Sara Sweeney in my life.... Let's go to the beach and drive the men crazy." Sara gleefully asked, "Aren't all men crazy?"

Kathy and Sara were enjoying dinner at Chalet Suisse when Todd and Amy came in with two other people. Benny seated them right across from the girls and Sara was very uncomfortable and suggested to Kathy about changing tables. "Nonsense. Be yourself and go say hello to him." Sara got up and approached Todd and his companions.

"Hello Amy. My name is Sara Sweeney and I'm from Ohio. I'd like to apologize to you for my immaturity earlier in the week. I had a big crush on your fiancée when I was fifteen years old and I was hoping he would remember me. I'm sorry that I disturbed your dinner." Sara reached out for Amy's hand, but was refused. Sara still continued to smile and said, "Goodnight" and walked back to her table.

Kathy was proud of Sara and told Juaquin to bring two more raspberry cosmos and dessert. The other guy with Todd came over and introduced himself. "Hi. I'm Amy's brother Sean.... What's the name of that dessert?" Sara gushed, "Hot Framboise Kisses."

Sean boyishly replied, "I'll bet they are.... You are without a doubt, the most beautiful woman I have ever seen. Would you care to join me tonight for a moonlit walk on the beach?" Sara looked over at Todd and then approved, "Sure Sean. I'd love to go. Meet me at Costa Linda Beach at eleven o'clock. You'll find me under a front row palapa."

As the two girls began to leave, Sara stood in front of the very quiet Todd allowing him to view her body highlighted through the white toga and she looked like a Greek Goddess. She lustfully said, "I'll see you later, Sean!" and blew him a kiss.

Kathy held back any comments until they were in the car. "Oh, my dear niece.... You have stirred the pot and you might be serving the dish if that guy shows up tonight." Sara devilishly grinned. "I hope he shows up hungry!"

Sean eagerly arrived before eleven and easily found Sara still wearing the white toga. She stood and took her panties off while explaining, "I am not in the mood for a walk." Sara began to take off the stunned man's shorts and kneeled in front of him.

"Relax, Sean and let me enjoy my last night in Aruba." She began to serve Sean the "erotic dish" until he finally paid his bill, twenty minutes later. Sara gave Sean a quick peck on the lips and grinned. "Thanks for the wonderful walk." She picked up her panties and flip flops and Sean watched her every move as Sara slowly strutted off the beach.

On the flight back to reality, Sara had a long talk with her aunt about her urges and needs. "I'm not waiting for a guy to sweep me off my feet anymore. I can now appreciate your attitude towards men. I like when they desire me…. I really do and I'm going to be the one breaking their hearts next year in Aruba." Kathy listened before warning her. "Be careful to know the man before you break his heart…. Next year should be very interesting, Kiddo."

COVID

Next year was very interesting, but for all the wrong reasons. Covid came knocking on the world's door and everything, including Aruba, was shut down. Kathy dealt with her stressful job, as Malone University was forced to provide more online learning while struggling to adjust to the "new" world. She worked late nights trying to keep her university functioning properly and rarely spent quality time with her niece.

Sara's sparkling personality was broken into a thousand pieces over the next two years. She was now learning at home and working eighty hours a week in the hospital during Covid. She saw people of all ages and races die before her eyes. She saw families, rich and poor, destroyed by this deadly virus.

Sara always wanted to be a nurse because she enjoyed helping people, but she wore down, fighting a losing battle in a hopeless situation. She felt so helpless holding a wife after telling her the horrible news of her husband's passing. Most days, Sara would come home and cry herself to sleep and then start the day over again.

Kathy was worried about her niece and booked a last minute trip for late June of 2020. She sent Sara a text. "PLEASE. Take a week off and be my guest at Marco Island…. We need a break." Sara texted back, "Can't wait…. Can we leave today?" They both now had something to look forward to as they struggled to get through Springtime.

Few people at the airport and an uncrowded flight were a constant reminder of Covid. Masks were mandatory and everybody social distanced themselves as protection. As soon as they got off the plane, the girls realized that they weren't in Aruba. It was hot and muggy and they were sweating by the time they got to their rental car.

After checking into the Marriott, Sara and Kathy put on their bikinis and sprinted toward the ocean. Reality set in the closer they got to the water. The beach had white sand, but it was filled with rocks and broken seashells, making it uncomfortable to walk on. The crashing waves were bringing in seaweed, and a red tide was evident along the beach.

The lifeguard advised them not to enter the ocean and they dejectedly returned to the overcrowded pool and tried to get two lounge chairs together. As they finally got situated and were peacefully sunbathing, Sara stated the obvious, "Aruba has spoiled us forever, Auntie." Kathy agreed, "I guess this trip will make us appreciate Aruba more…. Let's hope this pandemic will be over soon and we'll be sunning ourselves on Eagle Beach next year."

Suddenly, lightning filled the sky and the heavens released a downpour on them. Sara and Kathy began laughing hysterically as they sang the Aruba National Anthem while running for cover!

Florida was a much-needed break for the hardworking pair. They did a dolphin tour, found many pretty shells on Tiger Tail Beach, and watched several 'average' sunsets. The biggest plus was they finally got to spend some quality time together. After seven days, they were relaxed and ready to go home.

BRIGHT FUTURE

Sara's hard work paid off as she got her BSN in a little over three years and began working full time at Mercy Hospital in the Pediatrics Wing. It was a needed change after her stressful stint in the Intensive Care Unit and she was very excited about her future. Sara loved children and the staff was very kind to her, teaching her the ins and outs of the department. Although Covid was still at its peak, Sara no longer dreaded coming into work.

A popular doctor would joke and flirt with Sara as he made his rounds visiting the children. She thought he was cute, but didn't know anything about him and always played "hard to get". One night the shift went out for drinks after work and the young doctor was at a booth with a few friends and Sara introduced herself. "Hi Doctor Rockich. Who are your good looking friends?"

The young doctor laughed and countered back, "These guys are way too old for you, Sara…. And please call me Dave." Sara shyly smiled and said, "You have a good night, Doctor Rockich" and slowly walked back to her friends at the bar, showing off those "painted on" jeans.

Dave Rockich was ten years older than Sara, but he was determined to sway the young girl. He asked her out every day for a month and was turned down each time. He sent flowers to her weekly and had all the other nurses endorse him until, finally, Sara said yes.

Kathy was happy for her and remarked that he came from a wealthy family and then joked, "I wonder if his parents own at Costa Linda?" Sara countered, "Maybe they own a house on Malmok Beach?" Sara chuckled, but was very nervous about a relationship with any doctor that might sidetrack her career.

The night of the date, Dave pulled into Kathy's driveway driving a BMW Gran Coupe and got out of the car to present Sara a large bouquet of roses. Kathy was very impressed, but Sara thanked him for the flowers and handed them to her aunt. As she walked towards the passenger door, she sarcastically commented, "Wow…. It looks like you make a whole lot more money than I do." Dave grinned and opened the door for his stunning date.

He took her to Gervasi Vineyard for dinner at the Bistro and was immediately seated by the Maître d'. Sara looked intently at Dave as he ordered an expensive bottle of wine and she blissfully asked, "Do you always take your women to places like this on the first date?" Dave gazed into her blue eyes and answered. "Only the special ones."

They drank, ate, and laughed the entire night as Dave told her all about himself. His family owned a book publishing company in New York City. But he wanted to become a doctor and help young children in need. He graduated from Columbia School of Medicine and did his residency at the Cleveland Clinic. Sara asked if he was a fellow Cleveland Browns' fan and he replied, "I'm a Jets fan so I guess we both root for losers."

As the dinner date continued into the wee hours, the flirting increased as the alcohol continued to flow. They were having late night cocktails, when Dave became flustered and confessed, "I don't think I can drive home…. I'm wasted."

Sara suggested taking a cab home, but Dave had a better idea. "I can't leave my car here. I'll see if there is a room available on the property." He was on the phone for only a minute then paid his tab. He escorted his very unstable date to his car, drove them to a villa, and helped her inside.

Sara was too tipsy to question his decision making and began to undress before she passed out. Dave quickly stripped and then held her as he began to explore her naked body. His lips and tongue quickly wore down Sara's resistance, and she moaned with great pleasure. The two lovers were now entangled in heated passion, and Sara was numb to the outside world. Dave collapsed from pleasure on top of her and cuddled there until morning.

When Sara awoke from last night's fantasy, her breakfast was waiting for her in a wicker basket. Dave stopped gazing at her in bed and handed her a robe. "Let's eat outside on the terrace." She quickly texted Kathy to explain what had happened last night and then joined Dave for a romantic breakfast.

Sara giggled during their conversation. "I guess you seduce all your first dates this way." Dave took a rose from the table centerpiece and handed it to her and answered, "Only you." As they were finishing breakfast, Sara feverishly smiled at Dave and suggested, "I'm going to take a shower…. Would you care to join me?" Dave followed her back into the villa and they stayed there until late morning check out.

For the next nine months, Dave and Sara were inseparable, and their romance blossomed into a loving relationship. They worked together, laughed together, and at night, they slept together. Dave wanted Sara to move into his home, but she always concluded, "Sorry Honey, but I won't leave my aunt."

Dave became jealous of Kathy, but never revealed his emotions to Sara. He didn't want to ruin the special bond the girls had between them. Dave needed Kathy to be an ally and when he brought Sara flowers, he always had a bouquet for her aunt.

HAPPY RETURN

Covid began to ramp down as the world strived for normalcy. The hospitals were still filled with patients, but the vaccine was proving to be successful. Restrictions were now being lifted and Aruba was once again opened to travel.

Kathy began planning their trip and was looking forward to spending precious time with her niece. She rarely saw Sara much on the weekends and missed their insightful conversations. Kathy understood that Sara was in love and was happy for her, but deep in her heart, she felt that Sara was rushing into a relationship. Kathy kept her feelings hidden and always supported her niece.

As June got closer, Sara began to spend more time with Kathy as they prepared for their annual trip. She always felt guilty about no longer sharing their lives together, but she was madly in love with Dave and enjoyed his company.

Aruba was now the magnet that reunited their fun loving spirits together. They hadn't walked on Eagle Beach for almost two years and were anxious for their return. Sara was so excited as the day of departure approached. "I can't wait to run down to Amsterdam Manor on that soft white sand." Kathy added, "I'm looking forward to watching that first sunset with you in the water…. And tasting that chocolate mousse in my mouth." Sara grabbed her aunt's shoulders and happily shouted, "HOT FRAMBOISE KISSES!"

Dave was less enthusiastic than the girls. He wanted to go with them, but was firmly rejected by Sara. "Aruba is our special place. My aunt means so much to me and I really need to enjoy our time together…. Please understand that and respect my wishes." She kissed Dave and continued, "You can take me any place in the world that you desire, but Aruba belongs to me and my Aunt Kathy."

Dave suggested, "If I take you to Hawaii, can we make love under a waterfall?" Sara deeply kissed him and then whispered in his ear. "If you take me to Hawaii, I'll make love to you anywhere you like."

The last week leading up to the trip was filled with stress and suspense as the two girls waited for the results of their Covid tests. Sara had acquired Covid around New Years, but Kathy never had developed any symptoms of the illness. They decided if one would test positive, the trip would be canceled. Neither wanted to go without the other; it just wouldn't feel the same. Luckily, both results came back negative and they were off to their "One Happy Island".

As they saw the island from the air, Kathy held Sara's hand and confessed, "I never realized how much I took this country for granted.... It's so nice to be back." Sara tearfully replied, "I never realized how much I took you for granted, Auntie.... This is a special week for us to enjoy each other, away from reality." Kathy and Sara held hands tightly as the airplane touched ground.

Hans was waiting for the girls with the rental car and happily welcomed them back to the island. He told about the hardships of all the businesses and resorts over the last two years. "It is very nice to see people coming back.... Thank you for not forgetting us." They drove through town with no traffic jam and saw only a few tourists on the once busy streets.

When they pulled up to Costa Linda, it still looked the same; it still looked like home. They gave hugs to Wilmer and Javier and checked in with Lina at the front desk. The room wasn't ready, but they didn't care. They changed into their bikinis at the beach bathroom and sprinted onto the soft sand and dove into the crashing ocean waves.

The girls laughed and skipped rocks across the water as a child would do, forgetting about the time of day. When they were chilly from their horseplay in the blue sea, the girls would expose their shivering bodies to the blazing sun. Kathy and Sara ended the first day the way they always did; holding each other in the water while watching the sun make its glorious exit. Kathy just sighed and repeated her famous line. "How can anything top this…. I could die a happy girl now."

It was dark when the girls finally arrived at their suite, but instead of unpacking, the two sat on the balcony and admired the beautiful property of Costa Linda. Kathy observed, "The magic of this island has always filled me with amazement. I'm so happy to be able to share this with you, Kiddo."

Sara kneeled in front of her aunt and confessed. "You're more magical than Aruba. You saved a little girl from a fate that no one deserved and raised her as your own. You magically planted a seed and watched her turn into a successful woman…. I could never repay you for everything you've done for me." Kathy could say nothing as she tearfully hugged her loving niece.

Sara awoke with her mind set on going for a run down the beach. She put on a sports bra with a bikini bottom and enjoyed the stares and whistles along her trip toward Amsterdam Manor. As she jogged, Sara thought of the first time she met a boy from what seemed like a long time ago. "I wonder if he married that bitch? They were perfect for each other.... I'll bet she was from New York City." She laughed all the way back to her resort.

The girls planned on a snorkeling trip to Arashi Beach, but Hank quickly changed those plans. Sara heard the familiar moaning coming from Kathy's room and knew she would be tied up for a while. She pleasantly yelled, "Take your time.... I'll see you at the beach, Auntie."

Sara checked her phone messages on her way to the gym and saw that a strange number had sent a text with pictures attached. Several pictures showed Kathy and her watching last night's sunset and they moved Sara to tears. The last picture showed Sara jogging earlier this morning and she now knew the identity behind the mystery text.

Sara walked back down to La Cabana Beach and went fishing for Todd. She began to slowly remove her coverup in front of the rental hut for everyone to see her almost naked body and stood there as the "bait". Soon a voice observed, "You're certainly not a shy one." Sara grinned and replied, "I'm surprised Amy doesn't have you on a leash.... How's my buddy Sean doing?"

Todd's face got red with embarrassment. "I'm really glad you brought that up.... Was it necessary for you to fuck Sean to piss me off? Did you really enjoy that?"

Sara got right in his face and lustfully answered, "Let me remember…. Wasn't it you that ignored me at the beach and again at Chalet Suisse? Wasn't it you that said nothing while your fiancée embarrassed me? I fucked Sean to piss off his sister, not you…. And yes, I did enjoy it!"

Sara turned to leave when she heard, "Amy's not my fiancée anymore, but don't pat yourself on the back because you had nothing to do with it…. She found a rich lawyer who kissed her ass more than I did."

Sara quickly had a change of heart. "I'm sorry to hear that, Todd. I actually came down here to look for you and thank you for those pictures of my aunt and me…. They're priceless."

Todd finally smiled and told her. "I was hoping that you were coming down this year, so I snuck up to your resort and watched you two for an hour. I'll send you all of the pictures I took…. You're a beautiful model and I couldn't stop shooting you…. I'm so sorry I treated you like that two years ago, but I don't regret turning you away when you were a teenager."

A sudden warmth went through Sara's heart and she blissfully suggested. "I hear your resort has a pretty wild bar. Do you want to buy this girl a drink?" She reached out her hand and Todd gladly accepted

FORTY NIGHTS IN ARUBA

it. They walked across the street to have a cold drink together.

La Cabana had a young crowd who loved to party. It was happy hour and the bar was packed as the band was rocking. A couple of guys from Boston volunteered their seats so they could have a closer view of their new "eye candy".

It was hard to hear a conversation so Sara asked Todd to dance, but he rejected her request. She looked at him with those baby blue eyes and pouted. "If you don't dance with me, I'm going to cry." Todd saw the other vultures circling their sensual prey so he grabbed Sara's arm and led her to the front of the bar.

Todd could have fallen down and no one would have noticed; all eyes were on Sara and her stunning body moving in rhythm to the band. The concrete dance floor was filled with happy drunks yelling encouragement to the young man and Sara could tell he was embarrassed. She pulled Todd close and kissed him in front of the applauding crowd. The cheers turned into boos when she jumped into the pool and swam to the water slide with Todd following close behind.

They found an empty table and Sara began to tell him about Dave and their romance. Todd was happy for her, but disappointedly stated his honest opinion. "I just guess that we were never meant to be together."

Sara delicately agreed and got ready to leave. "I had a blast with you today. You're the 'Master' of afternoon fun.... Too bad I never got to try you out at night." She saw two very cute girls watching their every move, so she deeply kissed Todd and then whispered in his ear, "Thanks for the pictures. Whenever I see them, I'll remember you." As she walked by the curious girls, Sara grinned, "He's all yours, ladies."

Her beach walk back to Costa Linda was one of reflection. She always had feelings for Todd, but she was in love with Dave. She wondered why Dave hadn't called or returned her texts. Sara needed advice from Kathy, but was surprised to find her in a very perplexed mood. "What's wrong Auntie?"

Kathy rolled her eyes back and simply said, "MEN." It seems that Hank was planning on leaving his wife and asked Kathy to marry him. She thought he was joking and began to laugh. "I saw the hurt look in his eyes and realized he was serious, but he stormed out of the bedroom and disappeared before I could talk to him.... I really like Hank, but I don't want to marry him."

Sara wanted to cheer her aunt up. "Give him time to reflect and then go talk to him.... He'll come around.... How about we drive down to Surfside

Beach and watch the sunset together. Maybe we'll get lucky and watch a couple of planes land." Kathy perked up. "That sounds like a fun night. We can eat at Surfside Beach Bar and hangout with the locals." Tonight, both women needed to forget the men in their lives.

Sara decided to jog the opposite direction to Bushiri Beach on Sunday morning. She sat on the beach and threw rocks into the water, thinking about yesterday and her renewed feelings for a guy she hardly knew. She needed to stay away from Todd and clear her head, but that was now becoming harder to do.

A couple of local fishermen joined her and they had a nice conversation in Papiamento. Sara always prided herself on speaking the language when needed. The locals were happy to have the tourists back, but were nervous about the future of their island.

Kathy called to tell her that she had that "awkward" conversation with Hank and she was looking forward to a snorkeling date with her niece. Sara became excited and yelled into her phone. "Mangel Halto…. Grab my snorkel gear and a couple of towels and pick me up at Bushiri Beach and we'll snorkel the reef." Kathy didn't hesitate. "I'll pick you up in ten minutes."

The girls spent the next two glorious hours entangled with the sea life at their favorite spot. The sun's reflection showed the many blues of the ocean and they shared those views with the many locals who were also enjoying a day of fun. They waited in line at Zeerovers to enjoy a nice late lunch and drove back on 4B to sightsee Santa Cruz and then Sara climbed the Casibari Rock formations for a selfie.

They got back to Eagle Beach barely in time for a sunset picture by the famous fofoti tree near La Cabana. Sara nervously expected to see Todd, but he was nowhere around. After they arrived at Costa Linda, she started to tell Kathy about her feelings for him, but the conversation was cut off when fellow owner Amy began chatting with them as they walked toward their suite.

As soon as they walked in, the girls were shocked to see tropical flowers everywhere. They looked at each other and both saw a man sitting on the balcony. The closer they got, Sara became very confused and opened the balcony door. She dejectedly asked, "Dave…. What are you doing here?"

Her boyfriend rushed to hug her and admitted. "I wanted to surprise you and by the looks on both of your faces, I did a pretty good job." Sara smooched him, but was still confused. "We talked about this, Honey, and I thought you understood?"

Dave kissed Kathy on the cheek, ignoring his girlfriend's question. "I hope you like the flowers, Kathy, and I hope you won't mind putting me up for a few days." Kathy gave Dave a big hug and said, "You're always welcome here…. Let's show you around."

As they walked the property, Dave told the girls of his desire to come to Aruba. "I was curious about this beautiful country after listening to all your fond memories, and I wanted to experience Aruba with my own two eyes. I took a few days off and flew down here to join you. I wasn't trying to upset you; I just wanted to surprise you." Kathy insisted that it was a pleasure to have Dave as her guest, but Sara wasn't saying a word.

Kathy excused herself. "I'm meeting Hank for some late night cocktails at the Water's Edge. You're both welcome to join us." Dave thanked her for the offer, but said he was tired and wanted to go to bed early.

When Kathy left, Dave's demeanor changed. "Where in the hell were you? I waited here for three hours wondering where you were." Sara calmly stated the facts. "We went to the southern end of the island to snorkel and got some food…. That's what we do. We don't keep track of time in Aruba; everything is slow paced and relaxed here."

Dave apologized to his fiancée. "I know you don't want me here, but I really missed you." Sara sarcastically countered, "You missed me…. Dave, I was with you four days ago. You never called, you never returned my texts, and you tell me you missed me?"

Sara stopped before she started an argument and asked Dave to go for a moonlit walk on the beach with her. Dave picked her up and carried her into the bedroom. "We'll do that walk tomorrow night." Sara sighed, "I thought that you were tired?" Dave smirked as he undressed her and confidently said, "I'm going to be."

Sara awoke the next morning and gently rolled Dave's naked body off her. She went for her daily beach run and returned to mean-spirited questions. "Where did you go? I woke up and you were gone…. How long were you away?" Sara was in no mood for a debate. "Dave, I went for a run on the beach. You know I run at home…. I run here too."

The loud discussion brought Kathy out of her room. "Good morning, guys. Did you sleep well last night, Dave?" Dave sarcastically replied, "I guess I slept too well. My girl snuck away this morning without me even knowing."

Dave was not very receptive to Kathy's plans to snorkel for turtles at Malmok Beach. "You go if you want, but I think Sara and I are going to hang around the pool." Kathy's eyes told Sara to relax and breathe deeply, but her voice said, "I think I'm going to visit the Butterfly Farm today. You two have a wonderful day."

Sara bit her tongue when Dave told her, "You are NOT wearing that thong in public." She bit her tongue again when he was rude to Maria at the towel hut, but she could bite no more when Dave started flirting with two girls from New Jersey. He was so engaged talking with them, that he never noticed his girlfriend going back to her suite and re-emerging in the skimpiest bikini she owned. Sara walked behind Dave, wrote something on a napkin, and then left for the beach.

Dave was pissed when he read her note. "Honey, I went for a walk on the beach. Come join me if you like." When he saw ten guys following her almost naked body, Dave became furious and ran toward Sara. "What in the hell are you doing?" She kissed him in front of the crowd and shyly answered, "I'm showing you off to everyone" and then she deeply kissed him again. Dave's ego allowed him to believe the "bull" and Sara got a much needed chuckle.

Dave's flight was leaving one day earlier than the girl's and after three days of hanging around the pool, his upper body was sunburnt and he was ready to get back to Ohio.

He surprised Sara and Kathy with a romantic sunset dinner at Barefoot on Surfside Beach. Kathy had always wanted to dine there and was very excited about the invitation and gratefully told him, "That sounds wonderful, Dave. You should come down here more often." Sara was also pleasantly surprised and wore a long flowing "island" dress to impress her man.

After they were seated in the front row on the beach, Dave quickly excused himself and was gone for ten minutes. The girls were sipping on their cocktails when he arrived back at the table. Sara greeted him with a kiss and a "Chill" beer and they ordered their entrees.

All three were positioned to watch the gorgeous "ball of fire" fall from the sky when a young Aruban boy ran up to their table and presented Sara with a bouquet of roses. All eyes were on Dave as he kneeled in front of Sara and proposed marriage to her.

She was in shock and didn't even hear his romantic speech, but she still blurted out, "I'd love to marry you, Dave" and caressed him as the two passionately kissed in front of the admiring dinner guests. Dave kissed her again and joyfully concluded, "Now do you understand why I wanted to come down here." Kathy hugged them both. "What a wonderful surprise. I'm honored to be here and witness this special moment in my niece's life."

The three chatted and enjoyed each other's company all night. Dave was not shy about his passion as he said goodnight to Kathy and took his fiancée into the bedroom. Sara undressed herself and then slowly undressed her lover as Dave waited in anticipation. She began to kiss his body, but Dave omitted foreplay and quickly went for penetration. After their lovemaking was over, Sara tried to cuddle with Dave, but was politely rejected. "Oh Babe, my sunburn is killing me and I've got an early flight out tomorrow." He rolled over on his side and said goodnight to his new fiancée.

It was all business for Dave the next morning as he stayed in contact with the hospital about his upcoming workload. Sara tried to explain Aruba's unusual procedure of departure to the States, but Dave wasn't listening and she thought, "Boy, I hope he doesn't forget about his suitcase and miss his flight." He grabbed his bag, she kissed him goodbye, and pointed him towards the "departure" doors. Dave promised to call her as soon as his flight landed in Ohio.

Sara got back into the car and looked at her aunt, grinning as she howled, "Malmok Beach Auntie!" Kathy quickly drove back to Costa Linda where they snatched their gear, and then the two girls spent the entire afternoon snorkeling with the turtles.

As they watched their final sunset in the water at Eagle Beach, Sara thanked her aunt for easily accepting her fiancée and Kathy lovingly responded. "Dave's visit was a pleasant surprise and seeing you get engaged in person was very special for me. He's a part of our family now." The two embraced for a long time in the water and then got ready for their traditional last dinner at Chalet Suisse.

As soon as they arrived at the restaurant, Kathy noticed that Chalet Suisse was packed and they were seated in the same section as Todd and a large group of people. Sara walked quickly past Todd's table and hoped he wouldn't see her, but that was impossible because of the revealing mini dress she was wearing.

Sara looked over at his table once she sat and Todd was gazing directly at her. She got Kathy's attention when she blurted out, "Christ. He's coming over." Kathy observed, "He's a lot cuter than I remember." Todd stood in front of them and politely asked, "Good evening, ladies…. Haven't we met here before?" Kathy told Todd about their last night tradition, but she could tell that he was lost inside Sara's magical blue eyes.

Todd was a gentleman when Sara smiled sadly and raised her left hand to display her new engagement ring. "My boyfriend came down here Sunday and he proposed to me last night." She could feel his hand trembling as he congratulated her with a gentle shake. "I'm truly happy for you. He's a very lucky man.... I hope he's not from New York City."

Sara suddenly remembered their conversation about people from New York City from seven years earlier. She blurted out as Todd was leaving. "Was Amy from New York City?" Todd turned around and regrettably noted, "Unfortunately, she most definitely was.... Have a safe flight and have a wonderful life, Sara."

Sara could not get Todd's words out of her mind for the entire flight back to Ohio. Kathy could tell from her quiet demeanor that Sara was troubled so she tried to cheer her up. "Did I tell you Hank proposed to me again this morning?" Sara's eyes lit up. "NO WAY!"

Kathy cautiously explained, "I told him that you just got engaged and one accepted proposal a year for a 'Sweeney Girl' was the limit." Sara thought that she was joking until she saw the despair in Kathy's eyes as she continued. "I care about Hank, but I don't think I love him. If he does leave his wife, it won't be because of me." Sara quietly held her aunt's hand for the rest of the flight back home.

THE REAL WORLD

Dave insisted on Sara moving in with him and she reluctantly agreed. She left most of her sentimental belongings at Kathy's house and promised her that they would still see each other regularly. Kathy gave her blessing. "You're twenty-three years old now and it's time for you to spread your wings and fly."

Life moved fast for Sara. She was promoted at work and moved to another wing in the hospital. She would still run into Dave from time to time, but was no longer on his daily rounds. Sara began working towards her master's degree and hoped one day to become a Nurse Practitioner in Pediatrics. Dave was very supportive of Sara in her future pursuit. When they weren't rolling around in the sack, he was helping with her homework. They both wanted to wait until Covid was a distant memory before they wed and Dave's family desired a very big wedding.

Kathy remained under the gun at her university and was looking forward to retirement. She had accumulated enough wealth to live comfortably, but she was only forty-seven and still enjoyed her position at Malone. Kathy didn't like going home to an empty house so she began working longer hours and then started donating her time to charity work.

Kathy's goal was to retire at the age of fifty-five and then travel the world, but her partner was soon to be a spouse and she had no intentions of being a "third wheel". She missed Sara dearly and looked forward to their time together in Aruba.

Dave and Sara attended a black-tie affair for the Cleveland Clinic around Thanksgiving. They were enjoying the evening when he saw an old colleague on the dance floor with a beautiful blonde-haired woman. "My God. That's Jeff Peterson. Who's the gorgeous woman he's dancing with?" He wanted to get closer for an introduction and asked Sara to dance with him, but she stubbornly refused. Dave practically had to "drag" her to the floor and forced her to dance closer to Jeff and his date.

Dave politely smiled at the couple now dancing right next to them. "Hey Jeff. It's been a while…. Who's your beautiful date?" Before Jeff could answer, the mystery woman said, "Hello My Dear Sara. You look stunning tonight." Sara dejectedly replied, "Hello Stacey."

Jeff was surprised by the greeting and asked how they knew each other and Sara timidly answered, "She's my mother." Dave was blown away by the revelation and invited Jeff and Stacey to join them at their table against the wishes shown in his fiancée's glaring eyes.

The rest of the night was spent with conversations about Stacey and Sara. His buddy Jeff was an afterthought as Dave was infatuated with Stacey. "I cannot believe that you are Sara's mom. You two look like sisters." Stacey, always the flirt, replied, "You're so sweet. I was eighteen when I had Sara and she was an accident." Sara was embarrassed, but Dave kissed her on the cheek and proudly proclaimed, "She certainly isn't an accident anymore and I hope to add another beauty to your stable."

Stacey gently held Sara's unwilling hand and told Dave. "I'm very proud of Sara. She's worked hard to achieve her goals and stay focused in her life.... Sara told me she was engaged, but she never told me how good looking her fiancée was. Of course, Sara always dated good looking boys."

Sara's smiling face was holding back the tears of always taking a back seat to her mother. In high school, Stacey would rarely show at any of Sara's events, but when she did, Stacey always tried to outdo her daughter. The night she won Homecoming Queen, all the talk was about Stacey in her skintight miniskirt. For some reason, Stacey enjoyed stealing the spotlight from her daughter.

Sara was silent, listening to Dave's banter on the drive home. "I just can't get over how much your mother looks like you. Is she only seventeen years older than you?" Finally, Sara had enough and told him, "You know how I feel about my mom. She didn't want me and she never acted like my mother.... I love her, but Stacey never wanted to be a part of my life.... Can we please quit talking about her?" Dave apologized. "I'm sorry, I promise to not bring her name up again."

Every Christmas, Kathy would host a small party for her family. It was the only season of the year that Sara had to spend quality time with her father. After Eddy married Megan, Sara was no longer welcomed in her father's home and after she moved in with Kathy, Eddy rarely talked to her. Sara missed her dad and always looked forward to seeing him around Christmas. It was Dave's first time attending the "get together" and he was nervous about meeting her father.

Dinner was about to begin and Eddy and his second family were all "no shows". Halfway through the night, there was a knock at the door and Kathy rushed to greet Eddy. She was shocked when she found out it wasn't her brother, but his first wife. "My goodness, what a pleasant surprise. I haven't seen you forever, Stacey." Sara's heart stopped when she heard the greeting. "What is Mom up to?"

Stacey was always invited to the annual party, but never attended after the divorce. Sara was the last person to greet her mother and asked, "Why are you here tonight?" Stacey was hurt by her daughter's question and explained. "Sweetheart, I know that I haven't been a good mother to you, but I want to be involved in your life again.... You're getting married and soon, I'll be a grandmother."

Stacey took off her winter coat to reveal a "skintight" red velvet pants suit and Kathy immediately left the room. She was very upset that NOW, Stacey wanted to be a part of Sara's life.

Sara followed her aunt into the kitchen as the male family members gathered around her mother. Kathy was washing dishes and Sara wrapped her arms around her aunt. "She's never been a mother to me and suddenly she wants to be a grandmother to my child."

Kathy continued to wash the pans and confessed. "I could never understand that woman. She birthed a beautiful healthy baby girl that any family would desire and gave her away." The more Kathy tearfully talked, the tighter Sara hugged and she finally interrupted her aunt. "Stacey's going to be really pissed when I name my daughter 'Katherine'.... You'll always be my mom." Kathy embraced her niece and whimpered, "Only six more months until paradise."

After the two girls composed themselves, they returned to the room and Sara overheard Stacey talking about the upcoming wedding. She approached Stacey and Dave with a fake smile painted on her irritated face. "Our wedding plans are no concern of yours, Mom. We don't even have a date set aside.... Dave and I are going to pay for it all so you and Dad don't have to worry about it."

Stacey was offended. "I would love to help you plan the big wedding that I was cheated out of.... I was hoping Eddy would be here tonight so that we could discuss helping you out financially. Where is he anyway?" Stacey began to laugh, "The only time Eddy ever 'came' early was the night we made you." Sara and Kathy were furious, but Kathy threw water on the fire. "Dessert is on the table, if anyone is interested."

Dave defended Stacey to a silent Sara after the party ended. "Your mom seems like a nice person. You really need to make an effort to understand her side of the story and get to know the person she has become now.... She's going to be the grandmother of our children."

Sara went into the bedroom to avoid an argument with Dave, but he followed behind still spewing advice out of his mouth. She interrupted him and angrily asked, "When you grew up in New York, did your mother ever forget about you at Christmas and then tell you that Santa didn't bring you anything because you were a bad boy?" Dave shook his head sideways and Sara angrily stated, "Well…. My fucking mother did!"

Three weeks later, Kathy received a phone call from Megan. "I'm sorry to tell you that Eddy passed away last night." Kathy screamed in disbelief and began to cry, knowing that her only sibling was now dead. Megan said matter-of-factly, "Please control yourself so that I can continue with the story…. Eddy got infected with Covid a month ago and was put into the hospital after his lungs failed to work properly…. He never got better and he died yesterday."

Kathy was now clear minded. "He's been in the hospital for a month and you chose not to tell me?" Megan coldly answered, "I didn't want to ruin your holidays. Besides, you two haven't been close since your parents died in that car crash ten years ago and I know how Eddy really felt about you and Sara…. Eddy wanted to be cremated with no services, so there is no need for you to do anything…. Unless you want to help me pay for the burial?" Kathy's response was silence. Megan concluded, "Please tell Sara the bad news and my family will take care of everything else."

Kathy composed herself, called Sara, and asked her to please come over to her house after work. As soon as Sara saw her aunt's face, she knew something was wrong. Kathy sat her down and held her hands. "Sara darling. Your father passed away last night." Sara was numb as Kathy struggled through the details of his death.

Sara lowered her head and whispered. "That's why he didn't come to the Christmas party. I knew we weren't close, but Dad always enjoyed being with us at Christmas…. Now, I'll never see him again." Kathy hugged her niece and told her. "I know Eddy wasn't much of a father to you, but he fought to save you from being aborted. He was proud of that…. He was proud of you." The two women held each other tightly and cried for what seemed like an eternity.

Sara called Dave with the bad news and told him that she was going to stay with her aunt for the next two days to comfort her. Dave was not very understanding and suggested that Sara should bring Kathy to his house. Sara calmly responded. "No Dave…. Kathy needs me here and I'm staying until she feels better…. Dad was her younger brother and she is hurting badly. Please, don't challenge me on this matter." Sara stayed with her aunt for the next three days and the only thing that made them blissful was talking about Aruba.

Dave was becoming impatient and wanted to wed in the summer, but Sara preferred to finish her master's degree. They compromised on an August wedding in 2023 in order to get the wedding venue they both desired.

Stacey was becoming more involved in Sara's life and was slowly melting down the frozen wall between them. She would text Sara old pictures of her, Eddy and Sara that showed they were an "actual" family when Sara was very young. To see her dad's smile as he was holding her was very heartwarming. Sara even let her mom tag along on some of her wedding planning excursions, but it was Kathy only, when she searched for the perfect gown.

As the trip to Aruba neared, Stacey suggested that she would like to make it a threesome, but Sara only laughed. "Mom, that's our special place…. You wouldn't even like Aruba. It would mess up your hair." Stacey was not happy to be rejected by her daughter. "We need to have our own special place too." Sara bit her tongue and smiled. She was doing that a lot since her mother came back into her life.

A WELCOME SIGHT

This year's trip to paradise was much needed. So much had happened over the past six months and Sara was stressed from school, work, and the wedding. Kathy was still grieving the loss of her brother and was now dealing with Megan's begging for money. Dave was firmly told to stay home and to not surprise his fiancée this year. He was not happy to be excluded and was becoming more jealous of Sara's close relationship with her aunt.

Hans was a welcomed sight, giving them their rental car and they swiftly sped off to their "second home". The eager girls quickly changed into their bikinis and sprinted towards Eagle Beach. As Kathy passed the Water's Edge Bar, she noticed Hank cheerfully standing up and pointing to his now devoid ring finger. She blew him a kiss and kept on going to the palapa. Hank knew better than to crash the girl's traditional first day on the beach and chose not to follow them.

While floating on the calm water, Kathy talked about Hank. "He's not married anymore. I hope Hank doesn't propose again…. I just want to relax and enjoy his company. I don't want to stress over our situation the entire week."

Sara understood and advised her aunt. "We've got an hour until sunset. Why don't you go over to the bar and talk to Hank…. Let him lay his cards on the table before you go crazy worrying about it." Kathy smiled at her niece and before she left, Kathy asked. "How did you get so smart, Kiddo?" Sara giggled, "I've got a brilliant aunt who taught me everything I know."

Hank met Kathy with a kindhearted smile and the two talked for an hour. Kathy opened up her soul to Hank and made him understand that marriage was not an option. He countered with a well thought-out proposal. "I love our time together here and I don't want to chase you away…. How about we pretend that we are in love this one special week for the rest of our lives." Kathy replied, "That sounds like a wonderful idea Hank, except I won't be pretending." She deeply kissed him and sighed, "I gotta go…. I've got a beautiful young lady waiting for me."

Kathy joined Sara in the water and they watched the glowing sun disappear into the ocean. Sara remarked, "It just never gets old" and Kathy chuckled, "Does it ever rain here?" Then she asked Sara for a big favor. "Is it okay with you if I ask Hank to go snorkeling with us? I'd like to spend more time with him on this trip." Sara gave her approval and held Kathy's hand tightly as they left the water. "That's a great idea. I'd really like to get to know him better."

Kathy went to Hank's suite for drinks and a lot of 'hanky panky' while Sara tried to contact Dave without any luck. She enjoyed soaking in the hot tub and thought about her fiancée's immature attitude. "Dave is such a mommy's boy…. He always pouts when he doesn't get his way. Sometimes it's hard to believe that he is a doctor." Sara remembered the warning she received about New Yorkers and giggled to herself while watching the stars appear above her.

FORTY NIGHTS IN ARUBA

Sara awoke to find Kathy absent from her room and decided to go for a run down to La Cabana. She was hoping Todd would run out from the crowd and say hi, but he was nowhere to be found. For the next five days, Sara would make that run in a bikini, hoping to fish out Todd, but he wasn't biting.

Hank and the girls went snorkeling everywhere on the island. He took them on a sunset snorkel on the "Black Pearl" and they had a blast drinking rum punches and eating the best grilled cheese sandwiches in the world. Two nights later, they were on the Jolly Pirates ship, drinking and swinging off a rope into the Caribbean Sea.

Sara grabbed Hank and kissed him on the forehead while laughing hysterically. "Where in the hell have you been for the last eight years…. I'm having so much fun!" Kathy playfully shoved Sara out of the way and warned her niece, "Watch yourself, Kiddo. He's all mine" and then she passionately kissed Hank while Sara videotaped it on her cell phone. Sara took a lot of pictures and videos of the two lovers during the entire trip.

On Thursday afternoon, the three amigos came back from a great snorkel at Tres Trapi and Kathy and Hank decided to "turn in for a nap" so Sara left the lovebirds alone and decided to walk to La Cabana. She walked through all the palapas wearing a bright red string bikini and was propositioned several times, but none of them were Todd. She took her show to the pool bar across the street and still no Todd.

A cute redhead approached her and said, "He's not here." Sara recognized the girl from Chalet Suisse a year ago and the girl curiously asked, "You're looking for my brother, Todd. Right? He didn't come down this year…. My name is Toni. Do you want to have a drink?"

Sara introduced herself and asked if Todd was okay. Toni rolled her eyes and replied, "He's fine other than having a broken heart." Sara asked what happened and Toni laughed. "Come on…. You seriously don't know that you hurt him?" Sara responded, "Me…. What did I do to him? I thought we were friends."

While Sara was defending herself, Toni was scrolling through her picture gallery and then showed Sara her phone. "Does that look like 'friends' to you?" Sara silently viewed several pictures of a man and woman lovingly enjoying each other by the bar. Toni waited until she finished looking at all of the pictures and then continued. "I've never seen my big brother happier the afternoon I took these pictures…. Then you 'crushed' him that night at Chalet Suisse."

Sara remained speechless, still staring at the picture of her, romantically looking into Todd's eyes before she kissed him and then she stuttered out. "I wasn't engaged when I kissed him." Toni chimed in, "Well, you were engaged when you broke his heart.... That's why he's not here." Sara asked Toni, "Could you please text me all of these pictures if I give you my cell phone number?"

Toni reluctantly entered Sara's number into her phone and rudely asked. "What do you want the pictures for? Are you gonna look at them when you need a good laugh? Like the night you screwed his fiancée's brother.... Did anyone ever tell you that you're a bitch!" Sara put her head down and before she walked away, she agreed. "You are so right Toni.... I am a bitch."

The long walk back to Costa Linda was filled with reflection. She cared about Todd, but she was in love with Dave. Sara didn't want to hurt Todd that night and she was honest with him about her engagement.

She saw her aunt and Hank playing in the ocean and took some pictures of the lovers. Sara took many pictures of them together and wanted to surprise Kathy with a photo display for her birthday. She chose not to talk about Todd and let Kathy fully enjoy her last day.

Hank joined the girls for their traditional last dinner at Chalet Suisse. Tonight, Sara dressed conservative and truly enjoyed the company of Hank and Kathy. "I've got to tell you, Hank.... You are a lot more fun than my fiancée. Maybe I should marry you?" Kathy laughed and observed, "Would that make Hank my nephew?"

Through all the laughter, Sara could see a table full of people staring at her and decided to confront them. She confidently approached and greeted the perturbed diners. "Good evening. It seems that your family has the same last night tradition as mine."

No one was impressed with her perky observation, but Sara continued on. "Mr. and Mrs. Powell; I would like to tell you in person what a fine job you did raising Todd and Toni. I had a very insightful conversation with your daughter today…. Please tell Todd that I missed seeing him this year. Have a safe flight home tomorrow."

Sara left the table with no acknowledgement from anyone. She sat back down with Hank and Kathy and collected her thoughts. Soon her phone began to accept many texts and she observed Toni staring at her with a slight smile. Sara waved and mouthed the words "Thank you" in appreciation of receiving those special pictures.

On the flight back home, Kathy was unusually tired. "Hank wore me out on this trip. I can't believe he's ten years older than me. He's like the Energizer Bunny…. He just doesn't stop." Sara agreed. "Hank's twenty-five years older than Dave and he can run circles around him."

After Kathy quickly dozed off, Sara looked through her phone and sadly realized that Dave never phoned or texted her the entire seven days. She knew he was mad about being left out and hoped that he'd get over it. Sara spent the rest of the flight staring at Todd and her together, while trying to sort out her emotions.

LESSONS LEARNED

Dave acted like a spoiled child when Sara returned home. He never asked her about her trip and criticized every move she made for a month. Sara was beginning to have doubts about her future marriage, but was still "possessed" under Dave's magical spell. She pleased him in bed every time he demanded her love and soon, he relaxed his temperament.

By Fall, they were once again enjoying their relationship and looking forward to their future lives together. After celebrating Christmas with Kathy, they spent the rest of their holiday in New York City with Dave's family.

Dave's parents wanted their only son to return to New York City and open a practice in the "Big Apple" so they always pressured Sara to relocate. The wedding was only nine months away and Sara wanted to avoid all confrontations so she just politely considered, "I'll really think about it after the wedding is over."

Dave began debating Sara at home about moving to New York City. "We could make a lot more money if we move there and buy a house in Syosset. My dad can get us both into a wonderful hospital that is located there…. It's a great place to raise our children."

Deep inside her soul, Sara was becoming conflicted. "Is our marriage going to be one of convenience or passion? Am I marrying him just because he's a successful doctor?" She tried to comfort herself by saying, "This is just bridal nerves unleashing before the wedding…. I'll be fine."

Sara was proud of herself for quickly gaining her master's degree in March of 2023 and she now had free time to finish her wedding plans. The venue, caterer, and entertainment were already booked so the last task was, finally, finding the perfect dress.

Sara and Kathy met at Abbott's Bridal Shop for Sara to try on more gowns. After four hours of futile searching, Sara came out in a stunning blush pink gown with a flowing train. Kathy's jaw hit the floor. "That's it…. You look like a fairytale princess!" The two adults began jumping up and down like children. Sara had finally found the perfect dress.

With three months to go, the dress was ready for the final fitting and Sara scheduled it at Kathy's convenience, making sure she would be the first person to see her wear it. She hugged Kathy at the front door and noticed she felt thinner. Sara asked if her aunt was on a diet and Kathy grinned. "It's bikini season in three weeks and I want to look good for Hank." Sara laughed, "If you lose any more weight, that bikini is going to fall off of you."

When Sara came out for Kathy's final approval, her aunt became overwhelmed with emotion. Sara ran to Kathy and kneeled in front of her. "Are you okay, Auntie" and Kathy tearfully pondered, "I wish your father could see you now…. Eddy would've wanted to walk you down the aisle." The Sweeney girls tenderly held each other all the way back to the fitting room.

The week of the Aruba trip, Dave started to become difficult. "Why can't you skip this year? In two months, we are going to be in Hawaii on our honeymoon…. Kathy can go on her own for once. Besides, Hawaii is more beautiful than that desert rock."

Sara's blue eyes turned into a raging ball of flames. "What Did You Say?" Dave saw his soon to be bride's anger and tried to talk his way out of an almost certain death. "I'm sorry. I was way out of line, Babe.... I'm just very nervous about this wedding. We've got a lot of our own money wrapped up in this event."

Sara squeezed Dave and whispered in his ear. "I love you, Dave, but don't challenge me on my ONE WEEK trip with my aunt ever again.... I'm going and you can't stop me." Sara walked past her somber fiancée and into the spare bedroom, locking the door behind her.

ANOTHER WEEK IN PARADISE

Kathy was quiet in her thoughts on the flight down to Aruba and asked Sara, "How about you drive around the island this year Kiddo? It's time you take off the training wheels."

Sara grinned and replied, "That sounds like fun Auntie.... I'll take us through Arikok Park and we'll hang out at that old house I like near Boca dos Playa." Kathy cheerfully warned her niece, "As long as you don't drive us off one of those cliffs."

The first thing Kathy did after they arrived at Costa Linda was to seek out Hank while Sara checked in at the front desk. He saw her approaching the bar and stood to greet her with a warm hug. Kathy cupped his cheeks with her hands and passionately kissed him in front of all his cheering friends at the bar. When she finished, he could barely hear her say, "I Love You Hank" but he saw the serious look in her eyes. He ordered two drinks and took his love to an empty palapa for a romantic talk.

Hank left to check into his room, leaving Kathy alone with her thoughts. She was peacefully watching the waves crash onto the white sandy beach, when Sara arrived enthusiastically wearing a blue string bikini. Kathy looked at her niece and glowed. "My God, Sara. You are such a beautiful woman. How did I get so lucky?"

Sara paused, puzzled by her aunt's compliment and then said, "I brought you down a bathing suit. Why don't you go put it on and we'll watch the sunset in the water." Kathy's face beamed for a long time and finally she agreed. "I'll change in the bathroom next to the bar…. You go down and play in the water and I'll join you there shortly."

Sara ran into the blue sea and began to float past the breaking waves. As she waited for her aunt to join her, Sara thought about the compliment and the strange way Kathy presented it. She hoped that this week would give Kathy the needed rest that she deserved. "I hope Aunt Kathy has a great time with Hank. I know she's looking forward to being with him." And then Sara grinned, "I hope Hank doesn't wear her out again!"

Her daydreaming was cut short when she felt a hug from behind. "Well Kiddo, we've got another week in paradise." Sara happily replied, "It looks like it's going to be another great sunset, Auntie."

The girls were so mesmerized by the sun setting that a rogue wave caught them by surprise and pulled them under. Sara reemerged laughing until she couldn't find her aunt. She panicked and pulled Kathy from under the surf and tried to balance her while Kathy struggled to stand up.

Suddenly two muscular arms wrapped around Kathy's waist and gave her the stability she desperately needed. She looked back at her hero's worried face and giggled, "My Prince Charming has arrived to save me."

Prince Charming looked at Sara as she gratefully thanked him with her magical blue eyes and he asked, "May I join you ladies for sunset?" Kathy happily gave him an invitation. "Todd, Honey…. You can do whatever you want with us ladies." Kathy then enjoyed the sunset exploding into a flaming orange sky as Todd and Sara remained by her side.

Kathy apologized for scaring her niece and Todd on their walk back to the palapa. "I'm sorry guys. I drank way too much on an empty stomach and got super tipsy out there…. If you will excuse me, I think I'm going to get some much needed rest. Please tell Hank that I'll see him tomorrow."

Soon after Kathy left, Sara forced herself into Todd's arms and passionately kissed him. Todd gently laid her on the sand as their tongues slowly danced inside each other's mouths. Todd pulled away to gaze into her eyes and run his fingers through her soft long hair. Sara's heart was pounding like it had never done before and she begged for Todd to make love to her in the ocean. "Please. Nobody will see us…. Nobody will know. I want you…. I've always wanted you!"

Todd realized that he was making a big mistake, so he threw cold water on the torrid fire. "I'm not taking advantage of you tonight, Sara. You're in a vulnerable state of mind…. Besides, you've still got that rock on your finger."

Sara was very disappointed and pouted, "I don't get you Todd Powell…. First you rejected me because I was underage, then you ignored me when you were engaged, and now you won't make love to me because I'm engaged. What in the hell is your problem!"

Todd stepped back and tried to calm her down. "My problem is that I'm in love with a woman I can't have…. You and I have been on different pages since we met and I'm always one step behind. If I would have been your first love nine years ago, would you have respected me today?" I would rather you respect me than love me for the wrong reasons."

Sara became clear minded and agreed with Todd, but asked, "Why were you here tonight?" Todd wasted no time to answer. "I wanted to see if you were still engaged and take some pictures of you and your aunt at sunset. Toni told me that you really liked the other ones I took…. I guess I was hoping I still had a chance with you."

Sara embraced him in a friendly manner. "Thank God you were here tonight. I couldn't get her to stand up and if she would have drowned in my arms, I would have killed myself…. Thank you, Todd, for saving her…. Thank you for being my friend."

Todd walked Sara back to the elevator, and she confessed to him. "I've never seen my aunt act that way in the water. She's an excellent swimmer…. It just doesn't make sense that she was drunk." Her eyes twinkled at Todd as she said goodnight. "You're my Aunt Kathy's Prince Charming…. You're my Prince Charming." Todd took her hand and kissed it softly. "You'll always be my Cinderella."

Sara's mind was traveling a million different ways. She went to get advice from Kathy, but she was sleeping soundly so Sara decided to wait until morning.

Sara decided to run on the walking path early on Saturday, trying to avoid Todd as she sorted last night out in her head. "I was overcome with gratitude towards him for saving Kathy's life. I had a weak moment…. This wedding is putting too much tension on my relationship with Dave…. Am I truly in love with him or do I just want to make him happy?" The morning run did little to replenish Sara's confidence in her future life with her "one and only".

Upon her return to their suite, Sara noticed that Kathy was still asleep. Her aunt's phone began to ring and she answered it quickly before Kathy awoke. It was Hank, wanting to know where Kathy was and the two gabbed while Sara sat on a balcony chair, enjoying the million dollar view. "She's still asleep, Hank. Auntie has been super stressed lately and you're all she has been talking about for months."

Hank was so relieved to hear that. "I was worried about her. She was supposed to come over for drinks last night, but she never showed. I called twice, but she didn't answer…. Kathy was so serious when I first saw her yesterday at the bar. I was beginning to think that she was coming here this year to break up with me." Sara reassured him. "Kathy is totally in love with you, Hank."

After her phone conversation ended, Sara checked a new text sent to Kathy while she was sleeping. She was so lost in disbelief while reading it that Sara failed to hear her aunt join her on the balcony. Kathy lovingly put her hands on both of Sara's shoulders and asked, "Is that from the hospital, Sweety?"

Sara stared at the blue ocean, unable to speak and Kathy revealed, "I'm sick, Sara. I just found out earlier this week. I didn't know how to tell you so I'm relieved that you read it first. I was going to tell you down here after we arrived.... The doctors advised me to not travel, but no one was going to cheat me out of my week here with you and Hank."

Sara put her head down and began to softly weep as Kathy continued, "The doctors have a plan and I'm going to beat this disease and we'll be laughing about it in no time. Sara broke her silence and asked, "What kind is it?" Kathy countered, "Does it matter?" Sara began crying harder. "WHAT KIND IS IT?"

Kathy now stood in front of Sara and kneeled to see the devastation in her niece's eyes. She held Sara by her hands and confessed. "I have Pancreatic Cancer, but I'm going to beat it. I prom...." Sara broke her aunt's grip and ran into her room, hysterically sobbing, "NO. NO. NOOOO!"

Kathy sat down on the warm chair and cried herself empty. She knew that she had to be strong for Sara. After twenty minutes of soul searching, Kathy joined her grief stricken niece in her room.

Sara's head was buried into a pillow, allowing her to quietly cry her tears of sorrow. Kathy breathed deeply and then forcibly rolled Sara over. She kneeled over top of Sara and commanded, "Sara Sweeney. Look at me! I'm still here and I've got no plans of leaving you…. You've got to be strong, Sara." Kathy hugged her niece and promised to never let go.

When they both calmed their emotions, Kathy explained her sad story. "Around Easter, I started to lose my appetite and food felt funny settling in my stomach. I started to lose weight around the time of your bridal sessions, but didn't think much about it. About three weeks ago, I started getting pains in my abdomen so I went to my doctor and he referred me to the Cleveland Clinic. They were really good to me and quickly discovered that I had cancer. I put off surgery until our trip was over…. I'm scheduled for surgery the Friday after we get home."

Sara regained her poise and told her aunt. "I can't lose you and I'm NOT going to lose you…. We're going to fight this battle together. We'll beat this cancer, Auntie. I promise you."

Kathy serenely smiled at her caring niece and asked for a favor. "Sweety, I desperately need your help this week. Last night in the water proved that I no longer can function free spirited…. I love you more than anything, but I'm truly in love with Hank and I want our time together this year to be perfect."

Sara handed her a hankie and they both wiped the tears from their eyes as Kathy continued. "Hank cannot know about our secret. I don't want his pity; I want his love…. I need you to protect our secret from him anyway possible. When I grow weak, you need to create a diversion and when I lie to him, you need to support the lie with your beautiful smile. I know I can do everything physically, but just in moderation. It will mean the world to me if you will be my partner in crime for the next six days."

Sara embraced Kathy tightly and sighed. "I'll do anything you want me to do this week, Auntie." Kathy's cell phone began to ring and she snickered, "And so, the lying begins…. Hello Hank. Where are we snorkeling today?" Sara could hear Hank say, "How about Mangel Halto" and Kathy replied, "Meet us out in the lobby in twenty minutes." Sara got everything ready while Kathy got dressed.

The snorkelers were enjoying some fun conversation during the drive to Savaneta, when Hank asked, "Who's the guy, Sara? I came down to get your aunt after sunset and you were rolling around on the sand with him."

Kathy turned around and big eyed her blushing niece who was sitting uncomfortably in the backseat. "Just a guy that I've known down here for a while." Hank countered, "Is that the same guy that didn't show up last year because he was in love with you?" Sara's silence most definitely answered Hank's question.

Sara knew the location of Mangel Halto's reef and was determined to give her aunt the easiest route there so she made a bet with Hank. "I'll bet you dinner tonight that we can beat you to the reef. We'll leave from the beach and you leave from the pier. Hank eagerly agreed. "We're going to El Gaucho's tonight and you're buying, Missy!"

The diversion gave Sara the time to get Kathy comfortably into the water. Sara knew that it was an easy swim to the barrier and then they would use the current to float to the reef. Hank had to swim harder to join them, but was the first one there as the girls took their time. Kathy was grateful for the detour and held Hank's hand as they explored the colorful fish swimming around the reef.

Sara's eyes were always on her aunt and when Kathy started to struggle, Sara signaled the two lovers. "I've got a bad leg cramp and I need to go to the beach immediately." Kathy took Sara's lead and instructed, "I'll follow Sara to the mangroves. You get the car, Hank, and meet us at the entrance."

Sara helped Kathy to the beach and she laid there in exhaustion. When she finally caught her breath, Kathy had a devilish grin on her face. "It didn't take you long to become a good liar, Kiddo."

For the next five days, Sara made sure their secret was safe and Kathy was enjoying herself. She plotted ahead on all the excursions, making sure her aunt was comfortable doing them. When Kathy was tired, Sara would tell Hank that they were going shopping, and then she watched over her bed as her aunt slept.

Sara would run in the early morning before she helped Kathy prepare for another adventurous day and at night when two lovers were together. The running kept her sane and focused. And her focus was on Kathy and nobody else.

Kathy desired to be alone with Hank for a romantic sunset dinner at Passions On The Beach. Sara wanted to surprise them by taking some romantic pictures, so she walked down to Amsterdam Manor and hid in a palapa, waiting for sunset. Suddenly a voice advised her, "If you want a perfect sunset picture of them, take your pictures now while the sun is glowing behind their table." Sara smiled and said, "Thanks, Todd" and the two quickly rushed to get the perfect picture.

Sara waved at Kathy and asked her and Hank to pose for the camera. After Sara and Todd pretended to be paparazzi, Kathy made a strange request. "Hurry, I want a picture of you two in front of our table." Todd instantly captured the beauty of the aunt and niece, holding each other at sunset and then he joined Sara at the table. Kathy positioned the young couple and demanded that Todd put his arm around her niece.

After Kathy finished taking her pictures, Todd and Sara moved closer to the water and watched the sky burst with orange and red throughout it. Kathy finally put her phone down and held Hank's hand as she watched her niece put her head on Todd's shoulder. Kathy looked into Hank's eyes and tearfully pondered. "That should have been us twenty-five years ago…. I love you, Hank."

Todd offered to walk Sara back to Costa Linda and she accepted. She apologized for not seeking him out this week. "I don't want you to think that I was avoiding you…. I've had a lot on my mind and this week has been a challenge. Todd stopped her and asked, "She's sick. Isn't she?"

Sara's chin was quivering and she pulled him close to her and answered, "YES." Tears that were suppressed for a week now rained out of her eyes. Todd held her tightly and then sat them both on the soft white sand and she begged him. "Please, you can't tell anyone about this…. Hank doesn't know and it would kill her if he found out…. Please Todd, I promised her." They continued to embrace each other while silently listening to the waves crash into the darkness of their future.

The last full day, the girls and Hank hung around the pool and Eagle Beach. Kathy camouflaged her illness by sleeping most of the afternoon under the shade of their palapa. Sara used up her last trick on Hank. "WOW. You must have worn Aunt Kathy out last night!"

Sara and Hank had a long talk about Kathy and what a wonderful woman she was. Hank said the biggest regret in his life was not meeting her when he was a young man. Sara added, "I've never seen my aunt so in love with a man." They both enjoyed each other's company and were becoming close friends.

Their traditional last night dinner at Chalet Suisse was a very special one for Kathy. They were again seated within viewing distance of the Powell family and Sara and Todd were gazing at each other like lovesick puppies.

Kathy was watching her niece and said, "I've had enough of this" and she went over to the Powell table and introduced herself. "Hello. My name is Kathy Sweeney. I'm Sara's aunt and I wanted to tell you both what a brave man your son is. He saved me from drowning last week and I would like it if you joined us for dinner…. On me." Mr. Powell thanked her for the compliment, but declined the dinner invitation.

Kathy concluded, "Goodnight" and turned to leave. Before she made a step, she felt a strong arm interlock with hers and Todd politely escorted her back to their table. He asked, "May I sit next to you Miss Sweeney" and Sara cutely answered, "I would truly love that Mr. Powell."

While they were all laughing, Todd's sister, Toni came over and asked, "Can I sit with you guys too?" Kathy remarked, "You're very welcome, young lady, but I think you two are going to be flying home on different airplanes than your parents."

The five diners chatted and chuckled the whole night. They all saluted the week's end with raspberry cosmopolitans and Hot Framboise Kisses. Kathy paid the bill and then she gave Joaquin a big hug. "You've always treated us so well here…. I remember the first time we dined here without a reservation and Benny got us right in. Thanks for everything."

Hank suggested a group walk along the beach, but Toni looked at her brother and declined. As they arrived back at Costa Linda, the two couples soon separated. Todd dragged two beach chairs to the water's edge and the two had a romantic chat as the waves crashed in front of them.

Sara was done flirting and shyly asked, "Are we ever going to make love?" Todd sighed, still staring into the roaring darkness. "You and I are strangers in the real world. I've known you for nine years and I don't even know what you do for a living…. We come to Aruba at the same time every year and enjoy each other's company…. Then we leave paradise after one week and I wait for another year to see your smiling face."

Sara began to realize the cold hard facts of their relationship as Todd continued. "I'm very much in love with you, Sara…. Since the day you seduced me near Alto Vista, I've dreamed of making love to you, but now I realize that I can't have you…. I don't want to stay up at night remembering a one night stand, so my dream will remain locked inside my mind and deeply inside my heart."

Sara listened intently to every word and sadly agreed. "You are always on my mind when I daydream of this magical island and I will always respect you as a man. I care so much about you…. Please remember that…. Please remember me." Todd held her hand, still staring into the darkness and asked his one true love, "How can I ever forget you, Sara Sweeney?"

Todd quickly got up and began to drag both chairs back to the palapa. Sara thanked him again for saving her aunt's life and for keeping the "secret" safe. Todd handed her a piece of paper that he had been saving. "They are doing great work in Mexico and their research might help Aunt Kathy. This is the phone number of a very good friend of mine. Feel free to use my name if you desire to call him."

Sara looked deep into his eyes and kissed him softly and gratefully whispered, "Thank you, Todd." He held her tightly and then passionately kissed her willing lips. His eyes twinkled as he said, "I'll see you next year" and then she watched him fade away into the darkness of the night.

Sara awoke on "travel day" to find Kathy not in her room and began to panic when Hank said she was not with him. Sara ran down to the beach to find her aunt peacefully gazing out at the distant horizon.

Sara quietly sat next to her aunt and Kathy reached out for her niece's hand. "You know Kiddo, we found a hidden gem here nine years ago.... I told Hank last night that I regret not accepting his marriage proposal and then we made love.... I sincerely hope to see him again next year." Sara squeezed Kathy's hand and reassured her, "You'll see him again. I promise."

It was a very hectic day at the airport departure terminal, and that took a heavy toll on Kathy. Sara handled the luggage transfers, but it was three hours of standing that wore her aunt down. Sara supported Kathy as they boarded the plane and Kathy slept the entire trip home. Sara was too busy writing down notes and questions to reflect on her trip. She was now focused on her aunt's health; Aruba and Todd were now distant memories.

STRUGGLING TIMES

Sara wasted no time telling Dave the bad news. She sadly detailed everything she knew as he patiently listened to her and then Sara revealed her plan. "I love you, Dave, but my Aunt Kathy means more to me than anyone else in the world. She raised me to be the woman I am today and I am not going to desert Auntie in her time of need."

Sara asked her fiancée the biggest request of her young life. "I am going to postpone the wedding until next year. I can't be a happy newlywed until Kathy is healthy and watching me walk down the aisle."

Dave sat in stunned silence as Sara continued. "I will contact everyone involved with the wedding and explain my situation to them. The invitations have not been sent out and we never finalized with the caterer. I'm sure I can move the honeymoon trip back a year.... Please, Sweetheart, I need your support now more than ever."

Dave broke his silence and expressed his opinion. "We can still get married and help your aunt out at the same time. I have a lot of connections that can be of aide to her.... My parents won't be happy about this and we could potentially forfeit a lot of money on deposits. Let's 'sleep' on this for a month until we know more about your aunt's condition.... Cleveland Clinic may have misdiagnosed her and she might not be that bad."

A controlled fire began to burn inside Sara. "Not bad? You're a doctor. Would you tell one of your patients that Stage One Pancreatic Cancer was not bad?" Dave fueled the fire. "You're jumping the gun on this whole affair, Sara. We need to wait."

She quickly replied, "I'm not waiting for anything.... I canceled the wedding venue earlier this morning, and they were very understanding. They charged my credit card a ten percent penalty so you won't be out a single cent.... The wedding is officially postponed."

Dave became irate and asked, "Don't I have a say in my own wedding? Who are you to control everything?" Sara sharply answered back, "I'm Kathy Sweeney's niece and NO.... You don't have a say in the matter." Dave stormed out of the house and yelled, "Nice to have you home, Sara!" She was very disappointed in Dave's demeanor, but was determined to take care of Kathy first and hoped Dave would soon come around.

By the day of the surgery, Sara was a ball of nerves. She took Kathy to her doctor appointments and blood tests, but her worries were now getting the best of her. Dave was of no comfort as he silently ignored her despair. Kathy was worried more about

Sara than herself and always put on a "smiling" face for her niece. When she was going into surgery, Kathy grinned and told Sara, "I'll see you in a couple hours, Sweety." Sara held her breath for the next three hours.

As the doctor approached her with post-op information, Sara started to cry. She saw the same look in his eyes that she saw daily while comforting the loved ones of Covid victims. She put her head down as the doctor confirmed the devastating news. He told her that the tumor was removed, but the cancer had spread. She breathed deeply and asked, "What are her options?" The doctor was very vague, saying that they would discuss that very soon.

When Kathy awoke, Sara was looking down upon her and holding her hand. She asked her niece how the surgery went and Sara answered, "It went fine; they got the tumor removed and will tell us what our next move will be in a few days."

Kathy watched her niece's bloodshot eyes and quivering jaw. She thought of Hank and Aruba when she noted, "You're becoming a very good liar, Kiddo." Sara squeezed her hand tightly and reassured her aunt, "I made you a promise and I'm keeping it."

Sara was in denial as the doctor painted the gloomy picture the next day. "We need to start radiation treatments as soon as your body has recovered from the surgery. We can do it as an outpatient or we can admit you into our cancer wing." Sara interrupted the doctor and announced, "I'm moving back in with her so we can arrange the treatments accordingly." Kathy looked into Sara's eyes and said "NO," but Sara stubbornly told her aunt. "I owe you the world.... It's time I start paying you back."

Sara urgently needed Dave's approval, so she planned a very romantic dinner to surprise him when he came home on Saturday. He was thrilled to see his fiancée in a sexy night gown serving his favorite dishes. "Is this what I have to look forward to when we're married?" As he was sipping his favorite pinot grigio after dinner, Dave remarked, "Fabulous food, Babe. What's for dessert?"

Sara shyly sighed "Me" and walked into the bedroom. Dave quickly drank his wine and ran in behind her to satisfy his sweet tooth and he was very hungry.

The couple spent the entire weekend trying to rekindle their love affair and Sara pleased Dave in so many ways. She was growing uncomfortable knowing that she had to "work" at being in love with Dave and knew the relationship was becoming unhealthy. Her focus was no longer on her cloudy future; it was on the present with her aunt. Kathy was soon to be discharged from the hospital and Sara knew she had to reveal her future plan to Dave quickly, not knowing how he would take it.

On Monday night, Sara laid her cards on the table and asked Dave for his support. "Honey, Kathy's getting out of the hospital on Wednesday, and she's going to struggle to take care of herself after receiving the radiation treatments. I can't juggle work, homelife, and taking care of her, so I've decided to move in with Kathy until this is all over.

At first Dave was upset. "Come on Sara. What about us? What about me? I get so tired of playing second fiddle to your aunt. I love you and I need you…. I'm so jealous of her."

Sara chose not to confront Dave and gently tried to persuade him by uncertain promises. "I love you very much, but my Aunt Kathy has very little time left…. You and I have a lifetime together." Dave toned down his attitude and supported her decision. "I'm sorry. I just don't like being away from you…. We'll make it work, somehow." Sara was content with his answer and could now focus on fulfilling her promise to her aunt.

Kathy was in Stage Two of her cancer when she began her radiation treatments in August. She was still recovering from her surgery, but the doctors felt she needed the treatments as soon as possible. Sara worked the daylight shift while home health care attended to her aunt and she took care of her the rest of the day. The two Sweeney girls would talk about their lives together frequently, and when Kathy slept, Sara searched the internet for a miracle.

HAIL MARY

Sara decided to call Franco Cortez in Mexico. He was Todd's friend who had research knowledge that she desperately needed. She called the number given to her and left her name and contact number on his voice mail and mentioned Todd's name. The next day she received a phone call from Oasis of Hope Hospital in Mexico.

"Hello Sara. My name is Doctor Franco Cortez from Oasis of Hope. I've been expecting your call. Todd Powell called me a month ago about your situation. Todd is 'my man' and I owe him dearly and he called in his 'favor' on your behalf…. What can I do to help you?"

Sara felt so relieved and told Doctor Cortez everything she knew about Kathy's case. After she finished her story, Doctor Cortez explained. "I will call Cleveland Clinic myself and request all of your aunt's charts. I know of Doctor Acierno and I'm sure he will comply with my wishes. Your aunt will have to sign a release form and then I will thoroughly look over her files." Sara thanked him at least ten times and told

Doctor Cortez that she would patiently wait for his call.

As soon as she disconnected, Sara found Todd's contact number in her cell phone and her heart stopped. She was so distracted that she didn't take the time to view the pictures that he sent her a few weeks ago. Sara never knew that he took a picture of Kathy and her gazing into each other's eyes at Passions restaurant.

She began to release six weeks of emotions and Kathy heard her crying. She came into the living room, asking Sara what was wrong and she answered her aunt, "Todd took this picture of us while we weren't looking." Kathy sat in silence and stared forever at the love of the aunt and niece captured by one picture. She finally looked at Sara and remarked, "That's the best picture that I've ever seen in my life." Sara, still sobbing, nodded her head up and down in agreement.

After Kathy fell asleep, Sara texted Todd a long romantic message and expressed her feelings for him, but remembered their talk on the beach and deleted it. Instead, she typed, "Thank you for caring about us, My Prince Charming" with six pink hearts attached to it. Thinking of Todd put a pleasant smile on her face and she fell asleep, knowing that he still "remembered" her.

Two days later Sara received a phone call from Mexico while working and she excused herself from the nurse's station to take the private call. She held her breath and listened to Doctor Cortez's prognosis. "I've talked to Doctor Acierno and we have agreed on how to attack your aunt's cancer. Kathy is going to be treated with Chemo Immuno Precision Injections, instead of radiation. Hopefully we will see some early positive results." Sara knew a little about the CIPI procedure and asked what Kathy's chances were.

There was a long pause on the phone and then Doctor Cortez delivered the troubling news. "Your Aunt Kathy has jumped into Stage Three of her type of cancer and it's quickly spreading to her other organs. We're hoping the CIPI treatments will slow down the cancer and help ease her pain. If I could treat her in Mexico, the outcome would still be the same. Pancreatic cancer is a very deadly disease, Sara…. I'm sorry to tell you that she has only six months at the most."

Sara sadly whispered, "Thank you for your help, Doctor Cortez" and sat down in disbelief. The last six months had been a roller coaster ride and now the roller coaster had flown off the track. Her faith was shattered as she thought, "This cannot be happening. Kathy is just a good person and God picks her…. Why?"

Sara asked to leave work early and went to tell Dave before she faced Kathy with the bad news. She went over to his house and he wasn't there so she called him and asked, "Where are you? I thought you were off today. I need to talk to you.... Please, can you come home?"

Dave answered with little emotion. "Sorry, Babe. I got called out and I can't get home for at least three hours.... I love you and I'll call you tonight." Sara felt so alone, and nobody was in her "corner" except her dying aunt and a man she meets once a year.

The drive back home felt like she was walking in the desert, desperately trying to find salvation. "How am I going to tell her? I can't believe this is happening." She cleared her troubling thoughts and tried to be strong for her aunt. "I want her to hear it from me, but what am I going to say?"

Kathy was awake when she arrived home and was eating some cottage cheese. Her appetite was slowly diminishing and she was losing more weight. The color of her once rosy face was changing to a shade of blond, but she was still smiling for her niece. "Bad day at work, Kiddo? Sit down and I'll make you some homemade cottage cheese." Sara and Kathy had a good chuckle; she always knew how to make her niece feel content and forget about her problems.

Tonight was not a good night to tell her and Kathy soon fell asleep on the couch. Sara knew that she had only two days left to tell her aunt before the treatments started so time was running out on her silence. She was looking forward to talking to her fiancée and getting some needed support and advice, but his call never came that night. Sara was very disappointed, but she realized how busy one gets working at a hospital as the work piles on. "I hope Dave calls me tomorrow."

Sara tried to unclutter her worried mind by studying her notes taken from her conversation with Doctor Cortez and learning more about the CIPI treatments. She googled his name and it confirmed his worldwide expertise in cancer research and she wondered why Todd's name unlocked the door to his help. "Who is this guy that I see once a year?"

Sara saw that Todd texted her back with one pink heart and she snickered thinking, "Boy.... Only one heart. I must not rank very high with him." She then googled his name and was "floored" to find out that her annual beach friend was a rising star in Orthopedic Surgery at Buffalo General Hospital. Sara was fascinated and read everything she could about him. He specialized in hand surgery and was one of the youngest doctors to reside at that prestigious hospital.

It was late and the wine bottle was now empty and that gave Sara the courage to text Todd. "Why didn't you make love to me? I wanted you inside me so many times and you were always a GENTLEMAN.... I wish you were like all the other guys."

Sara accidently hit send and was horrified to actually read the text and its contents, so she recklessly sent him another text. "Sorry. I'm very drunk and didn't mean what I said. Please disregard that message." Her eyes became blurry and she fell asleep next to her aunt.

Sara awoke late the next day and rushed to work. She had no makeup on and her hair was a mess. She saw her reflection in her review mirror and she looked "plain". The last two months had taken a toll on her. She was no longer running and was not eating properly. She looked more like forty than twenty-four and she didn't really care that her beauty was fading away. Kathy was the only thing on her mind.

Before lunch, Sara received an unexpected visitor. "What are you doing here, Stacey?" Her mother replied. "I just came to check on you. I know that Kathy has been sick and you are upset about it.... Would you like to join me for lunch?"

Sara rejected her offer and asked, "Why would you care about Kathy? That's not in your

DNA." Stacey became emotional. "I know I haven't been much of a mother to you, but I'd like to be your friend…. If you want me?" Sara let down her defenses and answered her mother. "I would love to have a friend right now…. I'll grab a quick bite with you."

Stacey listened patiently as Sara expressed all of her worries and fears. "I love Dave, but he's been of no help and sometimes I think he doesn't even care anymore. You know how I feel about Aunt Kathy and you know that I will never leave her to fight this alone. I wish he could understand that he's only making things worse."

Stacey sadly agreed with her daughter. "You need to be strong for Kathy. She and I have never seen eye to eye, but she will always be my sister-in-law and I do still have feelings for her. Stay with her and don't worry about Dave's feelings. He'll get over it soon enough."

Sara was so relieved and hugged her mother before she returned to the hospital. "Thanks, Mom, for hearing me out. I'm happy that you understand…. We need to do lunch again soon." Stacey replied, "I'd really like that. How about next week; same time and place? Call me if you need to talk to someone."

Sara kissed her mom on the cheek and replied, "I'd love to spend more time with you." Sara thought about her mother and her surprising compassion the rest of the afternoon. She hoped it was genuine and cautiously wanted Stacey to be back in her life. Sara needed a friend.

Sara left from work early again to have the dreaded conversation with her aunt. After the caregiver left, Sara asked Kathy to sit with her. "I'm not going to beat around the bush, Auntie.... I talked to Doctor Acierno and he said that they are going to start aggressive Chemo on you tomorrow. It's a 'Hail Mary' treatment that will prolong your life, but the medicine will take a heavy toll on you physically. I promise that I'll be right next to you for the whole process.... Please don't give up. I'm not going to.... Let's fight this together." Kathy smiled and told her niece. "We can't lose as long as we stick together."

REFLECTION

Summer turned into fall as Kathy struggled to live her life. It hurt her deeply to be away from Malone University and all her friends there, but they kept in contact to help keep her spirits high. She was suffering from reactions to the Chemo injections and had great abdominal pain that she hid from Sara.

Kathy knew Sara was wearing down from worrying nonstop about her and feared that she would have an emotional breakdown. Kathy decided to hire a full-time nurse so Sara could spend more time with Dave. Sara fought her on the idea, but the two women eventually compromised. Sara would stay with her aunt through the week and spend the weekends with her fiancée.

Dave was pleased that Sara was back, but was not happy about her weight gain. After a session of much needed sex ended, Sara cuddled tightly next to her lover. He embarrassed her by uttering out, "You're getting soft, Babe. I hope you'll still fit into your wedding gown by next August."

Sara politely defended herself. "Sorry Honey…. I quit my running to take care of Kathy. I'll start back up again real soon." Dave agreed, "That's a great idea…. Hit the road and sweat off ten pounds. I love to feel that tight body against mine."

When Dave awoke the next morning, Sara was gone. Dave was happy to read the note that said she was off for a morning run, but was very upset when she came back five hours later. "Where in the hell have you been?"

Sara sarcastically answered, "I've been running all morning, trying to sweat off that ten pounds, so you won't be ashamed of making love to a fat chick anymore." She was deeply hurt by his comment last night, but was grateful he said it. Running was a wonderful escape for Sara throughout her entire life and she never realized how much she missed it until that morning. Dave hugged her and apologized for the insensitive comment, but she just smiled and thanked him. "I'll be ten pounds lighter in two weeks."

Kathy was happy that Stacey was spending more time with her daughter. Kathy knew that Stacey needed to finally step up for Sara and fill the role that she could no longer play. She was never jealous of Stacey and actually felt sorry for her because Stacey missed out on watching her baby become a beautiful woman. Kathy prayed now that Stacey would watch and learn from Sara when she became a mother. "I just wished I could have seen her first baby born."

The treatments were only prolonging the inevitable and Sara was determined to make her aunt's last few months more enjoyable. She would take Kathy outside for a stroll in her wheelchair in fair weather. They would laugh and talk about the old times, never mentioning the darkness that was waiting for them. They were both at peace with the fact that Sara wouldn't be able to keep her promise. At night Sara would read her aunt's favorite poetry to her and Kathy would absorb her niece's words until she fell asleep. They cherished every last second together.

Kathy loved the holidays and Halloween was her favorite. Sara asked all of Kathy's friend's to surprise her aunt, by trick or treating her on Halloween night. Sara wrapped Kathy in a coat and blanket and wheeled her out on the porch to receive the children and pass out the candy.

Soon after the kids thinned out, a group of adults in costume ranging from the "Tin Man" to "Red Riding Hood" began to show up, requesting wine from the "Queen" of the household. Kathy was so elated to see her friends from Malone and she enjoyed the wonderful conversations of their lives together over a glass of wine. Kathy laughed hysterically when Stacey showed up, dressed as Marilyn Monroe. "You just don't ever give up.... Do you Stacey?"

Sara took a few pictures and then put her phone down to remember this moment in her mind. She watched as Kathy's friends honored her with admiration and kindness. Sara began to get emotional when she saw that famous sparkle shine once again in her Auntie's eyes. Kathy looked over at her niece and lovingly smiled, mouthing the words, "Thank You.... I Love You." Sara blew her a kiss and then left the room so her expected tears would not ruin the festive occasion.

After the party was over and Kathy was fast asleep, Sara tried to phone Dave and tell him how everything went, but he must have been sleeping after working a double at the hospital. She was disappointed in him for always avoiding her aunt. Sara always knew of Dave's jealousy towards Kathy and he distanced himself from her aunt ever since he surprised them both in Aruba.

Sara spent the next two months working continuously to satisfy Dave and Kathy. She ran every day to enjoy the silence of reality and it helped maintain her focus. The treatments continued, but Kathy's body was in decline. She could only eat mashed food and was no longer able to enjoy the outdoors in her wheelchair. Sara put up the Christmas tree after a sad Thanksgiving, knowing that it would be Kathy's last.

The Mercy Hospital Christmas party was being held on a Thursday and Sara decided not to go, but Kathy begged her niece to attend it with Dave. "Please Sweety, go and have some fun with your fiancée…. I'll be fine with a caregiver."

Sara finally gave in and told Dave that she would meet him at the formal function. She was looking forward to a fun night and rushed to his house to shower and dress. Sara opened their closet to look for her long red velvet gown that would be appropriate for a Christmas function.

As she was reaching for the gown, Sara glimpsed down to see a green nighty lying in the corner of the closet. "I don't have a green teddy?" She picked up the stained garment and examined it as her mind was moving at light speed. "What in the hell.... That son of a bitch.... So, he wants to play games.... I can play games too!"

She made a wardrobe switch to a more suitable outfit and drove to the function. Sara was furious with Dave, but took a deep breath and thought about her aunt. "There's no way that I'm going to upset Kathy right before her last Christmas. She cannot know about this."

As soon as Sara entered the hall, she saw her fiancée flirting closely with a very attractive brunette. She watched as Dave giggled and showed off like a schoolboy. "He seems to be enjoying himself.... I don't think he's going to be smiling in a few minutes." Sara went to check her winter coat and then strolled to the bar for a martini.

Dave was telling his woman companion a stale joke when he noticed a crowd forming by the bar. He began to awkwardly stare at a woman completely surrounded by a circle of men and he thought to himself, "Damn. I need to meet this chick before Sara comes." He excused himself to get more cocktails and confidently approached the bar. "She's half naked and what an ass on her." His cockiness quickly turned into horror as he entered the circle.

The CEO of Mercy announced Dave. "There's the man of the hour. We've been gabbing with your future wife.... I didn't know Sara had a master's degree. You're a very lucky man, Dave.... A VERY lucky man." Dave nervously agreed with his boss. "I know that I'm a lucky man. Sara tells me that every night…. I'm going to steal her away from you for a dance." All Sara's admirers watched her walk away in a white see through mini skirt that left nothing for the imagination.

The music was fast paced, but Dave pulled her close to him as if it were a slow dance. Everyone was watching Sara dance with her red-faced partner. Dave's teeth were grinning tightly when he quietly expressed his concern. "What are you doing Sara? Why are you dressed like that? That's the CEO and the whole goddamn board of directors you were teasing…. What are you trying to prove?"

Sara acted confused and shyly gushed to her fiancée. "I wanted to wear something sexy to show off that ten pounds I lost because of your support. I desire to be with you tonight, Honey."

Suddenly the brunette from earlier tapped on Dave's shoulder and he nervously told her. "I'm sorry, but I can't dance with you Elaine. This is my fiancée, Sara Sweeney. She's a nurse here at Mercy…. Elaine works with me, Dear…. In the lab department."

Elaine smiled at Sara, ignoring Dave and said, "I'm sorry, Dave. You misunderstood me. I don't want to dance with you…. I want to dance with your fiancée. Shall we?" Sara exchanged Dave's hand with Elaine's and accepted. "I would love to dance with you." As the two gorgeous women giggled while tightly holding each other, every man and woman were taking pictures and videos. Everyone but Dave. For the rest of the night, Sara's dance card was full.

Once the silent couple returned home, Dave read Sara the riot act. "I have never been so embarrassed in my life. You acted like a whore tonight.... You probably ruined any chances of me being promoted. I hope you're satisfied."

Sara wept fake tears. "I'm sorry, Honey, but I wanted you to make passionate love to me tonight and that was the only way to get your attention.... Why don't you take off all of your clothes and join me in the bedroom? I have a surprise for you."

When Dave joined Sara, she was wearing the green nighty that she found and Dave got a very disturbed look on his face. Sara lustfully pondered, "I found this teddy on the floor in our closet.... I forgot all about having it. I thought you wanted me to wear it tonight and that's what made me so 'horny' at the party." Sara laid on top of the stunned Dave and rocked him aggressively while never taking off the green nighty.

Dave awoke the next morning to the smell of bacon cooking and went into the kitchen to investigate. He saw Sara making breakfast and grinned, knowing that she was ignorant to the "real" owner of the green nighty. "What's yah cooking,

Babe?" Sara looked back at him and cheerfully said, "Omelets. I'm starved after you wore me out last night. Come and sit with me." They had a nice conversation about their upcoming trip to New York City and Dave was looking forward to spending New Year's Eve with his family.

Sara left after breakfast to go for a long run and clear her head. She saw the look on his face when she was wearing the green nighty last night and knew Dave was cheating on her. The most disturbing thing about his affair was that Sara didn't care. Dave was a good looking man, but he was looking "uglier" by the minute to her. She was determined to play his game until Kathy had passed to avoid all the soap opera drama. Sara was too devoted to her aunt to worry about Dave anymore.

Sara spent Christmas Eve alone with Kathy and they enjoyed a long chat. Sara brought in her traditional glass of eggnog with a touch of brandy in it. "Drink it slowly Auntie, I don't want you passing out on me." Kathy just laughed. "Just put a little eggnog in a glass of brandy for the next round." They were making the best of a sad situation and they were doing it together. Kathy demanded. "No tears tonight!"

Dave was supposed to join them on Christmas morning, but he was "unexpectedly" called out to cover a shift and couldn't make it. Sara told Kathy about him not coming and she observed, "Dave sure does work a lot of overtime." Sara was upset to be slighted again, but didn't want to talk about it on this very special day and quietly agreed. "He sure does like to work."

Sara sat on the couch and gave Kathy her Christmas present. "I know we said no presents this year, but I just had to get you this gift. I'm anxious to see your face when you open it." Kathy tore through the wrapping and stopped to stare at the scrapbook with the picture of Hank and her on the cover.

Sara sat close to her aunt and turned the pages as Kathy silently admired each picture that her niece had taken of the couple through the years. Kathy broke her silence while looking at an earlier picture of them from 2015. "He was a good looking man.... I wasn't too shabby either.... I should have married him." Sara's kiss on her cheek awoke Kathy from her dreamlike state of mind. "Damn you, Sara Sweeney. We promised that we would NOT cry today" and then they both started bawling like babies.

Kathy looked at the scrapbook three more times until she fell asleep on the couch, holding it tightly. Sara watched her eyes close and prayed that she was dreaming of Hank kissing her on Eagle Beach. She thought of the pictures that Todd took and then she thought of Todd.

Sara decided to text Todd and wish him a Merry Christmas, but she accidentally hit "call" instead. Before she could disconnect, she heard his voice. "Sara?" She was paralyzed with fear of rejection and her mouth froze shut. Again, she heard, "Sara, are you there? Is your Aunt Kathy okay?"

This time she responded. "Hi…. She's struggling, but we're both dreaming of Aruba right now. I'm sorry…. I meant to text you and I hit the wrong button." Todd laughed, "You really need to learn how to use a cell phone…. I was just thinking about you." Sara uttered shyly, "Oh sure, you're really thinking about me on Christmas day."

A picture immediately appeared on her screen of a man's hand, holding a framed photo of them dancing together at La Cabana and she started to warmly reminisce. "I've got great memories of our time together in Aruba. You have been so kind to help me with my aunt and I consider you a true friend…. I meant what I said on that text I sent you."

Todd quickly changed the conversation. "I hope you don't mind that Franco called me about Kathy and I'm sorry. You and your fiancée must be dealing with a lot of emotions right now." Sara's curiosity was now at its peak. "Franco Cortez is world renown in cancer research. How does he owe you a favor?"

Todd answered, "His son was rushed into our ER after his hand was crushed in a boating accident at Seneca Lake while his family vacationed there. I put Carlo's bones back together, and he's now throwing 90 mile an hour fastballs."

Sara quickly replied, "You never told me that you were a rising star in Orthopedic surgery" and Todd countered, "You never told me that you got your master's degree two years faster than I did…. In Aruba, we try to get away from all the bullshit of reality and just be ourselves."

Sara and Todd talked for over two hours about everything in their real lives. Todd asked to be kept in the loop concerning her aunt and before they said goodnight, Sara sighed, "I'm so happy to have talked to you, Todd…. It's a great Christmas gift for me to know my Prince Charming did not forget me."

Todd's voice began to quiver. "I could never forget you and I'm glad that you meant what you texted me that night. You know in your heart how I feel about you. Merry Christmas Cinderella." Sara finally had a day when she felt loved and wanted by a man and used those emotions to get her through the next three months.

The night before they were going to leave for New York City, Sara called her fiancée with bad news. "I'm so sorry Honey, but I'm coming down with the flu and there is no way that I'll be able to fly tomorrow. I know how your mother is with germs and I surely don't want to get on her bad side so close to the wedding. I hope you're not upset. Please give my love to everyone and don't worry about me…. I love you so much."

Dave was angry about the late cancellation and let her know about it. "I really wish you would go. Mother always calls you a 'runner' in a bad way and you always seem to prove her right." When Sara got off the phone, she was pissed. "Well, 'Mother' can kiss my ass!"

Kathy's pain was now revealed to Sara as her body continued to fail and her skin was now a shade of yellow. Kathy was only fifty years old, but she looked like ninety. This hurt Sara the most as she silently watched this horrific evolution. The doctors suspended the CIPI treatments after a bad reaction and wanted Kathy to be admitted to the hospital, but she wanted to be at home when it was her time to leave this earth.

Sara took a leave of absence from the hospital to grant Kathy her final wish. She was more than qualified to take care of her aunt and provide professional care. She fed and comforted her aunt intravenously and lifted her frail body to bathe her. Sara was in total "lockout" mode and was no longer aware of the outside world. Her phone contained many unanswered messages and Dave kept calling to complain of her disregard for him so she shut off her phone as her answer to his protests.

The Sweeneys were of Irish descent and Kathy always loved to celebrate Saint Patrick's Day. When she awoke that morning, Sara was affectionately gazing at her aunt wearing a very cute green blouse and she blurted out, "Top of the morning to you, Auntie!" Kathy cheerfully replied, "Happy Saint Paddy's Day, Kiddo."

Kathy was only awake for a few hours of each day so she immediately began her last long conversation with her niece. They talked about her life as she grew from a curious child to the president of Malone University. They talked about the young deaths of Eddy and her parents and Kathy observed, "You are soon going to be the elder of our Sweeney family. Try to become friends with your two half-brothers…. I think Eddy would want that." Sara squeezed her aunt's hand tightly. "I promise to always honor our family name." Kathy proudly smiled at her niece and simply said, "I know you will."

Sara blushed when Auntie started talking about her love life and that conversation led to Hank. "He was my one and only. I just wish we had met as teenagers so we could have spent more time together…. I am so glad we parted so perfectly and I never contacted him after Aruba. I didn't want him rushing here to save a lost cause and seeing me in this hospital bed as his last memory of me. You need to tell Hank that when you see him in June."

Sara began to cry. "I'm not going back to Aruba without you, Auntie. It just wouldn't be the same and I'd cry every time I saw the wonderful things that we shared together."

Kathy's face turned red with Irish fire and she demanded, "Oh YES, you are most definitely going back to Aruba…. This year's maintenance fees have been paid and you are the legal beneficiary of my timeshare and Aruba is in your blood…. I regret not traveling sooner in my life and working like a jackass…. What good did I get out of it?"

Kathy stared deeply into her niece's eyes and proclaimed, "Listen to me very carefully, Kiddo…. Don't waste your life hanging on to old regrets. Make new memories of your own and with someone you 'truly' love…. Not that asshole Dave. He doesn't deserve you and I'm tired of biting my tongue while he neglects you. Look at the pictures on my phone…. I've never seen you look at Dave that way and I know in my heart that Todd loves you."

Sara knew her aunt was right and revealed, "I just realized that I've never told Todd that I love him. I always begged him for sex, but I never realized that I love him." Kathy advised her niece. "It's never too late, Kiddo. Follow your heart and it will never lead you astray."

Kathy tried to squeeze Sara's hand harder and continued. "Please Sara, grant me these final requests. I want to be cremated and I want you and Hank to spread my ashes over the cliffs of Mangel Halto. That was our favorite snorkel spot and I will come to you as a beautiful parrot fish every time you enter the water.

Sara tearfully agreed to her aunt's requests and Kathy began to dive deep into their relationship. "Everyone always felt sorry for me for not marrying and having a family…. My family started the day you were born. I remember the sparkle in your shining blue eyes…. It was my greatest accomplishment and joy to watch that baby become the wonderful woman that I'm looking at right now. You are beautiful inside and out. Your kindness is your biggest strength and I could never thank you enough for what you have done for me this last year that we will share together."

Sara was crying uncontrollably and joined her Aunt Kathy in bed and hugged her fragile body as tight as she could. "You are not a part of my life. YOU ARE MY LIFE! What am I going to do without you…. What am I going to do?"

Kathy ran her fingers through Sara's long blonde hair and gave her answer. "You're going to live. You're going to love. You're going to find that guy and raise a family. I'll be the wind blowing through your hair in Aruba. I'll be everywhere to protect you and watch you grow old. I promise you.... I will always be there for you."

They lay on the bed joined together in a loving hug and Kathy soon fell asleep. Sara gently got out of bed and immediately grabbed her phone and texted Todd. "I have never told you that I love you. My mind is so clear now.... I'm in love with you, Todd." His return text was completely filled with red hearts. Sara wanted to call him, but didn't want to wake up Kathy. She knew her aunt's ordeal would soon be over and wanted her heart to be dedicated to Aunt Kathy.

Ten days later, Hospice was called in as Kathy's breathing became very difficult. She was now on oxygen and a morphine drip to comfort her pain. Whenever Kathy woke up, her niece was always there, holding her hand and tenderly smiling down on her. Although she could no longer speak, Kathy's eyes would communicate her love to Sara and place a beam of happiness on the grief stricken girl's face.

The two best friends parted ways on the first of April as Kathy took her last breath on a bright sunny day. Sara had been talking to her aunt nonstop for the last two days. She kept telling Kathy over and over again how wonderful their life together was and how she will always honor her spirit.

"Auntie.... I know you can hear me.... I'm ready to let go.... I love you so much. I'll see you soon in Aruba and we'll have that snorkel at Mangel Halto." At that exact time, Sara's hero exhaled her last breath and she lay next to Kathy for one final hug. Sara knew that she was all alone for the first time in her life.

LIFE'S SORROW

Sara spent the next two days functioning without emotion. She made all the arrangements for Auntie's funeral and wanted everyone to celebrate the life of Kathy Sweeney. Stacey was a big help with the preparations and stayed with Sara the night before the service. Dave seemed very somber, but was relieved that Sara's ordeal was finally over.

Sara was strong for her aunt at the service. She spent some quiet time alone with Kathy before the viewing started and admired her aged beauty. "You were a 'looker' Auntie. All the older guys were so jealous of Hank.... You're at peace now." Sara pleasantly greeted every guest who attended and accepted their tributes to Kathy. She was proud to be her niece and expressed that to all her friends.

Even her father's wife Megan showed up to pay her final respects and the two women had an interesting conversation. Megan told Sara, "Kathy and I never got along after you moved out during high school and that always bothered Eddy.... My kids were always jealous of you and Kathy going to Aruba every year. Are you going this year without her?" Her stepdaughter said "Yes" and explained her reasons why.

When Megan left the room, Sara wondered to herself, "That's the nicest Megan has ever been to me and she never talked about Aruba before. I wonder why she cares now?"

The burial service the next morning was a different story. The rainy day helped camouflage Sara's tears from the beginning to the end. The whole affair was numbing to her mind as the Priest gave Kathy's eulogy. She became faint as she looked into the casket for the last time. Sara held on to her aunt's hand and kissed her on the cheek, knowing that when the lid closed, she would never touch Kathy again. Dave and Stacey supported her physically as Sara's legs betrayed her after her final goodbyes at the grave site.

As the wake was ending, Sara told Dave that she was going to spend some quiet time at Kathy's house to reflect on this recent journey of faith. Dave insisted on Sara coming home with him, but she kissed him on the cheek and thanked him for his support. "I'll be fine, Honey. I just need some 'alone'

FORTY NIGHTS IN ARUBA

time with my thoughts. I'll call you tomorrow." Her fiancée was not pleased, but understood Sara's needs.

After she collected herself emotionally on Kathy's couch, she made a phone call. "Hi...." Todd knew from her long pause that Kathy was gone. "Are you okay.... I wish you would have called. I would have been there for you."

Sara softly replied. "I know.... My feelings are in a million pieces right now and you being here with Dave would have been too much for me. My Aunt Kathy never told Hank about her condition to spare him the grief. I guess I wanted to spare you from seeing me with my fiancée.... Please Todd. I need to sort this all out in my head. I know in my heart that I truly love you and I want to be with you, but it's very complicated."

Todd stopped her before she could say more. "I understand. I really do. I'll accept whatever you decide as long as we remain friends.... Somehow, I need you in my life. Are you coming to Aruba this year?"

Sara sighed as she answered. "At first, I didn't want to come, but Kathy had a long talk with me and now I'm going to count the days until I return. Please promise me that you'll be there, waiting for me.... I love you and I want to say that to you while I'm gazing into your eyes." There was silence on the phone and then Todd promised. "I'll be there, waiting impatiently for your answer and I'll love you regardless of your decision…. I can't wait to see you again. Goodnight Cinderella."

Sara spent the rest of April sorting out all of Aunt Kathy's affairs so she told Dave that she was going to reside in Kathy's home until everything was settled. "It's better if I stay here and sort through all the legal papers in case I need them. I hope you understand. This won't be a permanent thing."

Dave was surprisingly very supportive of her decision. "I completely understand. Maybe we could have a couple 'date nights' and get serious about the wedding once again…. Mother would kill us both if we canceled again."

Dave's comments about the wedding were unnerving. Sara didn't even know if she wanted to marry Dave anymore, but he had been very supportive of her lately. She loved both Todd and Dave, but Todd was a gentleman and Dave was not. Sara knew he had another woman at his home and hoped it was a one-night-stand, but he violated her trust. Kathy favored Todd over Dave and deep in her heart, so did Sara. She just needed a sign.

Sara returned to work in late April and was happy to be back into a routine. She began running again and would always think of Kathy and Aruba. And when Sara thought of Aruba, she always daydreamed about her Prince Charming. "He's the one. I saw the look in Auntie's eyes and the pictures of us together do not lie…. I can't wait to tell him, face to face in two months. I just hope Dave doesn't get ugly about it when I tell him." Sara was going to wait until Todd was onboard with her decision, but she decided to tell Dave as soon as possible. She just needed to find the confidence to do it.

One day, Sara walked back to the nurse's station and the two nurses stopped their gabbing in mid-sentence. Sara had an uncomfortable feeling that they were talking about her because they both looked away as she passed by. She was now curious about the subject matter so Sara asked her colleague, Cassy, about it and she answered nervously. "A lot of things have changed in the pediatric wing, if you get my drift." As Cassy quickly walked away, Sara thought long and hard about her answer.

Sara immediately called her old friend, Joan, who worked with her at the pediatric wing when she first started at Mercy. They remained close friends after Sara left the wing and Joan knew all the gossip that went on there.

Sara asked Joan for a lunch date with her and she responded, "I was expecting a call from you. How about drinks after work this Friday." Sara agreed and asked Joan. "So, you know what I'm calling you about?" Joan was quick with her reply. "See you at five at Bennigan's. Gotta go."

For the next three days, Sara was in a troubled state of mind. She knew what was going on; she just needed to hear it from Joan. The two friends embraced when they met inside of Bennigan's Bar. After they were seated, they ordered cocktails and Joan expressed, "That was a lovely service for Aunt Kathy. She would have been proud of the way you conducted yourself.... But you're not here to talk about your aunt. Are you?" Sara didn't beat around the bush. "What do you know about Dave?"

Joan sipped on her strawberry daiquiri and stated to her friend. "I know that he's a scum ball and you should castrate him.... He's been flirting with all the new girls and one of them is a real good looking gal who spends way too much time in his office. Doctor Rockich leaves in the middle of his rounds and comes back three hours later.... In different clothes."

Sara was very startled by Joan's observations. "It sounds like my fiancée is having affairs with multiple women. I need to catch him in the act." Joan quickly replied, "That won't be hard to do. Dave talks to one girl on his phone all the time and they always rendezvous at his house during the week. He's been leaving a lot lately."

Sara confirmed the cold hard facts. "I'm done with him.... I found a green nighty in our closet the night of the Christmas party. It was probably hers. Do you know how long this affair has been going on?"

Joan took a pause and sighed, "Right after you moved out to help Kathy. Almost a year ago." Sara put her head down in disbelief. "A year. I'm such a fool…. I actually believed that he loved me. He always told me that I was his 'dream' girl…. He's such a phony."

Joan apologized for not telling her sooner. "I knew what was going on, but I didn't want to upset you while you were stressed with Kathy…. He's a horrible man. He met with that woman the day they buried your aunt. I overheard him talking to her about it. He brags to the other doctors about how many women he's screwed…. You deserve so much better than that ass. Get away from him as fast as you can."

Sara was sickened to know that her soon to be ex fiancée would have sex with another woman while she was mourning the loss of her aunt. She became saturated with anger and asked her friend. "Please Joan…. Call me the next time you hear him planning a rendezvous at his house." Sara was ready to end this deceptive relationship and move on with her life, but she wanted the satisfaction of catching him in the act. Now, she just had to be patient until Dave made a mistake.

It was only a few days later when Sara received the call from Joan. "I just overheard Dave talking to her about leaving at his lunch break and meeting her at his house. He just left five minutes ago and the new gal followed him out the door, chit-chatting all the way.... Be careful when you confront him, Sara. He's a loose cannon and you don't know what Dave's capable of."

Sara responded to her warning. "Thanks for the information, Joan and don't worry about me.... Dave doesn't know what I'm capable of either."

Every mile she drove, the more outraged Sara became. "That bastard took advantage of me, knowing that I would never walk in on his affair because of Kathy. He never liked my aunt and used my love for her to conveniently screw his stable of women.... I hope he enjoyed his little game.... I'm going to enjoy videoing his face when he sees me." Sara parked in front of his house and prepared for the confrontation. She wasn't going to listen to his excuses and was looking forward to throwing her engagement ring at his face.

Sara quietly unlocked the door and approached the bedroom. She could now hear the groans of two people engaged in heated sex. She took a deep breath and then entered the room with great rage.

Sara screamed loudly, dropping her phone as her knees hit the floor and watched in horror as the two lovers continued without hesitation. She couldn't move; her body became frozen in time. Sara needed to throw up from the sickness in her stomach, but nothing came out of her mouth as the other woman moaned from climax in front of her.

Sara began to sob uncontrollably as her eyes forced her to stare at Dave and her mother dressing. Stacey gave Dave a quick kiss and walked over to her devastated daughter. "I'm sorry you had to witness the hard reality of life, Sara…. I gotta go. You two have a lot to talk about."

When the front door slammed shut, Dave calmly sat on the bed in front of her. "What did you think was going to happen? You leave for a year to be with that 'witch' who had you under her spell since the day I met you…. I have 'needs' you know and if you can't provide them for me, I'll look elsewhere. Don't worry. Your mother's not the only one, but she's a better fuck than you ever were…. Are you going to say anything, or are you just going to sit on the floor, crying like a baby?"

Sara struggled to get up and silently walked out of the house of pain, her mind clearly in disarray. Dave made no effort to follow her and smirked. "She'll be back. They always come back to me."

Sara had great difficulty driving home as the stream of tears blurred her vision. She lay on her bed, clutching the scrapbook that she made for her aunt and staring at the ceiling. She blurted out loud while still sobbing. "Aunt Kathy, I need you so badly now.... You were right all along about Dave. He never loved me.... I was his trophy girl to do with as he pleased.... He screwed my mother on the day I buried you!"

Sara started to cry harder. "Why does she hate me so much? I watched her and dad fight in front of me. I was always looked down on by my friends because of her whoring around. She acted like I was her competition and not her daughter.... I never hurt her and I always felt deep down that she hated me, but I don't know why.... I don't give a damn about Dave, but why does Mom hate me so much that she would screw my fiancée?"

Suddenly, a comforting feeling came into Sara's soul and her breathing calmed down as the waterfall of tears stopped. While she rubbed her eyes dry, Sara knew Kathy's spirit was watching over her and she felt that her aunt was listening to her cries of despair. For now, Sara didn't feel alone.

THE FINAL STRAW

The next work week was miserable for Sara as she was the center of the hospital gossip. Dave made no effort to hide the story of Sara and her mother, but he still begged her to come back to him through his sent texts. Joan told Sara that Dave was still seeing the girl on the phone and asked, "My God Sara. Is it true? Was that asshole sleeping with your mom?"

Sara was strong and firmly answered, "He was doing 'more' than just sleeping with her…. Joan, I need a big favor from you?" Sara revealed the favor in great detail. "I need you to video Dave flirting with his coworkers on company time without revealing yourself. Just send me whatever video you can safely take and I'll do the rest." Joan happily agreed to help her. "Most of the girls think he's a creep, but don't want to get on his bad side. I'd love to help you screw him…. It sounds like fun."

Sara was summoned to the office of Robert Presly, who was the CEO of Mercy Hospital. It was around the end of her shift and she feared she was going to be terminated. "Dave must have lied to Bob and he's going to fire me. I need to get a lawyer." Sara composed herself and started her trek to his fourth floor suite. "I'm going to record this conversation for my lawyer. I've done nothing wrong."

She was ready for a fight when she asked Presly the reason for the official visit. "Hello Bob, it's nice to see you. Is there something we need to discuss?" Bob was smiling when he wistfully answered. "You looked stunning the last time we spoke at the Christmas party and I've looked into your profile…. The hospital has an opening for a potential employee advancing to become a nurse practitioner. I'd like to offer you the position, Sara."

Sara was overjoyed and told her boss. "I would love that opportunity and I know that I will be an asset for the hospital." Bob walked closer to her, still intensely smiling. "I'm sure you will be a great 'asset'. I heard about your current situation with Doctor Rockich and I thought you might enjoy a little 'revenge fling' to pay him back."

He put both hands on her hips and feverishly declared. "I noticed your desire for me at the Christmas party and I'm also very fond of you. Dave told me that your mother outperformed you in the sack. I'd like to find that out for myself…. I think that request is a fair trade off for a prestigious position at this hospital."

Sara was bewildered by the CEO's request and forcibly took his roaming hands off of her hips. "What are you saying, Bob? I have to screw you to get the job. My hard work means nothing to you…. How dare you take advantage of me when I've just been embarrassed by my fiancée. I'm not a measuring stick for my mother so why don't you just go screw her…. And you can go to hell!"

As Sara was storming out the door, Bob threatened her. "Not a word of this to anybody or you'll end up being a nurse in a grade school…. Just remember who you're talking back to."

Sara turned back towards him with fire in her blue eyes. "I'll remember that I just talked to an old pervert who wanted to screw me for a job…. Have a nice day ASSHOLE!"

Sara had passed her breaking point and was no longer going to be anyone's patsy. She could never dream of a year so miserable and anger now replaced her sorrow. She got an idea on her drive home and got online to check flights going to Aruba.

Sara was done with Dave and her mother. She was done with Presly and Mercy Hospital. Sara wanted out of this crazy life that she called home and desperately desired to be on Eagle Beach. She needed to test Kathy's theory and snorkel with her spirit.

For the rest of the night, Sara researched her plan. She found a last minute availability on American Airlines to Aruba on May 19th and booked it. Now she was arriving over a month earlier than planned and had no lodging reserved until the last week of her new trip itinerary. She had a lot of work to do and only four days to accomplish it. Most people would have been petrified to rush to a foreign country, but Sara embraced it as the adventure of a lifetime.

Dave sent her flowers at work with a "makeup" card; Sara threw the card in the trash and gave out all the flowers to the patients. Before lunch, Sara went to Human Resources and filed a sexual harassment charge against the CEO of Mercy Hospital and turned in her resignation; effective immediately. She asked for and received her last paycheck and walked out the door forever. Kathy begged Sara to enjoy her life and she was now on a mission to do that.

As soon as Sara got home, she called Tropic Rental Cars and talked to Dennis about getting a car for forty one days on very short notice. Unfortunately, Dennis could not help her, but suggested that his friend in Seroe Blanco had well maintained used cars for rent at a very reasonable price. "His name is Ricardo and I'll text you his address and phone number. I'm sure he'll take care of you." Sara thanked Dennis and reassured him, "I'll see you next year."

On Thursday, Sara met with Kathy's attorney, John Di Albert, to discuss the will and he informed her that she was the sole beneficiary of her aunt's estate. She was happy to hear the news, but had more crucial things to discuss with him. "Mr. Di Albert, I need your legal team to represent me in a sexual harassment suit I filed against my former employer. Will you take the case?"

John Di Albert accepted her request. "Kathy was a good friend of mine. I'd be honored to represent you." Sara gave Di Albert the recording of her meeting with Presly and explained in great detail the abuse she was taking at the hospital. He was very receptive and Sara left his office with a confident demeanor.

Dave called again later that night, but this voice mail was not of remorse. "Jesus Christ Sara, have you lost your mind?" First, you quit your job and now, you're suing the hospital.... Presly just called me and he is furious.... I could lose my promotion because of you and your 'petty' actions. You'll never win the case so why piss everyone off? You're acting like a little baby over a few meaningless affairs.... Get over it."

Sara spent most of Friday at her bank, closing her current accounts and terminating her credit cards after being advised by Di Albert. He wanted her to eliminate anything that Dave had access to. When she left the bank that afternoon, all Sara had for her trip was two thousand dollars in cash and one credit card with a twenty five hundred dollar limit.

Sara spent three hundred dollars at Walmart on provisions for the trip and was thinking about her resources on her drive home. "I've got a budget of one hundred dollars a day.... That's crazy." She was still very excited and ready for her big adventure.

Sara was organizing her clothes for the trip when a knock was heard from her front door. She looked out the window and saw Dave's shiny black BMW parked in front of her house. Panic set in and she quickly double locked the door. Dave heard the clicks and politely requested, "Come on Babe, let me in. I need to talk to you." Sara replied to her fiancée behind the locked door. "We can talk from here."

Dave began to beg. "Please open the door. I need to hold you and tell you how truly sorry I am. I realize now that you're the one for me.... You hurt me deeply by always choosing Kathy over me and you forced me to be with your mother. I always pretended she was you.... Stacey tricked me into the affair. I love you, Sara, not your mother."

Sara wasn't fooled, and questioned him. "You love me? Why didn't you stop screwing her when I started crying? Why did you tell everyone that she was a better 'lay' than me? Is that how you judge women? Is every woman that you screwed better than me? I wasted three years of my life kissing your ass and I'm not wasting a second more."

Dave started his pretend sobbing, "Please, Sara, open the door. I know that I'm a sex addict and I promise that I'll go to therapy and become monogamous. All those women never meant a damn thing to me. My heart is breaking and only you can heal it. I need you…. We're engaged to be married. Don't throw away our future."

Dave listened closely for her icy reply. "My name is Sara Sweeney. I live at 2701 Sunset Boulevard. There's a man trying to break into my front door. Please send a squad car quickly before he kills me."

Sara disconnected and smirked. "You've got about ten minutes to tell me what you really want before the cops come and arrest your worthless ass…. Wouldn't 'Mother' be upset to see your face in a police lineup?"

"Open the goddamn door, Sara. OPEN THE GODDAMN DOOR! I want that ring back. I spent twenty thousand dollars on that engagement ring on your finger. It's mine and I want it back…. OPEN THE GODDAMN DOOR!"

"Your parents paid for this ring so don't think I'm stupid, mommy's little boy…. Tell 'Mother' that she'll get her ring back when I'm fucking good and ready!" Sara was relieved to hear the BMW speed away, but she knew Dave wouldn't stop until he had the ring.

Sara spent the entire Saturday locked inside her home, preparing for her big trip. She tightly packed everything she could think of inside two suitcases and the rest of her needed items went into her carry-on and purse. Her excitement was subdued when she carefully arranged the sealed container with Kathy's ashes inside. She told the container, "We're going home, Auntie."

Sara went to bed early and set two alarms to go off at 1AM. After she awoke from their blaring echoes, Sara turned off the main water valve and locked the house securely. She had one more stop to make before she drove to the airport.

Sara parked her Mazda a block away from Dave's house and began her final task. She turned off his security system with her phone and quietly entered his house. Sara heard the moans of two lovers engaged and went directly into the garage. Twenty minutes later, she reappeared and put her engagement ring and an envelope on the kitchen table and quietly left Dave and his house forever.

Sara parked her car in the long term parking lot and rolled her luggage into the airport to begin her tense wait for the American Airlines ticket counter to open. Once through security, she nervously lingered before she boarded her plane and when the airplane's wheels lifted off of the runway, Sara finally exhaled. She had pulled off a perfect "getaway" and then Sara contently fell asleep, dreaming of her aunt and their fun times together in Aruba.

While Sara was sleeping peacefully, Dave was now waking up. He went to make some coffee for Stacey and was shocked to see the ring on the table. "That little bitch snuck in here last night. She was so terrified of my threats that she couldn't face me to give back the ring."

After admiring the ring, he finally opened the envelope and read her letter….
"Dave, Thanks for opening my eyes to the world of 'men'. You made me think that I loved you by wining and dining me, so shame on me for being so stupid. You are a beautiful man with an ugly heart. I will never forget or forgive you for screwing the horrible woman that I am ashamed to share the same blood with. You two deserve each other so give her this ring and have your August wedding. Your family probably wouldn't even know that she wasn't me. You called my real mother a 'WITCH' and I should have killed you for it, but I am above that type of behavior. Please tell 'Mother' that her ring is also a very useful tool."

Dave was happy to get his coveted ring back, but was confused about what she meant. He and Stacey got a chuckle out of Sara's letter and Dave dressed to go get them breakfast. When he entered the garage, he screamed in horror, "SARA!"

Stacey quickly rushed into the garage to find Dave crying like a baby next to his beloved BMW. She was shocked to see the entire car deeply scratched, with the words 'MOTHER' and 'WITCH' covering every panel. Dave embraced her as he continued to weep and Stacey laughed silently to herself. "Sara's finally getting it."

FORTY NIGHTS

Sara was now wide awake and was delighted to officially put everything and everybody in Canton behind her. For the next forty one days, only Aruba would be on her mind.

She began talking to an old man and his wife, who shared her row, about their fond memories of Aruba. As the plane began its approach, Sara asked the man if she could lean next to him to view the west side of the island. "My Aunt Kathy and I loved watching Aruba from the air."

His wife gave her permission. "Al would love that, My Dear. Just don't give him a heart attack before we land." Sara became very emotional when she saw Costa Linda and told Al, "That's my second home right there." She thought to herself. "I've got thirty three days until I check into Costa Linda and I have no clue what adventures lie ahead of me."

Sara was smiling from ear to ear as the plane touched down at Reina Beatrix International. She called Ricardo and took a taxi to his car lot. He was kind enough to meet her there on his day off. Ricardo was accompanied by his son, Juan, who became infatuated with Sara. He spoke to his father in Papiamento, "She's very attractive" and Sara smiled at him and said, "Danki". Ricardo was impressed and asked her if she spoke Papiamento and Sara answered, "I try" in his native language, so they made the entire transaction speaking Papiamento.

Ricardo showed her the available cars for rent, but another vehicle caught Sara's eye. "Is that van for rent? I'd be interested if it's safe and reasonably priced." Ricardo told her that it was an old taxi that he used to haul stuff around in. "It's ugly, but it runs great. I just put new tires and shocks on it.... If that is what you desire, I'll let you have it for one thousand US dollars." Sara quickly shook his hand and paid him cash.

Ricardo and Juan showed her how to operate everything on the van. Ricardo even threw in a sleeping bag and two blankets after he understood her plan. Sara was so happy and thanked them both. "Your country is full of so many kindhearted people and I hope to meet them all."

Juan invited Sara to join him and his friends at Surfside Beach, but she politely asked for a raincheck. "Maybe next Sunday? I have plans tonight." She stored Juan's phone number in her cell and took off for sunset on Eagle Beach.

Sara was comfortable driving the bigger vehicle around Aruba and she had no problems finding Costa Linda. She discovered a secret hiding place for her money and passport and stored them inside the van. She changed into a bikini and cover up and quickly walked through the front lobby, but saw no familiar faces anywhere.

Sara quickly found an open palapa, removed her coverup, and sprinted for the water before the sunset occurred. The cruel reality of the past year settled into her soul and Sara began to cry while watching the beautiful fireball disappear into the ocean. The only thing on her mind was Aunt Kathy as she stood in the water quietly weeping alone.

Her first night sleep in the van was surprisingly comfortable and Sara awoke well rested. She went for her morning run on Eagle Beach and pieced the next month together in her mind. "I know I don't have enough money to last the whole trip so I need to pace myself and make a financial journal. I'll use my credit card on everything until I max it out.... I'm glad I brought all those energy snack bars with me because I'm going to be living on them."

Sara heard someone whistle at her as she approached La Cabana and immediately thought of Todd. Everything changed so fast in her life since they last spoke and she developed a negative attitude towards all men. Sadly, she included Todd into this group. "With my luck, he's probably married or a serial killer.... I don't even know this guy very well and I really don't think I ever loved him. It was just a phase I was going through.... Who knows? He might have slept with my mother too."

Armed with her new outlook towards the opposite sex, Sara filed Todd deep into her memory and looked forward to the next month. "I'm going to live my life like Kathy asked me to. I'm not hanging on to old regrets. I'm going to make new memories and enjoy the next month ahead of me. I might not meet Mr. Right, but I'm gonna have some fun looking for him."

Sara returned to Costa Linda and began to reminisce as she slowly toured the property. "That's where Auntie and I beat those two 'hot' guys from Rhode Island in pool basketball and what fun we had playing volleyball.... There's the bar where Kathy and Hank first.... Hank, My God. What am I going to say to him? How am I going to tell him?"

Sara became emotional as she walked towards the van, but was intercepted by Wilmer. "Are you okay Miss Sweeney? Where's your mother?" Sara started crying and told him the sad story and then she quickly left in tears.

The van was very hot inside as she got in and composed herself. Sara ate an energy bar and drank some cold water. She knew that Aruba had the best drinking water in the world and that fact alone was going to save her a lot of money. She planned to fill her sports bottles everywhere she went and drink from them when she was thirsty. Sara even brought Gatorade powder to give her much needed electrolytes. She enjoyed the taste of Aruba water whether it was hot or cold and it was easily available at all the resorts.

The van doubled as a perfect bedroom, giving Sara the privacy and security she needed. She changed into a bikini and headed up the coast to Arashi Beach for a much needed snorkel. She drove past the crowded parking lot, and turned left onto the less populated beach area and parked near the water. Sara and Kathy learned many tricks and shortcuts from the previous nine years vacationing in Aruba. This year, Sara needed to use them all.

PALM BEACH PLEASURE

After a great first snorkel, Sara drove to Palm Beach and parked near the beach tennis courts. She snuck into the Holiday Inn property from the beach and used their pool to clean the salt off of her. After an enjoyable swim, Sara went fishing for lunch. She strutted down the beach and asked every guy alone if he would share his palapa with her.

The seductive angler finally got a "catch" in front of the Hilton when Jeff invited her to join him. They had a playful talk and Sara slyly said. "It's been great hanging with you, Jeff, but I'm really hungry…. Gotta go."

Sara slowly got up and showed her "assets" to him and Jeff suggested, "Let me flag down a girl and I'll order some food and drinks for us." Sara graciously accepted. "That would be great. You're so cute and I really enjoy your company." Sara's big catch fed her and she knew Aunt Kathy was grinning down at her.

Sara spent the next few days around Palm Beach and snorkeled on her favorite "Arashi to Boca Catalina to Malmok" trip. She spent the night at Boca Catalina's small parking lot and at first daylight she walked barefooted to Arashi Beach and began snorkeling down the coast to Malmok, seeing several turtles and a lot of colorful fish along the way. When she came up to locate her position around Tres Trapi, she saw all the tour boats at the Antilla Wreck and knew it was time to go to shore.

Sara sat on a rock to dry off and drink a Gatorade. As she watched all the boats surround the cove she fretted. "I've never seen so many tourists here. I never paid any attention last year because of Kathy's illness, but even driving around this year has become crazy. I pray that all the new resorts they're building won't take the 'charm' out of this beautiful island."

She drove up to the Lighthouse and it was a "zoo" with tour buses everywhere. The line to get a refreshment was very long so Sara decided to check off a bucket list item and climb the steps to the top of the California Lighthouse. She and Kathy always wanted to do that since it reopened, but never got around to it.

Sara stood atop in the driving wind, staring at Aruba's beauty and could see the snorkel route she took earlier. "WOW…. It's so peaceful up here even with all the people around me. I can easily see Hooiberg…. I'm going to try to run the steps up to the top this year."

Sara didn't consider herself a tourist because of her perspective of the island's nature and people. She always swam with a net bag to collect any debris she might encounter and picked up any trash she found on land. She noticed more trash carelessly being discarded each year since she had been coming and wished everyone would realize the beauty they were privileged to share together. She fondly sighed, "I do love this country."

Once back on the ground, Sara got hungry. "I think I'll go 'catch' some lunch" and off she went towards the Highrise. She "fished" around Pelican Pier in a white string bikini and "brought in" three guys from Michigan.

Sara cutely uttered "Hi" to Steven who was the best looking one. He quickly asked her to join them for lunch and started a fun conversation. When the boys found out Sara was from Ohio, they playfully insulted her favorite college football team and she enjoyed teasing them back.

Steven was smitten with Sara and invited her to go parasailing with him. She became very excited. "Hell yeah. I'd love to go with you…. Let's do it!" Sara always wanted to do exciting things in Aruba, but Kathy grew afraid of dangerous sports.

As the two lifted off the boat together, Sara could feel her heart pounding faster the higher they went. She felt like a seagull with the wind blowing in her face and she felt the presence of her late aunt's spirit as they peacefully viewed the big hotels from the air.

Once back at the beach, Steven invited her back to his room. Sara smooched him on his cheek and politely refused. "You're going to have to do better than that, Stevey.... Call me sometime and take me out for a nice romantic dinner, and you might get lucky."

Steven gave her his cell number and stated, "I'm here for the next ten days so call me when you're hungry." Sara deeply kissed him and looked into his sparkling green eyes. "You know I'm going to call and when I do, I'm gonna have a very 'big' appetite." She left Steve in awe as he watched her strut away, swinging her hips slowly.

Sara wanted desperately to wash the memory of Dave from her soul. She wasn't looking for love anymore; she was only looking for a good time. Sara needed to be with a man and Stevey fit the profile. "He's good looking, nice, has a room, and he's going to feed me.... What else could I ask for?"

Sara decided to celebrate her first week on the island. She spent Saturday afternoon hanging around the Marriott pool, pretending to be a guest, and was friendly to all the staff. Kathy always advised her to "act like you belong" and that advice was working fabulous at the Marriott.

She snuck into the "transition" room and had her first real shower since she left home. The hot water felt amazing and she stayed under it for a very long time, soaking her sun drenched body and thoroughly shampooing her long blond hair. Sara felt like a million bucks when she left the Marriott and walked to her van, parked behind Moomba Beach Bar.

Sara wasn't ashamed of using her body as a way to support herself, especially after the disrespect she received by men recently in Ohio. "If they want me, they're going to pay for me. I'll let them feed me and save my funds for doing fun stuff for myself." She let her sensual stimulation shut out any pure feelings she had for Todd. "I'm going to take advantage of their desires and have some enjoyment while doing it."

When she exited the van, Sara was dressed for a night out, wearing a flowing dress that highlighted her dark skin. She had a cocktail at the Vue Roof Top bar while watching the sun retire for another day. Then she began her trip to Paseo Herencia Mall and enjoyed the children performing their traditional dances. Sara joined them in the jubilant finale and then sat quietly watching the "dancing water" show as she thought of her aunt.

As Sara walked around the mall she saw a sign advertising a new show, called RCC and curiously went to the second floor to check it out. She peeked into the door to see a bunch of "hot" guys and gals doing sensual acrobatics and lustfully noted, "This show is now on my 'must do' list."

Sara bought two purple magnetic hearts off a street vendor to spruce up her mobile home. "They're going to look so cute on my van." She continued her shopping trip all the way to Soprano's Piano Bar, always looking but never buying.

Most of the people she passed were looking too, but Sara knew that they were staring at her for the wrong reason. She was a beautiful woman walking the street alone and that is a rare occurrence in the limelight of Palm Beach. Sara merely nodded at her spectators and waved to the children. She was content to be alone.

Sara stopped for a drink at the Bohemian and was immediately stimulated by the romantic atmosphere. She passed an elderly woman sitting at a table by herself and smiled at her as she was seated at the bar. Before she could even order a drink, a "Dave" character approached her and quickly began telling his life story. Sara politely declined his offer for a free drink, but the arrogant man wouldn't take no for an answer. To avoid an embarrassing scene, the elderly woman walked up to Sara and delicately said, "Our table is ready, Evelyn. Excuse us sir." She took Sara's hand and they walked back to her table.

Sara expressed her gratitude. "Thank you very much. That jerk reminded me of my ex.... Who's

Evelyn? The woman sipped her martini and answered, "I'm Evelyn and believe it or not, that used to happen to me a lot. Please, join me for dinner."

Sara wasted no time accepting her request. "I'd love to Evelyn. My name is Sara and I'm from Canton, Ohio. It's a real pleasure to meet you." The two ladies spent the rest of the evening becoming friends and storytelling about their favorite place on earth.

Evelyn listened patiently as Sara finally confessed the entire drama of her last year to caring ears. She was so grateful to say it out loud and Evelyn observed, "It sounds like life threw you a helluva curveball, but keep swinging and you'll eventually hit that homerun."

As they ate, Evelyn told her story. "You're Aunt Kathy reminds me of myself. I was an executive with Polaroid for thirty years. It would have been forty, but I refused to sleep my way to the top. I worked hard and refused to fall in love until I met Mike. I was forty one years old when we wed so children were out of the question, but we had each other for twenty eight wonderful years until he passed away two years ago…. We own a timeshare at Playa Linda and we always looked forward to coming here every year so now I come alone and reminisce about our life together."

Sara gave Evelyn condolences for her loss, but the sassy host refused to accept them. "Don't ever cry for me. I've had a blessed life and you'll have one too. Just don't give up.... Don't ever give up."

Sara got up and kissed Evelyn on the forehead. "You're my angel. I believe my Aunt Kathy sent me to you tonight.... I really do. Thanks for telling me your story." Before they parted ways, they exchanged phone numbers and Evelyn embraced her tightly. "I'll be here for another two weeks. If you desire a clean bed to sleep in.... Please come and visit me." Sara promised, "I will most definitely come. Thank you, Evelyn, from the bottom of my heart."

After Sara walked Evelyn back to her resort, she took the beach boardwalk towards to the Holiday Inn. She lay in a hammock and thanked the shining stars above her. "You were right, Auntie. You are here with me.... I can feel you in the evening breeze and I can see you smiling at me near the Big Dipper. I miss you." And then she fell asleep staring at her aunt.

EXPLORING THE ISLAND

Sara was awakened early by the determined crowd of palapa seekers who were filling the beach at 5 AM and she discreetly left for her van. After Sara got her morning run in, she called Juan and told him of her plans to be in his area. "Do you know of any good snorkeling spots near Surfside?"

Juan was thrilled to hear from her. "You're in luck. I'm off today and I'd love to show you around. Park near the airport runway fence and I'll pick you up at 1PM. Sara eagerly replied, "It's a date, I'll see you at one."

Sara put her "heart magnets" on the van and took off for Surfside Beach. Traffic started slowing down as she neared Oranjestad and three huge cruise ships towered over the right side of the town. She was stuck in traffic with "boat people" walking everywhere and wondered. "Why is the government allowing so many ships now? It used to be fun walking the fishing harbor to see what everyone caught, but now it's chaos."

She barely made it to Surfside Beach on time and couldn't find Juan anywhere. She began walking the beach searching for him when she heard a loud yell. "Sara. I'm over here." She looked into the sea and found Juan grinning boyishly in a small boat. "You can swim to the boat. Come on. Let's go!"

Sara went back to her van, got her snorkeling gear, and swam towards a new adventure. Juan helped her into the boat and was disappointed in her wardrobe. The sun was brutal this time of day so Sara had on a one piece bathing suit covered by a UPF 50+

rash guard. She was the one now staring at his dark muscular body. Juan was six years younger than Sara, but certainly didn't look like a teenager.

She asked him where they were going and he just answered, "Not far" and aimed his boat for Renaissance Island, thrilling his passenger. "Oh My God! I've always wanted to go to Flamingo Beach. I thought it was a private island.... Are we allowed to go there?"

Juan just kept grinning. "It is a private island closed to the public, but I work there so we're going snorkeling today." Sara jumped up and down, then kissed Juan as he anchored the boat close to shore. She couldn't wait to see the flamingos.

Sara and Juan spent all afternoon chasing turtles and parrot fish around in the water and walking the beaches with the other guests, while admiring the beautiful pink flamingos. They enjoyed a wonderful lunch, courtesy of his best friend who was working at the Papagayo Bar and Grill. Later in the day, they watched yachts and sailboats come and go from Bucuti Yacht Club. Sara was also fascinated by the commercial airplanes landing so close that you could almost touch them.

Sara and Juan remained behind, as the resort boats removed all the guests and staff from the island. They snuck into the first luxury hut on the adult side and romantically watched the sunset.

Sara was overcome with happiness. "Oh Juan, This is perfect. I don't think I've ever seen a more beautiful sunset. Thank you for sharing this with me." She took all kinds of pictures and selfies to remember this day and then she caressed Juan as the sky continued to burst with many colors.

Sara put her phone down and made the first move. She seductively kissed him while running her fingers through his jet black hair. Her gentle touch knew he was ready so she undressed and anxiously waited for him on the lounge. Juan took off his swim trunks and Sara gazed at his Adonis body in front of the fiery sky. She watched intently as he began to make love to her and she was hypnotized by the sky behind him. She softly moaned as the vivid heavens turned to gray.

Sara wanted to cuddle afterwards, but knew they needed to swim back to the anchored boat before darkness fell. They collected their belongings and stored them in Sara's watertight pouch and began their swim. Juan was silent the whole trip back and anchored as close to shore as possible.

Before Sara jumped into the water, she romantically kissed him and gushed, "You're the first real man that I've made love to in a very long time.... Thank you for the wonderful day." Juan still remained speechless as Sara disappeared into the night.

Once she was on shore, Juan flashed his lights and quickly sped away. Sara dried off and got into her van after deciding to sleep there for the night. She was happy, but confused about Juan's reaction to their lovemaking. "I know we both enjoyed it, but he was so quiet afterwards.... I'll never figure out men."

Early Monday morning, Sara chose to go down to Baby Beach for a sunrise snorkel. As she drove through Savaneta, she avoided stopping at Mangel Halto because of her fond memories with Kathy. "I'll snorkel there next week" she thought, trying to suppress the anxiety.

Sara was getting excited as she made the right at the big red anchor and headed for the Caribbean Sea. She hadn't snorkeled at Baby Beach in two years and was shocked to see the progress being made on the Secrets Resort. "Oh No! That place is going to be huge.... Where are they going to put everybody?"

She felt guilty for the locals, who didn't want too much change and realized that she was partly to blame. Sara and Kathy always endorsed trips to Aruba, and once you go to Aruba, you always go back. "People like us helped create this vacation monster."

Today, she got there early and spent the first half hour picking up trash from the day before. Then

Sara decided to get in the ocean before the crowd arrived and she took advantage of the calm water, making it easier to swim up the channel against the current. She had a wonderful snorkel, but every time she came up, she could see the ugliness dominating the hill above the beach. "Secrets Resort is going to be a problem."

By 11AM, the beach was packed, and Sara was ready to leave. She made a "rock heart" with Kathy's name inside it and said a prayer for her aunt. Her next stop was Rodger's Beach where she tried to snorkel with a school of parrot fish, but they quickly swam away from her. "I guess Auntie isn't one of them," she snickered.

Sara spent the whole day exploring the southern tip of the island. She hiked the cliffs and watched the magical waves, as she reflected about her amazing life with Kathy. She ate lunch at Rum Reef, and hopped into the pool to rinse all the salt off of her body.

As she drove the rough road up the coast, Sara noticed that the huge windmills were turning faster as the winds were picking up. She turned around and followed a large group of ATV's back to Boca Grandi Beach to watch the windsurfers glide across the crashing waves.

Sara sat on the beach in amazement of how exciting and difficult this graceful sport was. She always wanted to try it, but Kathy put her foot down and wouldn't allow her. She was always fearful that Sara would get hurt.

A voice shattered her meditation. "Hey. Can you give me a hand here?" Sara looked back to see a cute guy struggling with his sail and quickly went over to help. He thanked her and explained, "The winds are crazy good, but I'm having a hard time getting to the water…. My name's Luis." She joyfully replied, "I'm Sara" and they dragged the sail safely into the waves. Sara spent the rest of the afternoon helping all of the windsurfers.

Luis came over and sat with her and suggested, "The wind is perfect today and we're all surfing until dark and then camping out. My family owns one of those huts down there…. Would you like to join us?" Sara was very flattered. "That sounds like fun. Thanks for thinking of me."

The surfers finally wrapped up and relocated to Luis's hut. Five of them joined Sara around the fire laughing and telling their interesting stories. Luis and Sara were engaged in a conversation. "Have you ever tried kitesurfing, Sara?" She responded, "No, but I'm going to do it someday."

Luis offered to teach her. "I work as a server at the Flying Fishbone and I'm a part time kitesurfing instructor on Hadicurari Beach. I'm working up there next week on Tuesday and Wednesday.... Stop after four o'clock and I'll give you a free lesson."

Before Sara could reply, she overheard a conversation about her in Papiamento between Luis's girlfriends, Rosa and Vivian. "She's very beautiful, but still a crazy American for being out here alone. She doesn't even know us.... If I was a man, I'd screw her."

Luis realized that Sara understood the dialogue and tried to shut Vivian up, but it was too late. Sara stood up and walked seductively toward Vivian and then she bent down and kissed Vivian's startled face and said in perfect Papiamento, "I'm so sorry Sweetheart, but you're just not my type." The other four surfers laughed hysterically and Vivian kissed her back. Sara hung out with her new friends for the next couple days in Seroe Colorado.

SEARCHING FOR HER PURPOSE

On Thursday, Sara went to visit Evelyn and then decided to take a jog down Palm Beach. Soon a man was jogging right next to her and asked, "Are you trying to duck me?" Sara kept running and replied, "No. I'm just trying to work up an appetite." Steven countered, "You better get hungry quick. We're leaving Sunday morning.... How about tomorrow night?" Sara asked, "Where are you taking me, Stevey?"

Steven was getting out of breath and could barely talk. "How about Ruinas del Mar…. Meet me out in the Hyatt lobby at nine and wear something sexy." Then he stopped running and put both hands on his knees to catch his breath.

Sara turned around and jogged back to him, "You need to be in better shape tomorrow night, Stevey Boy or you're going to get worn out…. Are all Wolverines pussies?" She circled Steven a couple of times snickering and then she was gone.

Steven was waiting patiently for his date to show and Sara was fashionably late. She entered the lobby in a lavender toga and Steven was speechless. She gave him a peck on the cheek and began to walk past him. "Come on. We're going to be late and I'm starved." Steven was frozen in place as his mind was still processing that all Sara had on was a toga.

Sara ate like a horse as Steven watched her every move and her two cocktails loosened her up even more. As they were finishing dessert, Sara suggested going for a walk on the beach, but Steven wanted to go back to his room. Sara seductively asked, "Why don't we start on the beach and finish in your room?" Steven quickly paid the bill and was off to the beach to enjoy his nightcap.

Sara pleased him under the shining stars and helped him up afterwards. She liked to tease Stevey and did so all the way up to his seventh floor room. They made out in the elevator, but Steven insisted on finishing in his room.

Once inside, their clothes were soon taken off and the passion became nonstop as the two lovers rolled from position to position. Sara truly enjoyed the meaningless sex, knowing she would never see this guy again. As she was rocking on top of Steve, she felt the hardness of a man behind her and jumped off the bed.

Steven's two buddies were hiding in the bedroom closet and now, one was naked and ready to enjoy Sara while the third guy was videoing the whole sex act on his phone.

Sara shouted, "What the hell are you doing, you frickin bunch of perverts!" She grabbed her dress, purse, and shoes and made a quick getaway. As she was leaving, Steven yelled, "Ohio State sucks and so do you" and the other two Wolverines began to laugh at her expense.

Sara ran to the next resort, found her new friend's room, and frantically knocked on the door. "Please Evelyn, I need to see you…. It's Sara." Evelyn opened the door and Sara grasped her. "I screwed up real bad 'Auntie'. I just had sex with a guy whose friend videotaped us from the closet."

Evelyn poured Sara a shot and listened to her story. When Sara finished, Evelyn questioned her like a lawyer. "Do they know your last name or phone number? Were the lights on in the bedroom? Was the closet close to the bed? How big was he? Sara answered "No" to all the questions, but the last one, she was confused and just uttered, "Not very."

Evelyn poured herself a drink and sat down across the table from Sara and began to explain her theory. "They aren't going to post that anywhere on social media. With the lights off and the phone so far away, there is no way the video would be identifiable…. Probably a bunch of college punks trying to enjoy an orgy." Sara was relieved, but still confused. "Why did you want to know how big he was?" Evelyn displayed a devilish grin. "I was just curious?"

They both started to laugh as Sara finally calmed down and then Evelyn continued. "You're playing a very dangerous game, Sara. American men your age have no respect or courtesy towards anyone. A one night stand isn't what it used to be and the next time you might get hurt…. Who's Todd that you're so worried about him seeing the video?"

Sara sighed, "He's a guy I met down here ten years ago and I only see one week a year. I really like him and I hope to hang out with him when he gets down here next month." Now Evelyn was confused.

"You care about him, but you're sleeping with strange men?"

Sara put her head down and sadly confessed. "I don't understand either…. Sometimes I feel like I'm a slut and I'm turning into my mother and that sickens me…. I better go now."

Evelyn declared, "You're not going anywhere. Tomorrow morning, I'm going to get you a parking pass and a card for my room…. You're staying here for the next six days."

Sara didn't want to bother her hostess and declined the invitation, but Evelyn wasn't taking no for an answer. "I'm going to make you work for your keep…. I've been coming here for twenty years, and Mike never rented a car. I still haven't seen the natural bridge or Arikok Park. You know your way around this island pretty well and you're going to be my tour guide for the next six days."

They both walked together to the second bedroom and Evelyn told her grateful guest. "Get a goodnight's sleep in a clean bed and we'll straighten this all out tomorrow…. And the next time you go on a blind date, wear a bra and panties."

Sara's sad eyes looked at Evelyn and her long hug said thank you. She went into the shower to wash Steven off her body and regrettably knew that she was as much to blame as he was. The fact that she was becoming Stacey scared her. "I'm not my mother" consumed her thoughts as she cozied her body underneath the sheets and got a well needed rest. She had been very active for almost two weeks and it was still early in her trip.

Sara awoke late to find Evelyn gone and a note saying, "Good Morning. I am at breakfast with my girlfriends. Put on these clothes and bring your vehicle back here and park it in the garage below us. We're at Dushi Bagels if you'd like to join us."

Sara put on her makeshift wardrobe and retrieved her van. She made two trips up the elevator with her gathered belongings and sorted her stuff out in her new room. She went out on the balcony to enjoy the view and realized that Playa Linda was very similar to her "sister" resort that Sara called home on Eagle Beach.

Sara took advantage of this quiet time to calculate her finances. She'd spent another hundred bucks over the last week and was comfortably ahead of her budget. She decided to write a travel journal on her phone. Before she left Ohio, Sara had purchased Verizon's International plan and had unlimited access to the internet so she took this time to finally review her many texts.

She was threatened by Mercy Hospital, accused of vandalism by her old fiancée, and Joan had produced valuable information that Sara immediately forwarded to her lawyer. Di Albert sent several informative texts, but there was nothing from Todd. "I guess he's not interested in a relationship anymore and I'm not calling to find out why. I'll find out soon enough."

Evelyn entered the balcony and asked her guest what she was involved with and Sara explained her journal and again gratefully thanked her host. "I'm your 'slave' for the next six days. Where does my queen wish to go?"

Evelyn joyfully commanded, "Today, your queen will show you her kingdom and you'll slow down your fast pace.... I want to show you off to my friends. They've been introducing me to their family members for years. You are the guest of honor at Azzurro tonight.... Please wear something that isn't see through."

As Evelyn talked, Sara could see Kathy in her eyes. She was more direct and sarcastic in her demeanor than her aunt was, but Evelyn's free going spirit was very similar to Kathy's. Evelyn was 71 years young and could have been her grandmother, but she acted like a thirty year old.

They spent the rest of the day walking the property and relaxing at the pool. Evelyn insisted on buying her guest the perfect dress for dinner so they spent the heat of the afternoon on a "cool" shopping spree inside the air conditioned fashion stores.

Evelyn was having more fun than Sara, and Sara was having a blast.

The two new friends purposely showed up late and entered with all eyes staring at them. They were both wearing white, but Sara was wearing it so much better. As they slowly approached her friends' table, Betty stood up and exclaimed, "My God Evelyn. Where did you 'buy' her at?" When Marge said, "I used to look like that", Louise laughed, "You never looked like that in a million years!"

The five lady's enjoyed each other's company as all the men passed slowly by, staring at Sara's stunning beauty. Betty remarked, "We've never had this much attention in all the years we've been down here…. Sara Sweety, you need to visit us next year." They all enjoyed their pasta while the men enjoyed their view.

Evelyn announced, "Tomorrow, Sara and I are going to the Ostrich Farm for their monthly farmer's market. Who wants to join us?" Marge was onboard, but Betty and Louise were in their eighties and declined because of the heat.

The four elders split the check and Marge begged the guest of honor. "Sara my dear, would you please walk out by yourself…. Slowly…. We want to watch everyone's reaction." The four friends were giggling like schoolgirls when all their fellow owners came running to their table asking Evelyn who the "goddess" was.

Sara looked like a cab driver the next day as the three girls headed to the Ostrich Farm. They had fun talking and shopping with the locals. They all bought handmade miniature "Cunucu Houses" from Naomi and enjoyed learning her unique perspective of Aruba.

After two hours of walking, Sara shuffled Evelyn and Marge into the air conditioned van and they were off to see the Natural Baby Bridge. The parking lot was packed with tour buses and ATVs, but the girls still got out to get a closer view. As the strong wind blew the spray of the salt water onto their faces, the older women were amazed by the pounding of the waves against the cliffs. "How did we not come here sooner in our lives?"

Sara continued driving slowly up the coast while her friends stared out the windows and watched the "power" of mother nature. Sara sadly explained, "When Aunt Kathy and I started coming here, we could climb down that ladder over there and swim by ourselves in a small pool of water protected by the rock inside those crazy waves. Now, you can't even park your car near it…. We used to drive into the park on this road, but the ATVs have destroyed it…. I'm happy for the local businesses who profit from it, but I'm sad for the locals who love this side of their island."

After a refreshing cold drink at the Bushiribana Gold Mill Ruins, they started their trip back home. Sara stopped at the Glassblowing shop and they browsed the beautiful works of art. Sara narrated as her van passed through the Casibari Rock Formations and the town of Paradera.

Marge and Evelyn were really delighted with the tour, but were very tired from the excursion. They napped the rest of the afternoon while Sara joined her windsurfing friends, Vivian and Rosa, at the Flip Flop beach concert. The three girls had a blast listening to the music and hanging out with the carefree locals.

Evelyn and Sara spent the next four days together, touring the island in the early day while eating and shopping at night. Sara called Luis to confirm the Tuesday kitesurfing lesson and then informed Evelyn, who replied, "Have some fun, but don't kill yourself." She sounded just like Aunt Kathy.

Sara walked over to Hadicurari Beach early in the afternoon and watched the kitesurfers play in the water. Luis saw her and asked her to join a very nervous teenage girl who was struggling to follow his instructions. He introduced Sara to the confused girl.

"Mandy. This is Sara and she's from Ohio too. Sara has no clue at all how to kitesurf so you two are going to work together on your balance." Sara began chatting with the young girl about her hometown while she moved her back and forth on the practice board. Soon Mandy became comfortable and started making progress as Luis gave her more instructions.

When her time was up, Mandy asked to stay. "Can I practice more on the board? I'm staying at the Ritz next door and my parents know where I'm at." Luis looked at Sara who cheerfully agreed, "That's a great idea, Mandy. Maybe you can give me some pointers." Luis instructed the two girls for almost three hours and then they sat on the beach together and watched the sunset.

Mandy was sitting in the middle and was very excited. "This is so romantic.... I mean fun. I'm an only child and my parents both work a lot. I don't like to crowd them when they can have some alone time together."

Sara put her arm around her young friend. "I am an only child too.... I know exactly how you feel." Mandy put her head on Sara's shoulder while they watched the sun begin to disappear. Sara held her tightly and thought "Mandy is me when I first came to Aruba and right now, I feel like Auntie."

Sara walked Luis to his truck and winked at him. "She's got a crush on you, Mister." Luis was confused, "Mandy? She's only sixteen.... You're joking?" Sara confidently answered, "Nope. I was fifteen when I fell in love with an older man in Aruba. That's why she's so nervous around you. Be nice to her tomorrow.... See you next Tuesday."

Mandy was waiting for Sara and they had a heart to heart talk as they walked to the Ritz. Mandy told her about her struggles in high school. "I wish I was as pretty as you. No guys ever look at me." Sara held her hand and squeezed it tightly. "You are a pretty girl and guys are going to start noticing you.... Just be patient."

Mandy asked if Sara was coming to her next lesson and was disappointed when Sara answered, "I'm sorry Mandy, but I'm going to a vineyard with my good friend tomorrow. How long are you staying here?" Mandy replied, "Two weeks" and Sara promised her, "I'll see you for sure next Tuesday and maybe we can go snorkeling if your parents are okay with it." Mandy was very excited when the two parted ways at the Ritz. As Sara walked back to Playa Linda, she got emotional about her new friendships with Evelyn and Mandy. "I feel like I'm watching a rerun from 2014."

Evelyn was very excited about touring the Alto Vista Winery and Distillery. She had heard about it from the resort concierge. She booked two tickets and begged Sara to go. "None of the girls are interested, but I would love to see a vineyard in this desert." They left early so Evelyn could view the Alto Vista Chapel and its magnificent view of the coastline.

Sara and Evelyn arrived for the crowded 6 PM tour and were very impressed by the entire operation. The tour was very interesting and the tasting room was beautiful. They met two girls from the Netherlands who sat with them at their tasting table. The four women had a great time chatting away while sampling Aruba made rum and wine paired with cheeses.

Heidi and Ingrid lived on the island and worked at Bingos restaurant and both spoke very good English. They asked Sara to go out partying with them and Evelyn gave her blessing, but Sara declined. "I'd love to, but I'm spending the next two days with Evelyn. I'm going to be here for three more weeks…. Can we exchange cell numbers?" Heidi gave her phone number to Sara and warned her in advance. "When we go out, we party hard, like real Europeans!"

The last day before Evelyn left was very bittersweet for the two friends. Sara finally made the trip to Mangel Halto and they sat on a picnic table while their eyes absorbed the many blues of the Caribbean Sea. Sara reminisced about Kathy and Evelyn remembered her love filled life with Mike.

Evelyn appreciated her time with Sara. "Thank you for taking the time to show an old gal around the town.... You've shown me places that were always at my fingertips that I never tried to grasp."

Sara stared straight into the blue sea, avoiding any eye contact with her host. "Thank you Aunt Kathy for sending me an angel to watch over me. Evelyn took me in and protected me just like you did, twenty years ago. I love you Auntie." Sara turned her quivering chin to see Evelyn's head refusing to make eye contact and her older friend insisted. "Why don't we just enjoy this spectacular view without me crying like an old fool."

When they returned from Mangel Halto, they both packed their luggage after Sara washed her dirty clothes. Then the ladies socialized late into the afternoon. Mike and Evelyn's final night tradition was always dinner at Azzurro. She booked a table just for two and requested a favor from Sara. "Would you please, wear the pretty pink dress that you just got." Sara tenderly agreed, "I knew you liked that one the best so I was saving it for tonight."

They entered the restaurant hand in hand as if they were walking the red carpet and nodded to their friends. After ordering drinks, Evelyn revealed a secret. "Do you know the man I appreciate the most?"

Sara had no clue so Evelyn refreshed her memory. "That jackass who was flirting with you at the Bohemian…. I got up to save you from him, never realizing that you would change my outlook on life. I will NOT cry in public so let me finish…. I want you in my life and I'd love it if you would visit me sometime. I figured Watkins Glen is only six hours away from Canton and maybe we could meet in Erie."

Sara listened with a glowing beam on her face and told Evelyn, "You've been the best thing that's happened to me since my aunt passed away…. There's no way you're going to get rid of me!" Evelyn quickly changed the emotional subject. "Ernesto is playing Mike's favorite song…. That old hoot used to make an ass of himself on the dance floor."

Sara took the lead, standing up in front of Evelyn with her hand out. "May I have this dance Mrs. Reed?" They joyfully gazed into each other's eyes dancing the whole time Ernesto was playing guitar.

Before she fell asleep, Sara wrote down the events of tonight's dinner in the notebook that Evelyn bought her. Sara enjoyed writing about her life in Aruba and promised herself to record the entire trip. "Maybe I'll write a book someday" she tittered.

On the way to the airport, Sara gave Evelyn a present. "Open it up, I can't wait to see your face."

Evelyn opened the box to see a shiny necklace with the many blues of the Caribbean Sea. She was admiring it when Sara proudly bragged. "That's the same necklace you liked at the Ostrich Farm.... I snuck back and bought it for you so you won't forget me." Evelyn laughed. "How can I ever forget you!"

Sara got Evelyn's bags to the front door of the airport and said a quick farewell. Before she got back to the van, a middle aged couple started putting luggage into her vehicle. Sara was startled and asked, "What are you doing?"

The woman snapped back. "We are doing your job." Sara realized that they thought she was driving a taxi and tried to explain, but was rudely cut off again by the woman. "Take us to the RIU and be quick about it." Sara chuckled and said, "Yes Mam" and off they went.

Sara asked if they had a nice flight and the woman replied, "When did young American girls start driving cabs? This country is going to the crap house. These seats are dirty and musty, don't you people clean…. I have allergies, you know." Sara firmly inquired. "Are you from New York City?" And the woman laughed, "Yes…. Are you from Kentucky?"

Sara made a left at Ling and Sons and found the first available bus stop. She stopped and began taking their luggage out of her van. The couple followed her out with the woman screaming at her.

Sara declared, "Yeah. I'm from Kentucky and I'm allergic to your thousand dollar perfume." As she drove away, Sara could hear the husband yelling at his wife. "Nice job Nancy…. When will you ever learn!"

Sara parked her "musty" van in the Arashi parking lot and snorkeled all day. She then locked herself in for the evening. This was the first night that she slept in the van since last Friday so she needed to get reorganized. The first thing to do was check on Aunt Kathy's ashes and calculate her remaining finances.

She saw a picture taken a year ago on her phone and began to think about the photographer and his kind heart. "Todd was always so sweet to me and respected me as a woman. I thought I really loved him, but now I realize that I don't even know what true love is. He probably feels like I do and that's why he won't text me…. I guess I'll find out where I stand with him in a couple of weeks."

Sara scrolled down through her texts to see if Evelyn was back home and stopped when she saw Juan's old message, so she sent him a text and just typed "Hi" and wondered, "What did I do to upset him?"

Her phone suddenly rang and she quickly picked it up, thinking it might be Evelyn, but a woman's perky voice gushed, "Hello Sara Girl. This is

Heidi…. RCC is having a 'Magic Mike Party' tomorrow night. It's great fun with half naked men everywhere. Ingrid and I go almost every week…. Do you want me to get a ticket for you?" Sara didn't waste a breath, "Hell Yeah. I've been wanting to see them since I got here."

Heidi eagerly told Sara to meet them at 11PM in front of the elevator at Paseo Herencia. "We party hard, Girl. Wear something sexy that's easy to take off!" Sara laughed and said, "I'll see you there" and when she got off the phone, she wondered, "What did I get myself into?"

Sara was in the water by daybreak and snorkeled her ABM route until the tour boats flooded the area around 11AM. She snorkeled against the current all the way back to Arashi Beach and was very tired when she got out. Sara's intention was to visit a friend so she drove down to Hadicurari Beach. She changed into a new string bikini that Evelyn bought her and walked to the Ritz. She knew the only way to get past their security was to show a lot of skin.

Once past the guards, Sara started looking for Mandy. She ignored the catcalls and whistles; Sara wasn't "fishing" today. It took a while, but she finally found Mandy reading a book all alone. "Aren't you too young to read romance novels?"

Mandy looked up over her book and screamed, "SARA. What are you doing here!" Mandy jumped up and gave her friend a great big hug. "I was just thinking about you.... The heroine in my book reminds me of you. Can you hang out with me for a while?" Sara grinned at her and gushed, "That's why I'm here, Kiddo."

As the girls chatted away, Mandy watched the men circling their palapa. "Those guys have been walking past here since you came and sat with me." Sara asked if she wanted to play a fun game with a bunch of boys and Mandy replied, "I'd love to, but they won't play with me."

Sara gave her a stern look. "The first thing you need to learn is confidence. You're a beautiful girl. You need to act like one.... Follow me and do what I do. This'll be fun."

Sara got up and played with her long blonde hair and then slowly walked into the water as Mandy emulated her every move. They started laughing and floating on the salty sea water as the men soon joined them, pretending to throw a football and accidently wading into them.

Sara saw the time was right and instructed her young friend, "Get on my shoulders and start giggling" which drew more "wanted" attention to them. A crashing wave took them under and Sara came out squeezing her triangle bikini top tightly and winked at Mandy. "Let's go get some lunch."

They slowly strutted to the beach bar, arm in arm and Sara observed, "See that boy over there, Mandy. He's not looking at me.... He's looking at you." Mandy embraced her in front of their audience and whispered in Sara's ear, "You're the best." They spent the rest of the day together on the beach, driving the men and boys crazy.

Sara snuck in the "hospitality suite" and showered for the Magic Mike Show. She met Mandy's parents as she was leaving the Ritz and asked their permission to take her snorkeling next week and they both okayed it.

Her mother, Denise, was a lawyer and thanked Sara for befriending her daughter. "I can see why Amanda is so fond of you.... The resort has snorkeling gear as a courtesy so that won't be an issue next week.... Thanks for wanting to help her out. Her father and I are trying to work out a few things and I hate to say it, but we've neglected her on this trip." Sara said goodbye and got ready for her big night out.

The girl from Ohio looked like an "escort" from San Nicolas when Heidi and Ingrid arrived after 11PM. She had on a white halter top and a thin red mini skirt. The show had already started, but the girls still managed to get a table near the front.

Ingrid bought the first round of whiskey as they enjoyed the erotic performers in action. Ingrid made a toast, "To our first night out together.... I hope it doesn't turn out like the Kukoo Kunuku Party Bus." The Dutch women laughed as Sara's throat started to burn and she yelled over the loud music playing, "What kind of whiskey is this" and Heidi replied, "It's called 'Fire Ball' and it's got a cinnamon flavor to it."

Sara confidently confirmed, "It's got a kick to it.... What happened on the party bus?" Ingrid answered as one of the RCC guys came over to dance for Sara. "We were wasted halfway through the bar stops and started hitting on two brothers and one of their wives got pissed when Heidi started groping her husband.... When we came out of the bar, the bus was leaving early and the wife was laughing while flipping us off with both hands."

Heidi added through the roaring laughter, "A couple of months ago, we were at Aruba Ray's Comedy Club.... We sat in the front and Ray enjoyed making us a part of his act. He said what a great view he had so we both took off our tops and I asked him how the view looked now.... Ray liked it, but I guess security didn't and they escorted us out of the place."

After another round of shots, another dancer came over to Sara and began to perform in front of her. "That's Rafael. He's very good in bed.... They're all coming over here to check out the 'fresh meat' and see who's going to get lucky.... Looks like we're getting the leftovers tonight, Heidi."

As Eduardo began his act, he immediately swaggered to their table and began to sexually sway Sara with his moves. Heidi observed, "Eduardo wants you badly.... That's why we invited you Sara. These guys love new 'eye candy'.... Let's get another round."

Sara was aroused by the erotic show being performed for her approval. Two hours and God only knows how many shots of whiskey later, Sara was sitting on the stage as the performers took turns grinding their hips into her flushed face. She was wasted and was caught up in a dream of sexual fantasy.

Sara awoke the next morning aching from the pounding of her head. She was naked and lying next to Heidi on a bed. "What the fu.... OH MY GOD. What did I do?" Her question awoke Heidi and she got out of bed and put on some clothes. Sara's blood shot eyes saw Ingrid enter the room and she asked Heidi, "Did you and I have...."

The girls sat down on the bed beside Sara, and Ingrid handed her a cup of tea. Heidi answered, "No. We're not into girls, but we love to watch and you are one crazy American." Ingrid laughed, "I thought I was the wildest blonde on this island, but I'm not even in your league!"

Sara took several sips of tea and lay back down, staring at the ceiling. "The last thing I remember was dancing on stage." Heidi smirked, "You did more than just 'dance' on the stage. I know everyone got their money's worth last night.... I'm afraid all those shots of 'Fire Ball' did you in."

Sara was in disbelief of the night. "I can't remember anything and my whole body is throbbing with pain. What did I do?" Ingrid replied, "It's more like 'What DIDN'T you do'.... I've seen some kinky sex in my life, but last night takes the cake.... Who's Todd? You kept moaning his name all night.... I could hardly concentrate on my guy because of your loud moans."

The question triggered Sara's emotions. "Evelyn warned me about doing something careless like this. How could I have driven here as drunk as I was?"

Heidi quickly answered her question. "Eduardo drove you to our apartment in your van, Rafael drove us back in our car, and Carlos followed us in his truck. They left after the sex was over around an hour ago."

Sara began to think how disappointed Kathy would be of her and then screamed in horror. "Oh My God. Aunt Kathy!" She quickly put her clothes on and sprinted toward her van as Ingrid and Heidi looked at each other in confusion. Sara was frantic.

"All my money and belongings are in that van. Aunt Kathy's ashes…. What have I done?"

Sara was so relieved to see the keys still in the ignition and the inside of the vehicle untouched. She smiled slightly when she read a makeshift note on her driver's seat. "You are one wild American woman. Thanks for a fun night…. Eduardo."

Sara grabbed the keys and rejoined the girls for breakfast and explained her mad run to the van. Heidi understood and Ingrid told Sara, "We know all those guys…. We wouldn't invite a creep back to our apartment. We all just like to screw each other!" Sara and the girls began laughing and Ingrid suggested, "I'm tired…. Let's go back to bed and 'sleep' in it for a change."

Sara stayed with the girls for the weekend and enjoyed talking about their life in Aruba. She learned about the Netherlands and found out that Heidi was a celebrated tennis star who just got burnt out from the grueling lifestyle. "I escaped to this island paradise and I'll never go back to that stressful regimen again."

Sara promised to stay in touch with them but was finished with the crazy nightlife. "The next time we go out, I'm staying away from Fire Ball whiskey." Her two new friends roared in their agreement and welcomed Sara back any time.

As Sara drove to the beach for her kitesurfing lesson, she thought about Heidi and could relate to her desire to relocate to Aruba. "I'd love to just stay down here and start a new life. Nobody would miss me anyhow."

Her thoughts of becoming her mother unnerved Sara. "How can I befriend a teenager and then sleep with strange men on the same day? It just doesn't make sense…. I don't ever want to be like Stacey." So many thoughts cluttered her mind as she pulled into the parking lot on Hadicurari Beach.

Luis was working with Mandy in the water, trying to get her up on the board. Mandy saw Sara coming to them and yelled, "Hi Sara. I've got my snorkel gear over there. Are we going soon?" Sara saw Luis behind her just shaking his head in frustration and then told her young friend, "We're going to leave as soon as you balance yourself on that board" and then Sara swam over to join them.

It took Sara three attempts, but she finally balanced herself on the board and then challenged Mandy. "It's your turn now, Sweety." After Sara vacated the board, Mandy quickly balanced herself and stuck her tongue out at Sara, confidently gushing to her astonished teachers. "Let's roll."

Mandy ran to get her gear, wearing a very revealing bikini bottom that made Sara comment, "WOW! Look at you in that sexy swimsuit" and

Mandy proudly replied, "Mom took me shopping yesterday. She said this type highlights my 'butt' so she bought three suits for me."

Sara happily agreed. "Your mom's a smart lady. I'm glad the two of you got to spend time together." Mandy started clapping her hands. "I think mom's jealous of you after I told her about our fun Saturday on the beach…. Please Luis, come and snorkel with us."

Sara observed that Luis didn't have any equipment and that offended him. "You don't need all that stuff to swim with the turtles." Sara, always up for a challenge, countered. "I'll bet you dinner that I'll find a turtle before you do." Luis shook his head and said, "You're on." Sara drove them to Boca Catalina and she and Luis began teaching Mandy the basic lessons of snorkeling.

After Mandy was comfortable with her breathing, Luis got Sara's attention and yelled to his masked competition. "On your mark, get set, GO" and he took off for the turtles. Sara signaled for Mandy to return to the shore and then she took off after him. Luis swam along the coast toward Tres Trepi and Sara snorkeled farther out toward the Antilla. Twenty minutes later, Sara joined up with Luis and gave him a thumbs up and he dejectedly asked, "Where do you want to go for dinner?"

They returned to the shore to find Mandy talking to two boys her age and their parents. Sara yelled, "I won the bet, in case you're interested" and Mandy introduced her new friends. "This is Jake and John from Maryland and this is my big sister Sara and her boyfriend Luis. We're going back in the water to snorkel.... Tag along and we'll show you where all the good stuff is." The two boys followed the confident Mandy into the saltwater and her "Big Sis" gave them a special tour of the cove.

Forty minutes later, the snorkelers returned to shore. Jake, John, and Mandy were giddy after seeing the amazing world under the sea. Jake kissed Mandy and shouted out, "That was wild! Can I get your cell number" and she happily gave it to him as his family was packing up to leave the beach.

Sara saw the glow on her young friend's face and hugged her tightly. Mandy became emotional and whispered in Sara's ear. "That's the first time I've ever been kissed by a boy.... Thanks for going along with my lie." Sara cheerfully disagreed, "You didn't lie Kiddo. I'm officially your big sister."

On the short trip back, Luis told the two sisters that he was playing beach tennis at Moomba with his partner at seven o'clock and had to get going. "We've got a league match tonight. Why don't you guys come over and watch? It's a fun sport."

Sara walked hand in hand with Mandy as she giggled about the "greatest day" of her life. As they approached the Ritz, Mandy saw her mom and dad romantically kissing on the water's edge. "I never thought that I would see them do that again.... This island is magic." Denise waved to them and Mandy ran into her mother's arms. Sara stayed behind and captured the family watching the sunset together with her camera.

Sara began to walk away when Denise caught up to her and asked if they could have lunch together on Thursday afternoon. "They have a wonderful sushi bar here. Would four o'clock be okay? I really need to talk to you about an important matter." Sara agreed and asked Denise's permission to take Mandy down to the beach tennis courts near the Holiday Inn and Denise intensely grinned, "That would be heavenly."

The two girls made it in time for the last set of Luis's match. They stopped dead in their tracks and watched Luis's partner dominate HER rivals. Mandy rolled her eyes and uttered, "Looks like you got competition, Sis."

His partner was a gorgeous dark skinned woman with a well-toned body. The crowd's eyes were on her as she effortlessly moved back and forth. Their match ended in a victory and Luis introduced his partner.

"Ladies, this is my girlfriend, Anna…. We just won the match and I still have an hour remaining on my court reservation. Would you both like to learn how to play beach tennis?" Without asking, Mandy volunteered. "Hi. I'm Mandy and she's my sister Sara. We'd love to play."

Anna looked up and down Sara's body and then looked at Luis. "So, this is little Sara!" Anna then stared at Sara and smirked, "We'll show you the basics and then play a fun practice game…. How about Luis and Sara against me and Mandy?"

When the "fun" game started, the ball was flying and the remaining crowd was drooling. Sara caught on quickly and every wicked shot aimed at her was returned back the same way. Luis and Mandy were no longer involved in the flow of the game, so they retired and watched like the rest of the growing crowd.

Suddenly it got ugly and Anna called Sara a 'bitch' in Papiamento, not knowing Sara understood the language. Sara rushed the court and yelled, "You don't scare me 'bitch' so bring it" in Anna's native language. The cussing continued through each volley as the adversaries tried to decapitate each other.

Finally, Anna missed her shot and threw her racket at Luis and called him several ugly names. She stormed off the court to the crowd's ovation for the American. Sara grabbed Mandy's hand and while still talking Papiamento, told her embarrassed partner, "Thanks for the fun night, Asshole!" Mandy waved goodbye to Luis as she was being led away.

The walk back to the Ritz was thankfully short and Mandy had nothing but questions. "What were you saying to her? Did you see her eyes when you whooped her butt? Are you going to break up with Luis?" And then she asked if Sara would like to come up to her suite.

The hotheaded blonde quickly remembered the look on Denise's face and calmed down, trying to give Mandy's parents some much needed "alone" time. Sara suggested, "Let's go sit on the beach and listen to the waves crash together."

For the next three days, Sara was devoted to making the rest of Mandy's stay fun. She kept her van parked stationary in the public parking lot and commuted from it daily. She was very civil at Mandy's kitesurfing lesson as Luis remained very quiet. Sara and Luis had one thing in common; they both wanted to see Mandy travel some distance on the kiteboard before time ran out on her vacation.

Thursday morning was Mandy's last lesson and chance to complete her task. Luis and Sara were struggling to help Mandy maintain her balance as the wind moved the kiteboard back and forth. Sara saw Denise watching her daughter from afar and asked for her help. Once she joined the group, Sara revealed her plan. "If each one of us holds the board stable on both sides, front and rear, Mandy can get on and then we just let go and see what happens."

The three helpers fought the waves as Mandy struggled to get into position. Soon a gust of wind caught the kite from behind and Luis yelled to let go. They excitedly watched Mandy quickly sail one hundred feet before she fell off. Everyone acted like Mandy had just won the Olympics and she started screaming, "I did it! I did it!"

Mandy's achievement completely satisfied her and the lessons ended on a high note. Denise caressed her daughter and as they were walking back to the Ritz, Sara overheard the excited girl say, "I can't wait to come back next year!"

Luis came over and broke his silence. "You were a good friend to Mandy. You should be proud." Sara thanked him for the compliment and calmly stated the facts. "For the record. I don't care that you have a girlfriend, but she called me a 'bitch' for no reason and I don't take that lightly."

Luis tried to explain his situation. "Look. I don't really have a steady girlfriend. There are four women that I have relations with and we all get along. Anna was furious because I told her that you were chubby. She is very jealous, but very good in bed. I probably won't see her anymore because of you, but that's life.... I'm not interested in a wife; I like to play the field and they understand that. I hope you do too."

Sara smiled at Luis and concurred, "I totally get it and I'm starting to feel the same way myself…. See you next Tuesday and you still owe me dinner."

Sara met Denise at Divi Sushi Bar later that afternoon. As she was seated, Sara asked where Mandy was, and Denise answered, "Amanda took Frank snorkeling this afternoon. She wanted to show her father the turtles…. You've been so kind to her these last two weeks, and I can never thank you enough for what you did for my family."

Sara acknowledged her gratitude. "Mandy has been a breath of fresh air in my life. She reminds me of the first year I came to Aruba with my aunt ten years ago. That's the year my eyes opened wide to the real wonders of life."

They ordered drinks and a sushi sampler and Denise began to explain her situation. "Frank and I are very career driven. I'm a partner in a successful legal firm and Frank has just been promoted to Chief Surgeon at the Cleveland Clinic…. It's a funny coincidence, but I remember you in a black gown at a fundraiser a couple of years ago at the Renaissance Hotel; you were simply unforgettable."

Denise became serious and admitted, "Frank and I have dedicated our lives to becoming the best in our professions. Unfortunately, we have distanced ourselves from each other over the last ten years and to be honest with you, I was going to ask Frank for a divorce when we returned home. We have both had affairs through the years, only thinking about ourselves."

Denise sipped her martini and continued. "I was very jealous of you and became very irritated hearing the word 'Sara' constantly coming out of Amanda's mouth and then I met you in person…. I was floored that a beautiful woman would pay so much attention to my daughter when I don't even know who her friends are at school…. Do you understand what I'm trying to say? Frank and I have been so consumed in our crazy lifestyles that we've pushed the best thing that we ever did together out of our lives…. Seeing Amanda gazing at you slapped me in my face and opened my eyes. I wasn't a mother to her anymore."

Denise composed herself while trying a piece of sushi. "That is so delicious. I hope you enjoy it…. Frank and I were getting nowhere in our reconciliation until you showed up. After seeing my daughter admiring a stranger, I confessed my sins to Frank and begged him to join me in becoming the best parents that we could be and to do it together…. While you've been enjoying your time with Amanda this past week, Frank and I have been rekindling our love in this magical paradise. We've taken long walks on the beach, talking about our past and dreaming about our future. We made love for two hours Tuesday night…. We haven't made love for two hours combined since Amanda was born."

Sara was touched by her honesty. "I really appreciate you sharing this with me and I'm thrilled for Mandy. She's a great young lady and she needs you desperately over these next five years. I would've been lost without my Aunt Kathy's support as I became a woman. I'm very happy for your family and I'm jealous of you too…. I would love to stay in contact with Mandy if that's okay with you?"

Denise became delighted. "That's why I invited you to lunch today…. To ask that favor from you. Amanda loves you, Sara. She needs you in her life…. These past two weeks, I've watched her go from reading books alone to being a confident young woman who isn't afraid to fail. That's all because of you, Sara, and I can never thank you enough. If you ever need my help, please give me an opportunity to pay you back for saving my family."

Sara's blue eyes sparkled with delight and she asked Denise, "There is one thing I would like you to do…. My Aunt Kathy and I always spent the first night of our trip in Aruba, holding each other in the water while we enjoyed sunset together. It's what I remember most about her. Tonight, I want to pass that torch onto you and Mandy so she can always have that special memory of you."

Both women were emotional and Denise promised to keep the tradition alive. Sara got up to leave and lovingly smiled at her host. "Thank you for this wonderful lunch. I hope we can do it again in the near future.... Please tell your precious daughter that I'll meet her on the beach at seven tomorrow to say our goodbyes. Enjoy the sunset tonight, Denise."

Mandy was already on the beach and waiting when Sara arrived on Friday morning and the young girl suggested, "Let's walk down to Pelican Pier and hangout for a while." They sat on the pier for an hour, watching the busy day unfold, and Mandy confessed, "This was the best vacation EVER! I don't want to leave here Sara.... Thanks for making me feel like a woman and for being my friend." Sara was insulted. "Friend? I thought I was your big sister?"

Sara gave Mandy a present on their walk back to the Ritz. "I hope you like it. Just a little something to remember me by." Sara opened her hand and put a ring on Mandy's finger. "It has many shades of blue like the sea in front of us and it'll remind you of Aruba on a cold Ohio night."

Mandy thanked Sara and began to weep. "I promise to keep your Aunt Kathy's tradition alive.... I Don't Want To Say Goodbye!" Sara whispered into her ear. "Then Don't.... Just say, I'll see you later."

She kissed Mandy on top of her head and said, "See ya soon, Kiddo" and then she walked away.

MANGEL HALTO

Sara composed herself inside the van and then drove south to finally face Mangel Halto. It was their favorite snorkeling spot on the island, but Sara had been avoiding it for the last month, not wanting to snorkel there without her Aunt Kathy. She parked her van overlooking the beautiful blue water in front of her. Sara took her gear and climbed down the ladder, thinking about what Kathy told her the last days of her life. "Well, I guess it's about time I found that magical parrot fish."

For over two hours, Sara was absorbed in the purity of the sea and its surroundings. The ocean was her church and the reef was her "altar" and she confessed her last year to the sea life below her. At first she looked for the parrot fish, but a cute puffy fish hypnotized her and Sara tried to follow it everywhere. She was at peace with herself when she left the water that afternoon and decided to stay in Savaneta for a few days.

Sara knew Coral Reef Beach Aruba was a small resort snuggled between the Flying Fishbone and Aruba Beach Villas from her previous snorkeling trips in that area. It had a small beach with easy access to the sea and it had a small room still available, so she booked the weekend there. Eric and Jenny were very kind to her and advised Sara the whereabouts of the turtles and other sea life. She relaxed on the hammock after the long day of snorkeling and updated her travel journal.

After a month into the trip, Coral Reef was the first place she had actually paid for and Sara was proud of herself. She was still in good shape financially and with two weeks left, she had already done so many wonderful things while spending very little money. As she was relaxing, Sara began to hear the hustling noises of the famous restaurant next door to her. She went to the end of Coral Reef's property and enjoyed an amazing sunset while observing the front row diners at the Flying Fishbone.

As the sky darkened, Sara was fascinated with the ambiance of the restaurant. It transformed into a fairytale location with people actually eating while the gentle waves came over the barrier wall and covered their bare feet with saltwater. The million stars were easily seen above, shining down on the bright blue rays projecting out of the water.

Sara began spying on the guests through the hedges that divided the two properties. She was surprised to see Luis waiting on tables and then remembered that he worked there. A devilish idea entered her mind as she retreated to her room.

Sara spent the next day playing in the water near Coral Reef working up a tremendous appetite. She watched another picture perfect sunset with honeymooners from Chicago who asked Sara, "Does it ever really rain here?" She smiled and answered, "NEVER" as she used their phone to capture the newlyweds enjoying their first sunset as man and wife.

Sara excused herself to get ready for her dinner date and again chose the lavender toga as her weapon of seduction. She waited until nine o'clock to approach the hostess stand at the Flying Fishbone and asked for a table. Within minutes she was kindly seated without a reservation.

Everyone, including Luis, watched her seductively stroll to a table near the water. Luis grasped Sara's plan and became very anxious, thinking about their dinner date. He approached her table and announced, "Hello, my name is Luis and I will be your server tonight. Can I start you off with a cocktail or maybe 'water' if you like."

Sara looked like an evil divinity when she said, "I'd like your most expensive cocktail to start." Luis nervously smiled and begged her, "Please Sara. Do you know how expensive this place is and they run every sale through their computer system.... I don't make that much here." Sara just grinned. "I saw a turtle before you did. I won the bet and you're paying up tonight, Buster."

Luis dejectedly asked what his customer would like and she said, "For starters, I would like the ceviche and the shrimp casserole looks yummy.... And Waiter, could you please snap a few pics of me next to that table right there?" Luis took her phone while she approached the front row table and started posing next to a startled couple who also started smiling for the camera.

Luis never became flustered as he treated his friend like a customer for the rest of the night and finally asked, "Would you care for dessert tonight, Miss?" Sara looked at him with her bedroom eyes and sighed. "I don't think so. I'm going to have my dessert later." Luis started getting aroused. "Is there anything else you care for tonight?" Sara finished sucking on the straw of her daiquiri and lustfully answered him. "Only you."

The dining area was nearly empty of customers when Luis brought the check to her table and inquired. "I hope you enjoyed your experience tonight." Sara took the receipt book from his tense hand and remarked as she looked over the check. "I'm not sure I can answer that question right now" and then she looked directly into his eyes, "Ask me again tomorrow morning."

Luis frantically went back to the kitchen and counted only eighty two florins in his wallet and tried to borrow some money from his fellow waiters to pay off the expensive bill. When he returned to the dining area, Sara was gone. Inside the black book was one hundred and fifty dollars in US cash and a note. "Meet me where you took my picture as soon as you close. I won't wait a second if you're late."

Luis went to all the workers and asked if they saw the woman in purple leave, and no one had a clue. He quickly finished his duties and hid in the bathroom until he could hear the manager lock the door. When the coast was clear, Luis quickly went to the dining area and Sara was sitting on the table waiting for him. He wasted no words as he passionately kissed her body and made love to her on top of the table. Sara could feel him move to the flowing of the wind as she watched the sparkling sky above them. She moaned loudly as the seawater gently sprayed their naked bodies.

After they drained their passion, Sara led Luis around the hedges and towards her bedroom to "finish her dessert". The two lovers didn't even notice the astonished honeymooners watching them the entire time. Sara was unaware of anything other than her fiery desires.

Sara woke up the next morning and Luis was gone; no note, no flowers, no nothing. She wasn't upset that he took off in the dark; Sara expected it. "That's probably what I would have done. Leave before you say something stupid and give the wrong impression to a guy that might break his heart…. Luis was true to his word and I respect him for that, and he was very good in bed." Her light hearted observation quickly transformed into a sobering thought. "My God…. I am my mother."

The next two days, Sara stayed around Savaneta and snorkeled from Aruba Beach Villas all the way down to Villa Fillipe. Sara and the honeymooners took Coral Reef's kayaks over to the breaker island and looked for shiny sea glass. The clear sunny day allowed them to see the mountains of Venezuela, nineteen miles to their south. Sara checked out of Coral Reef and thanked Jenny for her kindness and drove to San Nicolas to enjoy the beautiful city murals.

That Monday afternoon, Sara hung out again with her friends Rosa and Vivian at Charlie's Bar. They had fun comparing notes of their experiences with Luis. Rosa delicately admitted, "We've all slept with him, but Anna is madly in love with Luis and I heard she wants to kill you…. Stay away from her. She's crazy and if she finds out you screwed him…. Oh brother."

Sara decided to reside above the cliffs of Mangel Halto for the next three days to find that elusive parrot fish that Kathy promised her. She snorkeled there twice a day, but the only parrot fish she saw eluded her as she approached them. She was frustrated, but still believed in the magic and kept her faith.

The only time she left Mangel Halto was for her kitesurfing lesson on Tuesday afternoon. She wasn't nervous when she saw Luis working with another beginner; she actually walked up to him and asked if he needed a hand. Luis smiled at his one night stand and calmly requested, "Could you help Harold focus on the board" and she helped Harold until his time was up and he was promptly led away by his jealous wife.

Sara broke the ice and promised her teacher, "You owe me one last lesson and I'll be out of your life for good." They were in the water and she was about to get on the board when he asked, "I know you can surf so don't lie to me.... Why did you come here today?"

Sara mounted the board and waited for a gust of wind. She joyfully gushed, "I came here so you could kiss my ass goodbye" and then she took off for her first kitesail adventure and almost made it to the turn before she wiped out. She got back on and almost made it back to Luis.

Sara got out of the water still laughing and hugged Luis. "That was incredible. The sensation of flying is awesome!" Luis tried to apologize about his bedroom escape, but Sara cut him off. "Don't. Let's not go there…. I would like to know about you and Anna?"

The question angered Luis and he swiftly brought the kite and board onto shore. Sara followed him and firmly insisted. "I think I have the right to know. There's rumors that she's trying to kill me?"

"She's not going to kill you. Who told you that nonsense? Ohhh, that's right…. I heard that you were with those two big mouths down at Charlie's yesterday. What else did Rosa tell you?" Sara sat down next to Luis as he was hastily putting away the sail and she calmly stated. "They told me that Anna is deeply in love with you."

Luis's emotions ignited with internal fire. He silently put the sail and board back and then sat next to Sara. "You and I met three weeks ago…. I've known Anna since we were kids. Anna and I share history. You and I don't. We see it all the time in Aruba. People like you want to change our world and then you leave…. Just because I screwed you doesn't give you the right to know my personal life. You better just get out of here right now!"

Sara stood up and before she left, she heatedly told Luis. "You're right. It is none of my business…. I thought you were my friend, but I guess that went out the window after you fucked me….

You're pissed because you're still in love with Anna. You big jerk!"

Sara drove off and parked at Bushiri Beach to reflect on what just happened and why it went so wrong. She never noticed her favorite part of the day as she desperately tried to sort her life out. "Luis was right. I should've never stuck my nose in his business. What is wrong with me?"

Sara called Evelyn and they talked for an hour until Sara's cell needed to be recharged. Before her phone quit Evelyn said. "Sara.... You have a big week ahead of you. Focus on Hank and your aunt's ashes. Focus on Todd. Quit playing games with these men." Sara thanked Evelyn for caring about her and then the phone died.

Sara stopped at the Pepe Nacho food truck on her way back to Mangel Halto. She ordered two tacos and a Chill beer and then sat down to enjoy a nice peaceful dinner. Sara looked up at the truck and saw Juan standing in line with a pretty girl. She smiled and waved at him, but he ignored her and sat down as far away from her as he could. Sara became distressed while eating her taco. "What did I do to this guy? We had a great time and he ignores me. Was I that bad?"

Sara let her curiosity get the best of her. She grabbed her Chill and when she approached Juan, he hastily intercepted her and walked Sara back to her table. "What are you doing Sara? That's my girlfriend and she doesn't know about us."

Sara was troubled by his attitude. "I'm sorry. I never meant to cause a scene. I just wanted to know why you've ignored me since that night?" Juan was very cold in his response. "You want to know why. I'll tell you why.... Guys do not like to be called other men's names when they're making love to a girl. Todd. Todd. Who in the hell is Todd?"

Sara didn't have a chance to apologize because Juan swiftly turned and walked away. She finished her Chill, grabbed her last taco, and sped away as fast as she could. Her hands were tightly clutched to the steering wheel until she arrived at Mangel Halto. She locked the doors and got back to her makeshift bedroom and stared at the van's ceiling in disbelief. "These guys think I'm a monster. I just wanted to have a good time.... I'm a slut just like Stacey."

The rest of the night was all business. Her phone was now charged and she replied to all her messages. Joan told her the hospital was in a witch hunt after the lawsuit was filed and she was very nervous about Presly finding out about Sara's plan. Di Albert had received the crucial new incriminating information and her lawyer was confident that Sara had a strong case. He also informed her that Kathy's estate was almost ready for the probate court.

All these texts, but none from Todd. "Why am I calling out his name when I'm screwing other men? I should have called him a long time ago, but I don't even know if we still want each other. I'll wait until I see his eyes in person and see if the spark is still there.... I'll know for sure then."

The next two days, Sara stayed put at Mangel Halto, snorkeling the entire area in search of the magical parrot fish. Sara enjoyed being in the water, but was becoming more frustrated by the minute as no parrot fish reacted to her. She was distraught when she came out of the water on Thursday afternoon, and drove straight to Costa Linda and spent the night thinking about her big day tomorrow.

HOME SWEET HOME ?

Sara wasn't giddy to be back "home" because of what lay ahead of her. She checked in early and headed straight for the "transition room" with her backpack and showered all the "dirt" off of her soul from the last thirty four days. The hot water felt like a thousand hands were massaging her tired aching body. The aloe shampoo softened her dried out blonde hair and the memories of the men she had been with began to fade away. An hour later, Sara was finally home.

Wilmer gave her a warm smile and checked her bags. She got two towels from Elizabeth and told her about Kathy's passing. All the regular guests and staff were sympathetic for Sara's loss. She found the closest palapa to the water and exhaled her anxieties away. The water looked so much bluer and the sand felt so much softer than it had been during her last visit on Eagle Beach over thirty three days ago.

It was around noon and this week's owners began to file in. Sara saw a few of Hank's buddies talking at the Water's Edge bar and knew that he would be joining them soon. She didn't want to tell him about Kathy in front of his friends so she went to the lobby and patiently waited for his arrival.

Sara saw Javier talking to a man and when he turned, Hank saw Sara grievously staring at him. His facial expressions immediately turned into a look of disbelief and he hurried over to Sara as she began to cry. Hank held back his emotions and asked, "What happened?"

Before she could tell him, Lina rushed over with a keycard. "Miss Sweeney. Your room is now ready in case you desire privacy." Sara thanked Lina and then she silently joined Hank on the elevator ride up to the third floor.

They sat down together on the couch and Sara began her story while staring straight at the wall. "I'd like to think you and I have become close friends over the past decade so please hear me out. I don't want to ever say this again.... Kathy passed away the first of April. She had been fighting pancreatic cancer for over a year."

Hank started to weep and asked Sara, "Why didn't she tell me? I could have been there to support her. She was sick last year. I knew it. She lost too much weight. I should...."

Sara begged Hank, "Please, let me finish.... I have thought about this moment since Saint Patrick's Day and I finally have everything scripted in my mind.... Aunt Kathy insisted on me coming here to tell you and I'm not going to deny her last wishes. Please, let me get this off my chest."

Hank quietly apologized and lowered his head. Sara reached out for his hand and continued. "Aunt Kathy loved you from the first second she saw you. She just didn't realize it until it was too late and she told me that on her deathbed.... Hank, I wanted to call you, but she objected so I respected her wishes. Kathy DID NOT want you to see her suffering. She didn't want you to remember her that way. Kathy was sick for over a year, but she was determined to spend one more special week with you last June. That's all she wanted and she took those memories of you to her grave. She BEGGED me not to tell you and I'm sorry that I deceived you that week."

A knock on the door suddenly stopped Sara's sad story and she excused herself. Wilmer quietly brought in her luggage and Sara immediately opened a suitcase and retrieved the scrapbook and Kathy's ashes.

She put them on the table and continued. "Aunt Kathy regretted not marrying you when you proposed to her.... She told me that many times. She wished that you two had met twenty five years ago. Hank, she told me during our last conversation that YOU were the ONLY one for her. I can still remember the sparkle in her eyes when she said that to me.... It was the last time I ever saw that sparkle."

Hank was drowning in his tears when Sara reached for the scrapbook. "I made this for Aunt Kathy and gave it to her on Christmas day. It was a great comfort to her until she passed. I want you to have it now." Sara handed Hank the scrapbook and he struggled to compose himself as she explained the book.

"You know how I love to take pictures.... Last fall I collected every picture of the two of you together and created this scrapbook. There are some very moving shots of you and Kathy lost in love and there's some pretty funny ones too; like when you two idiots jumped off that rope swing together."

Hank tried to laugh. "I thought I broke my back when I hit the water. I didn't want to act like an old man in front of her so I sucked it up." Sara began giggling. "She knew you were in pain. That's why she kept bringing you those rum punches."

Hank started to get emotional again when he saw the pictures of them at Passions the last night they were together. "I looked so old and she looked so thin, but together we looked beautiful. That's the last sunset we ever enjoyed together."

Sara interrupted his thoughts before they wandered off. "I have a big favor to ask you.... Aunt Kathy's last request was for you and me to sprinkle her ashes, in this container, over Mangel Halto. I need to do it as soon as possible. Can we go there tomorrow morning?"

Hank clutched the scrapbook in his arm and replied, "Absolutely. I'll meet you in the lobby at nine tomorrow morning.... I don't want to sound ungrateful for what you just did, but I need some alone time with this scrapbook.... You know how much I loved your aunt. I brought the ring down again to try one more time. We always said that for one week in Aruba, we would be 'married'. That was the best week of my year.... I've gotta go before I lose it again."

Hank left without saying goodbye, as Sara was lost in her own thoughts. "I did it, Auntie. I hope it's what you wanted." She sat on the couch, relieved that she finally delivered Kathy's love letter to Hank.

FORTY NIGHTS IN ARUBA

Sara stayed in her room for two hours, collecting her thoughts as she unpacked. She decided to put on a new bikini that Evelyn bought her and honor her aunt by playing in the water before sunset. Sara put on a happy face and said hello to everyone she knew as she returned to her palapa on the beach. She saw two men laying on her lounges and politely explained. "Excuse me, but this is my bag, and these are my towels. I believe you guys are in my hut."

One of the men looked up and down her body and then suggested. "Why don't you get between us and we can become a beach sandwich?" Sara respectfully refused. "That's a funny one…. I'll just grab my things and find another palapa. You guys can have this one." As she was gathering her items, the other man got up and confronted her. "What? We're not good enough for you, Rich Bitch?" He grabbed her arm. "You ain't going nowhere."

Before security could reach her, a young man swiftly approached the palapa and punched Sara's perpetrator in the face and threatened the other man. "You're next pal. If I were you, I'd take a hike." Security finally arrived and escorted the two men off the property.

Sara thanked her hero and put her stuff back while talking with him. "Those guys were real assholes. I don't even think they stay here…. Thanks for stopping them before it got ugly. My name is

Sara. I'm from Ohio." Her hero stated, "No problem. I was just reading and heard the commotion. I'm Chad and I'm from Boston.... Where's your husband at?"

Sara just giggled and revealed that she was single and Chad reassured her that he would keep an eye on her from his third row palapa. She was grateful for his concern and suggested, "Why don't you come over to my palapa and hang out with me. We can have a quiet conversation while you protect me."

They talked for a while and then Sara decided to go into water, followed by Chad. He started playfully throwing a ball to her and she finally started to release her tension from earlier in the day. Chad picked her up on his shoulders and crashed them into the waves and they came out of the surf roaring with laughter.

Sara was having so much fun that she didn't even notice the sad face staring at her. Todd had immediately rushed down to Eagle Beach after checking in at La Cabana to see Sara. He had been longing for this day since they last talked in April and was now in great dismay. His sad thoughts painted a very confusing picture. "She told me that she was over Dave and now she's here with him. Sara told me that she couldn't wait to see me. She said that she was in love with me...."

Heartbroken and embarrassed, Todd turned around, put the ring back into his pocket, and walked away. As he approached La Cabana, Toni could see the sorrow in her big brother's eyes and delicately asked, "Is she still engaged?"

Todd handed her his cell phone and regretfully answered, "Yup. I feel like the biggest idiot in Aruba. They were both playing and laughing in the water. I should have called her, but…. Take my phone and throw it in the ocean. I'm not going to need it this week." Toni was furious as she watched Todd slowly walk back across the street, knowing how much he loved Sara.

Minutes later Sara and Chad came out of the water and returned to the palapa. It was 6 PM and Sara politely asked Chad to leave. "Thanks for picking my spirits up and for being my hero today, but I'm expecting a dear friend soon and need to be alone with him." Chad said, "Sounds like he's a lucky guy" and left the beach.

Sara was now clear minded and was excited to see her Prince Charming. It had been almost a year since their last kiss and she desperately needed to see his face for her answer. "I hope when I finally see Todd, all my feelings for him will come back and all these other guys will disappear from my memory. I hope he feels the same about me."

Forty minutes later, Sara walked into the waves alone. She kept searching the beach for Todd and actually missed the sunset, right in front of her. She was hoping for a fairytale reunion, but that never happened. "Maybe his flight was delayed", so she sent him a text. "Hey. Looking forward to seeing you. Text me when you land."

Sara gathered her belongings and passed Chad at the bar. He observed she was alone and asked her. "Was your friend a no show" and she said, "Yup" and then Chad told her, "I'm here all week if you want to have some fun." Sara nodded and went back to her suite for a well needed rest.

Sara got up early for her daily run. She missed running alone on the soft sands of Eagle Beach and her thoughts always became focused during those runs. Today, she was hoping Todd would be waiting for her at La Cabana, but he wasn't. Sara walked the palapas and saw some familiar faces, but none were Todd's. He was nowhere to be found. She had to meet Hank at 9 AM, so she took off for Costa Linda.

When they met up in the lobby, Sara told Hank that she was driving, and Hank chuckled when he saw the van. "That's what you've been driving for a month?" Sara proudly replied, "This is my mobile bedroom. Do you like the heart-shaped magnets?" They were both in a much better mood today and were devoted to celebrating Kathy's life with happy stories.

Sara told Hank how she disguised Kathy's illness last year at Mangel Halto. "I made that bet with you to allow Auntie to easily get to the reef." Hank reflected. "You were always her partner in crime. I don't have to tell you what you meant to her. She was so proud of you, Sara."

When they got to Mangel Halto, Hank got an idea and rented a kayak off of a local for thirty bucks. "Instead of throwing her ashes off the cliff, let's sprinkle them all over the sea and talk about our love for Kathy."

They kayaked all the way down to the Spanish Lagoon and their uplifting stories helped cleanse each other's regrets. With Kathy's ashes now intertwined with the Caribbean Sea, Hank asked a favor of Sara. "Did I ever tell you how fond I am of you? I know we started out a little rocky, but I consider you a friend. Hell, I consider you family…. I don't want us to become strangers down here. I hope we can still do adventures like this…. Honestly, seeing you always makes me think of Kathy." Sara looked back at Hank and grinned. "I'd really like that."

By the time they returned the kayak, they could feel the heat of the afternoon sun and Sara challenged Hank. "This time let's race for real" and they took off snorkeling toward the reef. Sara won easily and when she looked back to gloat, she saw a school of colorful parrot fish following Hank.

She was in disbelief and pointed to Hank to turn around and when he did, all the parrot fish scattered, but one. Hank was staring eye to eye with a big blue parrot fish. Sara deliberately moved toward the fish and it still remained in eye contact with Hank. After they surrounded the blue parrot fish, it slowly led them from the reef to the sunken boat and then disappeared near the mangroves.

When they got back to the cliff, Sara started jabbering as soon as she removed her mouth piece. "Did you see that big blue parrot fish look at you? And then it led us to the boat. That was Aunt Ka.... thy's favorite place."

Sara didn't want Hank to think she was crazy, so she stopped. Hank was amazed also. "I thought the big blue parrot fish stayed around De Palm Island. I've never seen one here. He was a beauty. Did you get a good picture?" Sara was so excited that she never even considered taking a photo. "CRAP NO! I didn't, but 'she' will be back."

It was almost sunset when they got back to Costa Linda and parted ways for the night. Sara put a comfortable romper on and strolled up the beach to Passions and watched the lovers toast the end to a perfect day. Sara was so happy to find "Kathy" but still couldn't locate Todd on the beach and he left no messages. She called and there was no answer, so she texted him. "Hi. Did you make it down? I'm hoping to see you. I'm looking forward to talking to you. Please Todd. Call me."

After no returned message, Sara began to worry. "Why doesn't he want to talk to me? Did he see the porno that Steven took?" She decided to go across the street and ask some questions at the La Cabana pool bar. Sara looked everywhere for Todd and then she heard a girl's voice. "He's not here."

Sara went over to Todd's sister and asked, "Why didn't he come, Toni?" Toni ignored her and continued to flirt with two guys sitting with her. Sara repeated. "Why didn't he come? Is he mad at me?"

One of the guys joked around. "I'm not mad at you, Baby. Can I buy you a drink?" Toni uttered, "Don't waste your time; she's engaged."

Sara was furious and grabbed Toni by her arm. "What is your problem? I never did anything to you." Toni shook her arm free and fired back. "I'm tired of you screwing with my big brother's head. Just leave him alone and get the hell out of here."

Sara was not leaving and showed Toni her "ringless" finger. "What are you talking about? I called the wedding off last month, but your brother never made an effort to call me. Now, I'm the bad girl?" Toni remained on offense. "Sure, you are and

you'll always be a bad girl. So, who was the guy he.....
I saw you with yesterday?"

The argument was now escalating. "I was playing in the water with some guy staying at my resort. I made him leave so I could be alone with Todd, but he never fricken showed. He's here isn't he.... ISN'T HE?"

Before Sara got an answer, the security guard escorted her off the property as she violently yelled, "I waited a month to see your brother, and now he's playing games with me.... Tell Todd to go screw himself!"

Sara walked back to Costa Linda, cooling down the fire inside her and realized that she was her mother and there was nothing she could do about it. She ate dinner alone at the Water's Edge, thinking about her future. "I am so tired of dealing with men and they are tired of dealing with me. Forgive me Aunt Kathy, but I'm staying single.... Just like you did." Sara changed into a bikini and spent the rest of the night soaking in the hot tub.

Sunday morning came and Sara decided to run the opposite direction of La Cabana. She was on the running path near Divi when she was rudely pushed by a passing runner. Once Sara regained her balance, she saw the woman running away and began to chase her.

"I'd know that ass anywhere." They ran past Bushiri Beach, then through downtown Oranjestad, then past the West Deck, and then Anna turned into Surfside Beach as Sara was catching ground on her. Anna was running out of beach when Sara viciously tackled her from behind.

The two rivals rolled around on the sand until Sara held Anna down and raised her fist to punch her. Anna's beautiful face was full of tears and she screamed in Papiamento. "Go ahead…. DO IT. I know you slept with Luis." Anna started crying harder, leaving Sara an easy target, but she refused to hit her.

Sara got off of her and sat near the shore, watching an airplane land. "I was on one of those planes thirty six days ago, so excited to come back here…. Now I can't wait to leave…. Why do you hate me?"

Anna sat next to her and soothed herself as the two continued their conversation in Anna's native language. "I hate your beauty, I hate the way Luis looks at you, and I hate the way you look at him. He flaunts his women in front of me to torture me for a sin I committed five years ago. Do you know what it's like to love a man like that?"

Sara listened and quietly replied. "Two months ago, I caught my fiancée screwing my mother. Have you ever loved a man like that? Luis doesn't love me. We had a one night stand and I asked him a week ago about you and we had a fight. I know that he still loves you. I could see it in his eyes. Luis is a good man…. Beg him for forgiveness until he accepts you or you'll regret it forever." As the words were coming out her mouth, she thought about Todd and wished she would take her own advice.

The two women parted ways in a more friendly manner and Sara stopped at the Rennaissance Marina and watched all the people getting off the cruise ships and wondered about the future of the Aruban people. "Sunday is the locals' day to enjoy their island and it's packed today with foreigners. Even if I can speak their language and respect their ways, I'll always be a foreigner to them. Where will they go to escape us on their own island?"

Sara made it back to Costa Linda in time for pool volleyball and Chad made sure he was on her team. Chad was as competitive as Sara and the two made a winning combination in the pool. Sara took all her frustrations out on the ball that day to the delight of all the men who were playing and watching. Hank was playing against her and knew something was wrong.

After volleyball, Sara and Chad challenged Hank and his golfing buddy, Joltzy, to a corn hole match and Chad enjoyed taunting the old guys during the game. Hank asked Sara about Todd and she smirked, "Screw Todd" and Chad laughed, enjoying her insult.

Hank really liked Todd and was unsettled by Sara's remarks, thinking, "If I was thirty years younger, I'd shove that bean bag down that 'pretty' boy's throat." After they lost, Hank said goodbye to Sara and joined his buddies at the bar. He watched as Sara and Chad played "lovey dovey" in the pool and thought, "Kathy would not be happy."

Chad challenged Sara to a pool basketball game. "First person that gets to twenty one wins and the loser buys dinner." Sara took the ball out of his hands and accepted. "Madame Janette's sounds pretty good tonight" and immediately hit a long distance shot for a two point lead. The two competitors played aggressively. Chad muscled her with his strength and brushed against her breasts when he played defense. Sara became intrigued when Chad grabbed her hips several times after she shot.

When her game winning shot swished through the net, Sara handed him the ball and asked. "When are we leaving for 'MJ's' and Chad begged out. "Sorry, Babe, I've got a prior commitment tonight, but I'll make reservations for tomorrow at 8PM. Sara pouted and firmly reminded Chad. "I don't forget when I win a bet. I'll be waiting."

The next morning couldn't come fast enough as Sara quickly sped back to Mangel Halto alone, hoping to snorkel with Aunt Kathy's spirit again. "I'm not a religious person, but I do believe that was her, leading us to the boat. She wanted me to know.... I don't think I'm crazy."

As soon as she got in the water, Sara began her search for the big blue parrot fish and peacefully became lost in the wonder of sea life below her. There was no Todd or Anna in her serene mind, only sweet memories of her aunt. She would snorkel for a couple of hours and then find refuge underneath a beach palapa. By afternoon, there were no "Aunt Kathy" sightings, but surprisingly, she was not frustrated; only hungry. "I can't wait to taste that 'Bang Bang' shrimp at Madame J's tonight."

It was late afternoon when Sara went in for her last snorkel of the day. She didn't want to be late for her dinner date so she decided to make it a quick one. Once she neared the reef, Sara saw a school of vibrant parrot fish and they moved along as she snorkeled in the direction of them.

Now waiting for her was the big blue parrot fish and Kathy's spirit led her around the reef and boat. Sara was so mesmerized with the parrot fish that she lost track of her surroundings as "Kathy" led her into the deep ocean water and disappeared. Sara became disoriented and frantically returned to the shallow water.

On her drive back to Costa Linda, Sara tried to grasp why the fish reacted that way. "Was she trying to tell something about my life?" Then she started laughing at herself. "I'm losing my fricking mind!"

DATE NIGHT

Now, Sara was running late and after her shower, she heard a knock on the door and opened it slightly. "I thought we were going to meet in the lobby?" Chad confused her by saying, "I was waiting there, but I'm anxious that we're going to be late.... It's almost seven and someone told me it takes an hour to get to the Flying Fishbone."

That statement startled Sara as she wrapped a towel around her and let Chad in. "I thought we were eating at Madame Janette's? I guess I better hurry up.... Please Chad, take a seat.... I promise I won't be long." She hastily "put" herself together and in fifteen minutes she looked stunning. "I am so hungry. I hope you brought a lot of money tonight.... We better get going."

Sara asked for Chad's car keys. "Let me drive. We'll get there faster.... Newbies don't have a clue how to drive in Aruba." Chad threw her the keys and devilishly smiled. "Fine with me.... Now, I can enjoy the view."

Sara made it there with time to spare, but the parking lot was packed so she found a spot all the way down by Aruba Beach Villas. On their walk to the hostess stand, reality hit Sara and she thought about her last dinner there and the man who "served" her. "I hope Luis isn't working tonight."

Chad brought unneeded attention to them by complaining to the hostess. "I want a table in the water and be quick about it." As the hostess discussed the procedure, Sara saw Luis staring directly at her and she looked away in embarrassment.

After ten minutes, they were sitting in the water as Chad bragged loudly, "That's how you do it. These people need to be put in their place." Sara was grateful when another man took their order but was growing tired of Chad's big mouth and thought. "This guy is looking 'uglier' by the minute.... There is no way that I'm sleeping with him tonight."

Chad started ordering shots of whiskey and challenged Sara to a drinking contest, but Sara refused. "This place isn't Charlie's Bar, it's one of the top beach restaurants in the world."

Halfway into the service, Sara excused herself while Chad argued about the temperature of his steak. Luis cut her off on the way to the restroom and asked, "What are you doing here, Sara?" She looked at him confused. "What do you think I'm doing here? I'm on a dinner date." Luis was not happy. "With that asshole? Francisco is about to kill him.... Are you trying to make me jealous?"

Sara smirked at him. "NO. That's your style and you should talk to Anna about that.... Excuse me, but I need to go to the lady's room." She took ten minutes to calm down, put on a "happy" face, and then returned to her table discreetly.

Sara finished her dinner and declined dessert, but Chad had to try the Baked Alaska and all the attention that came with it. Sara just wanted to leave and was staring into the blue lit sea as Chad scarfed down his dessert. "I was here a week ago and made love on that table over there. It was magical then.... Why am I attracted to these good looking losers?"

Chad paid the $190 check with two one hundred dollar bills and told Francisco to keep the change. That was the final straw for Sara. Kathy always taught her to respect all people who served them and Chad crossed the line.

She gave Francisco a fifty dollar bill and smiled at him. "Thank you for the great service tonight. I'm sorry for any inconvenience we might have caused you." Chad was furious and after Francisco left, he expressed his displeasure. "Are you trying to show me up? That guy wasn't worth five cents."

Sara chose not to argue with him in public and left him at the table. Chad grabbed her hand and tried to be a gentleman by escorting her out the door. They quietly walked to the car and Chad tightly gripped her arm with his other hand as Sara demanded. "Stop doing that. You're hurting me…. What the fu…. Why is my van parked here?"

Sara panicked when she saw two men get out of her van. It was the same two guys who Chad threw out of her palapa four days ago. As the two men approached, Chad squeezed her arm tighter and sneered, "Looks like you're going for a swim tonight."

Sara hit Chad in the head with her cell phone and ran back to the Flying Fishbone. She could hear someone closing in on her from behind so she turned and violently swung her purse into his face. Sara kept running through the front door and then through the dinner crowd. She ran through Coral Reef's hedges and across the same path she took a week ago. Sara sprinted past Serene Resort and then quickly walked through the people dining on the beach of Aruba Villas.

Her pursuers were aggressively stopped by Francisco in the dining area. He escorted them out with security's help and told Chad. "Your dinner is OVER. Don't even think about coming back in."

With Francisco's help, Sara was able to gain valuable time and hid in one of the luxury huts still under construction. She shut off her phone and sat in the corner paralyzed with fear. She could hear Chad's voice giving instructions to the other men. "John, go to the beach and look for her hiding somewhere. Wally, go back to the van and watch the parking lot…. She's got no place to go. I've got her purse and we've gotta get her tonight."

Sara held her breath as she could now hear the footsteps coming close to her. Suddenly, she heard another voice ask, "What are you doing here?" And then Sara heard Chad nervously trying to explain. "I'm sorry Sir, but I'm trying to find my wife. She's very drunk and she wandered off while I was in the men's room. She's a blonde wearing a short black dress. Have you seen her?" The other voice responded. "No…. If you're not staying on this property, you are not allowed back here. Follow me to the dining area and we will talk to management about finding your wife."

While Sara was hiding in the hut, the employees at Flying Fishbone were closing for the night. Luis was cleaning the tables when he overheard Francisco telling Natasha about the ass who was chasing the "Hot" Blonde. "She gave me a fifty dollar tip and her boyfriend was so mad that he chased her to Coral Reef."

Luis came over and asked Francisco. "When did this happen?" Francisco told him that it was when he was in the kitchen, getting the food together for that big table of guests he was waiting on. "I grabbed the cheap bastard before he could catch her and threw him and his two friends out of here."

"Two friends?" Luis started to worry about Sara and sent her a text. "Are You OK" and got no reply so he called her and she never answered the disabled phone. Luis shrugged it off as a lover's quarrel and drove home wondering what she was doing with that loser.

Unfortunately, she was hiding from that loser and his friends with her mind only concentrating on survival. Around midnight, she tried to silently flee around Aruba Villas, but she saw Chad and the two other men spread out and guarding any potential escape routes.

She quietly snuck onto Serene's beach and borrowed a kayak and paddle. Then she became stealth in the water and allowed the current to take her to Villa Fillipe. When Sara saw the well-lit townhouse, she exhaled for the first time in three hours. She pulled the kayak onto the shore and turned her phone back on.

After she read the text from Luis, she called him and after two attempts, he decided to answer and heard her nervous voice. "Luis. Please don't hang up on me. I'm in trouble. Chad is trying to kill me." Luis was not amused. "Why are you bothering me at one in the morning? I have kitesurfing lessons to teach tomorrow.... Is he roughing you up in the sack?"

"No, goddamn it. He is trying to kill me and I don't know why? Please Luis. I know you hate me, but I'm begging you for your help.... Chad took me outside and two men got out of my van and they said they were going to take me for a swim, but I got away and hid, but they were still waiting for me so I stole a kayak, and I'm hiding at Villa Fillipe right now.... I'm terrified. I swear to God that I'm not making this up!"

Luis now knew that Sara was in serious trouble and tried to calm her down. "Stay hidden in the trees until I get there in my truck. Come out when I flash my lights. I'll be there in fifteen minutes." Luis hung up, quickly dressed, and got over there as fast as he could. When Sara saw his lights flicker off and on, she sprinted into his truck and burst into tears. He silently listened to her crying as they drove back to his house.

Luis brought Sara inside and sat her down on his couch. She was still crying and looked horrible.

Her dress was shredded and the cut on her knee was still bleeding. Luis wanted to know who Chad was and why he wanted to kill her, but she just kept crying. "I don't know why. I just met him four days ago and we went on a dinner date…. That's all I know."

Through the sounds of her crying, Sara could hear a soothing voice telling Luis in Papiamento, to let Sara sleep. Anna put her hands on Sara's slumped shoulders and promised her. "We will figure this all out tomorrow. You need to relax and calm your mind before you have a heart attack…. No one knows you're here."

Sara thanked them both. "I don't know what I would have done if you hadn't come. I owe you Luis" and he replied, "You don't owe me anything. Anna and I had a long talk yesterday after you attacked her. We've decided to try again because of your talks so I guess we're even…. Get some sleep, Sara. You're safe here."

The comforting words from Luis calmed down her emotions allowing Sara's mind to begin retracing her past year. "Who would want me dead? Are these three guys psychotic killers? It wasn't a random act. They had a plan. I've pissed off so many people lately…. Oh My God. Presly would want me dead. If I'm dead, the lawsuit would disappear and Dave knows where I'm at…. I ruined Dave's BMW and canceled our wedding and his family is very powerful. His Mother…. She despises me more than anyone…. I need to call Evelyn first thing in the morning." Sara fell asleep with so many questions running through her mind and so little time to answer them.

SEARCHING FOR ANSWERS

Luis awoke the next morning to hear Sara rambling on her phone to Evelyn and the two women were already starting a game plan. At first, Evelyn thought Sara was hallucinating, but quickly came on board the mystery train. Luis made some tea and handed Sara a cup as she continued to talk to Evelyn.

Anna came into the kitchen naked and passionately kissed an embarrassed Luis. "Let's go again, My Love. She's a million miles away from here." Luis gleefully denied, "Put some clothes on. She needs our help…. I'll make up for it tonight."

Sara got off the phone with Evelyn and again thanked Luis for saving her life and asked another favor of him. "Could you drop me off at Playa Linda when you go to work? Hopefully, I'm going to be staying with a woman I trust. My friend is calling her as we speak."

Luis wanted to take her directly to the police station, but she refused. "Somebody is seriously trying to kill me. If I file a report, it's my word against three men and nothing will happen. I've been talking to my friend for the last four hours and we're getting an idea who might want me dead. I'm sorry I got you into this mess and I don't want anyone to be hurt."

Anna came back into the kitchen fully dressed and told Sara. "I'll take you to Palm Beach and make sure you arrive safely. I like you. I see a lot of me when I look at you. Luis and I decided last night that we will give you aid." Luis crossly added. "I want a 'piece' of that pretty boy Chad."

Evelyn soon called back and confirmed that Marge was very happy to help out. "Marge thinks she's a 'Hardy Boy' and she's going to solve the case by herself so we'll let her have some fun, but DO NOT go back to your resort. The bad guys have your purse and key card and are probably waiting there for you. Stay inside at Marge's suite until you hear from me."

Luis left for work first and promised his American friend. "You have my number. Call me if you need help." Anna gave Sara a shirt and a pair of jeans to wear. "Go clean up, I think you're a size 5 like me. You need to blend in and act like us and not as a tourist. When you're ready, we'll leave…. I'm going to put some clothes in a bag for you to wear, but I want them back when this is over." Sara nervously sighed, hoping this nightmare would soon disappear.

Sara texted Juan on the way to the High Rise area. "Juan. Please don't disregard this message. I have a major problem with the van. I can't call Ricardo. I need your help." Within minutes, Juan called and angrily asked, "What is wrong with the van" and she quietly answered, "It got stolen last night."

Juan started screaming in Papiamento so loud that Anna could hear every cuss word. She grabbed the phone out of Sara's hand and started cussing him back as Sara listened intently.

Anna gave her back the phone and Juan very calmly apologized to Sara. "I'm sorry for acting like a child. I didn't know that you were in danger. I'll give you a couple of days before I tell my father because I know he will contact the police immediately…. I'm off work today so I'll drive up to Costa Linda and see if the van is there…. If you still want my help, I'll gladly give it to you."

Sara expressed her gratitude and asked Juan to stay in touch with any new information. After she got off the phone, Anna became curious, "What did you do to piss him off?" Sara blushed, "I called him another guy's name while we were having sex." Anna rolled her eyes and agreed, "I've done that a few times" and they both had a good laugh. As they continued past Super Food, Sara wondered briefly about the man whose name she kept moaning and why they never had a chance at love.

ONE STEP BEHIND

Todd was taking an afternoon off from his annual volunteer work at Horacio Oduber Hospital and decided to join his family on a Red Sail snorkel trip. When he came out of the water, Todd told his sister, "WOW, that Antilla Wreck is cool just like Sara described it to me."

That statement irritated Toni. "Will you PLEASE forget about her. I'm so tired of you moping around like a little puppy dog…. Get over Sara. She's a pure bitch! She told me to tell you to go screw yourself."

Todd was confused by the confession and became very upset. He was now the hothead and grabbed his sister's arm. "What do you mean, she told you? When did you talk to her?"

Toni broke free of his grip. "Sara came to La Cabana looking for you on Saturday and said that guy in the water was someone she just met. Then she had the nerve to say she waited all night for you and you never showed and some crap about her waiting here a month to see you.... We got into it and I had her thrown out of our resort."

Todd was crushed by this admission and hurt by his sister's actions. "You know how I feel about Sara and you never even told me about her looking for me on Saturday.... That was four days ago. Why would you do that to me, Toni?"

Todd left the heated debate and sat by himself on the catamaran's netting, looking out into the sea of another missed opportunity. "I guess I'm just not meant to be with Sara."

THE PLAN

Sara's thoughts were clear of Todd when Anna pulled in front of Playa Linda. Anna wanted to escort her up to Marge's suite, but Sara told her that she would be fine. "I don't want you to be late for work. Thanks for the lift and for helping me with Juan.... I'm really happy you and Luis are back together."

She walked quickly into the front lobby with her head down, went up to the second floor, and found the correct room number. Marge heard her knocking on the door and demanded, "What's the password" and she listened to the reply. "Come on

Marge, it's Sara. Please open the door for me."
Marge opened the door and Sara gave her a big hug while the older woman explained, "We've got to be cautious with murders on the island.... That's a great title for a novel."

Marge made lunch while Sara talked to Evelyn on speaker phone so Marge could hear every word. Marge was the "feisty" one of the older gals and Evelyn's best friend on the island. She was always up for an adventure.

Evelyn sent Sara a text, containing a picture of the information she had collected and Sara was impressed. "You've outdone yourself, Evelyn. "You have everything so clearly laid out.... What did you do at Polaroid?" Evelyn paused and then brashly revealed. "I ran it."

Evelyn was now the commander and Sara listened carefully to all her instructions. "I don't believe that this was a random act by three perverts so we need to find out more about them and where they are staying on the island. We need an inside man who can keep an eye on your room and the resort itself and that would be Hank.... You need to call him soon and explain everything. Once we locate these guys, someone has to infiltrate their group and it can't be you, Sara.... That's about it for now.... Any questions?"

Sara told Evelyn that she contacted Juan and he's out looking for the van and she'll call Hank immediately. "Luis, Juan, and Anna said they would help me so I feel a lot better now. I'm just worried that if I screw this up, I'll never find out who is really behind this plot…. Somebody might even get killed."

Evelyn agreed. "That's correct and NO cops. If these guys get arrested before we find the leader, he'll disappear into the night." Marge chimed in, "I've got a question…. Who's Hank?" Evelyn laughed and instructed Sara, "Look over the info carefully and write down everything you remember or thought was notable about Chad. He's the key…. Just don't do anything stupid."

Sara's next call was to Hank who was curious about her situation. "I thought we were going snorkeling today. Are you still with that loudmouth?" Sara tried to be direct with him. "Hank. Please listen carefully. I'm in big trouble and I need your help desperately. I need you to promise that you won't contact the police after this conversation is over…. My life depends on that."

Hank was listening to her while quickly finding some privacy on the beach. "What in the hell is going on, Sara? What do you mean 'your life depends on it'…. Where are you?"

Sara began to explain her nightmare. "Do you remember I told you about those two guys that Chad saved me from last Friday…. Last night, those same two guys and Chad tried to kill me. Please Hank, hear me out before you yell at me."

Sara then proceeded to tell Hank in great detail everything she knew about her situation. Sara could hear the hard breathing of his anger as she spoke and when she finished, Hank could no longer control his emotions. "I knew Chad was a piece of shit the minute I saw him. I should have never let you near him and this would have never happened…. I'm going to kill that 'son of a bitch'. I'm gonna go looking for him right now!"

Sara begged him not to do that. "Please, Hank. If you do kill him, the person behind all this will just hire someone else to kill me. I need to find out who this person is or I'm dead. I'm begging you…. Hank I need your help…. Just give me two days to figure it out and then I'll call the cops. I promise."

The crashing waves were all Sara could hear for what seemed like an eternity and then she heard Hank whisper. "What do you want me to do? You and I are family and family doesn't desert each other in times like this."

Sara told him about his role in her plan and he agreed. "It's going to be difficult to see Chad and pretend not to know about all of this, but he's all mine when this is over…. I'm driving down to see you after I walk the property…. Your aunt would kill me if I let anything happen to you."

Hank was nearing the fitness center when he saw Todd waiting for the elevator and nervously yelled his name. They shook hands and Hank asked what he was doing there and Todd answered. "I need to talk to Sara in person, but I can't find her anywhere so I'm going up to her room…. Do you know where she is?"

Hank knew that was a very bad idea so he detoured the lovesick man. "Yeah. She's snorkeling at Arashi today by herself. I'm going to pick her up in an hour. If you want…."

Suddenly the elevator door opened and Hank was looking eye to eye at Chad and heard him say, "Hey. What's up, old man…. Have you seen my Babe around today?"

Hank was now placed in a difficult predicament and chose to talk to Chad as Todd dejectedly walked away. "No. I haven't seen her at all today. How was dinner last night? Where did you go?"

Chad arrogantly replied, "We went to Madame J's last night and then came back to her bedroom for some fun and games; if you know what I mean…. She liked it so much that I'm staying with her now."

Hank wanted to punch him hard, but resisted the urge and laughed along. "Sara's a sexy woman. You're a lucky guy for sure…. I'm late for my golfing lessons so I'll see you around and tell Sara that I said hi." Hank no longer needed to investigate and drove quickly to Playa Linda with his new information on Chad's whereabouts.

Sara had just finished her long conversation with Denise who promised her full support after listening to the horrific story. The lawyer reassured her new friend, "Just get the names on their passports or driver's licenses and text me the info. I'll find out everything you need to know about them. You be careful…. Amanda sends you her love." Sara promised to be cautious. "I can't thank you enough, Denise. I can't wait to get home and see you guys soon…. I hope."

She was just getting ready to call Evelyn when her phone rang and it was Juan with good news. "Hey Sara, we found the van. It's parked behind the Talk of the Town Hotel. My girlfriend is with me and her uncle, Mr. Lopez works at the front desk and he told us that three guys were staying there from Texas. One of the guys matches the description of 'your Chad' and he wasn't with them for breakfast this morning…. This spying stuff is fun and it's making Maria horny."

Sara was too focused to be amused. "Could you please ask Maria's uncle to call you whenever they come or go? It's very important we know where they are at all times."

Juan was already one step ahead of Sara. "Mr. Lopez says they always drink at Sandra's Garden every night like clockwork. They also like to flirt with the women. Mr. Lopez told me that he saw them bring girls back to their room…. Maybe I should become a secret agent?" Sara finally laughed and agreed. "You would be a perfect spy…. You've been a great help today and please call me if you find out anything else."

As soon as she got off the phone, Sara got a brainstorm and instantly called Heidi. She once again told her tale of last night and asked her friend for help. "I need to get these guys' identification tonight before they get spooked and leave the country. I need you and Ingrid to seduce these men and take a picture of their IDs on your cell phone. Heidi feverishly responded, "That sounds so kinky and I know Ingrid would be up for it…. Are they good looking?"

Sara told Heidi that she would try to get Juan to take a picture of them, but she described each man the best she could remember. "Juan told me that they would be drinking at Sandra's Garden tonight and they like to flirt."

Heidi was getting excited just thinking about the night. "When we're through with them, they'll give us their bank account numbers! I'll call Ingrid at work and tell her about our new adventure.... We'll get to Sandra's after sunset and then the fireworks will start. Thanks, Girlfriend, for thinking of us; it should be a fun night of espionage."

Sara was on the speakerphone with Evelyn when Marge let Hank in and she remarked, "Wow. You're one 'hot' senior citizen!" Sara ran into his arms for a very long hug which depressed Marge. "Oh, I get it. You just like the young sexy chicks."

Once the chuckling was done, Hank revealed his significant information. "I just ran into Chad at Costa Linda and he said you two went to Madame Janette's last night. Chad is staying in your room."

Evelyn said with great pride. "Now we know where they all are so we have to act swiftly. Chad is the key. He's obviously the ringleader and we have got to know more about him. You said he was from Boston but had no distinguished accent. You have a few pictures of him on your phone, but that means nothing unless we have his real name.... We need someone to seduce him and it can't be you." Sara exhaled and realized she knew the perfect woman to pull off the seduction, but there was no way that Anna was going to do it.

It was almost four o'clock and Sara was running out of time so she called Luis before he left work. She asked to speak to him and Anna as soon as possible at Moomba's. Luis arrived first and Anna joined them about five minutes later.

Sara asked them to sit on the beach with her and began to explain today's events. "We've made great progress, but we are running out of time and I need a 'Hail Mary' as soon as possible.... We need to get Chad's driver's license or passport information and he knows me. I have two girlfriends who are going to seduce Chad's two partners tonight, but Chad is the one who holds the key to this mystery.... I need a very sexy woman to seduce Chad."

Luis got up in disgust. "I understand where you're going with this and there is no way that Anna's doing that. Not tonight. Not EVER!" Anna agreed, "That's crazy. I said I would help you, not screw some guy for you. Let's get out of here, My Love!" As they stormed off the beach, Sara's mind began racing. "Maybe I can wear a wig and glasses or pay someone...."

Ten minutes later, a hand touched her head and she looked up to see Anna smiling down on her. She knelt on the sand in front of Sara and explained, "You don't ask a proud man like Luis to borrow his woman for someone else's pleasure. You need to let him make that decision.... I let Luis talk himself into agreeing and I promised him that I would not have sex with this man.... Don't worry, I have a plan too." Sara embraced Anna tightly and thanked her for accepting this enormous favor.

Anna only had one problem. "I know a place where we can shop quickly for the right kind of outfit for tonight, but I don't have enough money to buy it." Anna left for Sextasy Aruba and Sara went back to Playa Linda to ask Marge if she could borrow her credit card.

"All my money and credit card are in my purse that they stole. I promise I'll pay you back." Marge went and got her purse and declared. "If I'm paying then I'm going too." Sara had no time to argue so she reluctantly agreed and they took a short taxi ride to Sextasy Aruba.

Sara was a little embarrassed when she walked inside the erotic Adult store and apologized to Marge. "I'm sorry. This is one of the few stores I've never been in and it looks pretty provocative." Marge picked up a sex toy and looked at it upside down. "What do you use this for?" Sara burst out in laughter and the sight of a seventy five year old woman playing with a leather whip was just what she needed to release her tension of today.

Sara found Anna toting a cart full of items and asked her, "Do you need all that stuff for tonight? We need to get going." Anna kept looking at the sexy lingerie. "I found everything I need for tonight, but I'm shopping for something special for Luis right now.... Relax and look around for a little while." Sara stood in silence and just shook her head. "This is the most nerve-racking day of my life and they're both trying on bunny ears!"

Sara finally got her two amused friends away from the adult store and Anna drove them back to the command center. The sun acted as an hourglass as Sara quickly prepared for the night ahead of her. She used the living room phone as a direct line to Evelyn and her cell phone as the means to reach her informants. As they prepared for the upcoming events, Anna used the second bedroom to shower and get dressed.

Juan called first. "Hey Sara, we see two of the guys crossing the street. Do you want me to follow them?" Sara replied. "Yes. You need to get a picture of them as fast as you can so I can send it to Heidi and Ingrid. Please hurry Juan."

Maria heard the conversation, grabbed her boyfriend's cell phone, and took off after the two men. She started giggling loudly which caused them to turn around and they observed a cute young girl waving at them. Instead of being cautious, the two merry suspects waved back and then they willingly posed for her picture. She cheerfully waved goodbye and ran back across the street to her stunned companion.

Maria proudly handed him back his phone and gushed, "I could be a secret agent too." Juan kissed his radiant partner, but Maria pushed him away. "Send Sara the picture right now and no fooling around…. This spy game is great fun."

Sara sent the received picture to Heidi as they were pulling into the parking lot near Sandra's Garden Bar. A few minutes later, Heidi called. "Hey…. These guys are cute. They're sitting at a table with three women. I'll keep you updated." Evelyn got very nervous when she heard the bad news, but Sara reassured her. "I've partied with these girls…. They know what they're doing, Evelyn."

Heidi and Ingrid slowly approached the popular table, both wearing thin lace rompers. Ingrid said hello to the two men and got sneers from their three female guests as she lustfully inquired, "Do you boys enjoy guessing games?"

They both nodded yes and then Heidi lowered her elbows onto the table and asked, "Which one of us is wearing panties?" Heidi raised up and the two Dutch 'assets' slowly walked to an open table and sat down. Twenty minutes later, Heidi sent Sara a text with three thumbs up and a smiley face.

It was after eight when Hank called from the bar. "Chad just left about ten minutes ago. I saw him talking on his phone to someone for around forty minutes, but I couldn't hear what he was saying…. I followed him to the elevator. I'm going to sit in front of the spa and make sure he doesn't come back down."

Evelyn was carefully listening to the conversation as she studied the situation. "His two partners were busy with the girls so Chad was probably talking to his boss. We need to get Anna in there now."

Sara opened the door to the second bedroom and was amazed by the gorgeous Aruban wearing a very erotic outfit. Anna appreciated Sara's stunned look and giggled. "Do you like it" and Sara just beamed, now understanding Anna's plan. Marge joined the two women and shouted, "Good Lord! You can't go out in public looking like that!"

Evelyn went over Anna's objectives while Marge got a jacket for her as a cover up. Sara was very nervous that the plan might backfire and tried to embrace Anna for luck, but Anna pushed her away. "You're going to mess up my makeup" and then she confidently smiled at her anxious friend. "Don't worry about me…. This should be a fun night and I'll be back before you know it."

Anna entered Costa Linda and nodded to Hank as she passed him on her way to the elevator. She found the room number on the third floor, knocked very loudly, and announced herself. "ROOM SERVICE". She heard movement and then a man firmly replied, "I don't need room service…. Go away."

She knocked again and enthusiastically declared, "You called for ROOM SERVICE" and he opened the door and irritably said, "I told you already that I…." Chad's mouth stopped moving as his eyes were staring at an island goddess in a "French Maid" costume. "Woooh! Who are you, Sweet Thing?" The maid answered, "I'm from the escort service in San Nicolas. This is room 3006, isn't it?"

Chad knew he was staying in room 3004, but he wasn't turning down this luscious dish for anything. "Yeah, yeah, yeah. Come on in. This is the right room. How much is this service going to cost me?" Anna put her lips close to his and seductively said, "That depends on what you are into? The show starts at twenty US dollars and continues up as we go."

Chad wasted no time taking out his wallet and giving her twenty bucks. Anna made a mental note of his wallet's location and continued her act. "Sit down and I will clean your room first." Chad was anxious and replied, "I better get more than a 'clean' room for my twenty bucks." Anna stood in front of her prey and nibbled on his ear. "Just relax while I start the show."

The French Maid bent down into Chad's drooling face and began dusting his pants. Then she asked, "May I pour you a drink, Sir" while taking her panties off. Chad was very aroused and accepted her request. "I would love a 'scotch and soda' and the bottle is on the kitchen countertop."

Anna slowly walked to the kitchen, "dusting" as she went. She made Chad a drink while her tongue played with a "lucky" straw and slowly approached him as he waited in anticipation. The French Maid put the drink into his trembling hand and toasted her prey as she slowly bent over. "Bottoms up" and then she kissed him after he quickly consumed his drink.

Anna instructed her horny client, "Take your clothes off, Sir, and I will give you a 'deep' massage." Chad stripped naked while watching the French Maid do an erotic striptease for him.

After five minutes, the maid was completely naked as Chad's weary eyes watched her slowly approach him. His legs were wobbling from his sexual desires exploding. Chad reached out clumsily to feel her breasts and Anna pushed his unconscious body onto the couch.

Anna giggled as she stood over the motionless body. "These 'Roofies' work every time." Anna quickly dressed and took Chad's wallet out of his shorts pocket. She took several pictures of his driver's license, took all of his cash, and carefully put the wallet back. She checked his cell phone for previous messages, but it was locked and she couldn't get into the home screen.

Anna found Sara's room still intact and did some shopping during the next five minutes. She quietly came out of the bedroom and saw Chad still passed out on the couch. Anna snuck out the front door and blew Hank a kiss as she passed him on her way to the lobby. Hank relayed her message by texting Sara a full screen of smiley faces and swiftly left for his room. Their team had pulled it off by ten o'clock.

Sara was overjoyed when she received the text from Hank and anxiously awaited Anna's arrival. Sara called Evelyn and told her the good news and Evelyn asked about Heidi and Ingrid. Before Sara could answer, Marge heard a loud knock on the door and let Anna in.

Sara saw her coming into the "war" room and rushed into her arms for a victory hug. They were like two silly children on Christmas Day as Sara honored her hero. "My God. You did it. You pulled it off without getting hurt."

Anna bragged, "It was easy. These Roofies work great. I keep a bottle of them in my purse at all times.... When I'm with a guy that I don't want to screw, I just slip him one and get away. I put three in his drink and he was out in five minutes. I hope he's not dead.... After I dressed, I got the pictures and double checked them before I left. I'll send them to you right now and make sure they are perfect before I go home."

Sara resent the pictures to Evelyn and Denise immediately and before Anna left, she gave Sara her backpack. "Your bedroom seemed untouched by him and your pack was in the corner so I took it.... Then I got greedy and took all of this."

Sara started to cry when she saw her passport and all her valuables that were locked inside the safe. Sara gratefully listened as Anna explained, "I used the combination number you gave me and it opened right up. He never even tried to open the safe.... It's late and I've got to go."

Marge and Sara asked her to stay the night, but Anna respectfully declined while grinning at both of them. "It was so erotic for me and I enjoyed teasing the American.... I need to get home before Luis leaves the Fishbone. I've got a surprise for him." Anna lustfully "flashed" the jacket open, gathered her belongings, and she was gone.

Sara had no time to rejoice as Evelyn noted, "We still haven't heard from Heidi and Ingrid. I hope they are okay…. I'm going to bed now, Sweety. We'll figure this all out tomorrow."

Marge also retired for the night and thanked her guest. "That was the most alive I've felt in years…. I can't wait to try out that leather whip. Goodnight Dear." Sara was now alone in her thoughts as she nervously waited for Heidi's text.

It was going to be a long wait because the girls were having way too much fun with their targets. They started doing shots of 'Fire Ball' at Sandra's Garden and decided to take the fun across the street to the Talk of the Town before they all passed out. Heidi even told Ingrid in front of Wally. "Hey, girl. We've got to get these guys' pants off so we can take some pictures."

Wally dropped his pants down and chuckled, "Take all the pictures you want" and the girls devoured him in the kitchen. Johnny felt neglected and took all of his clothes off and soon they were all naked and headed to the bedroom for more fun.

Heidi took a break from all the action and went back into the kitchen to photograph the two men's IDs. When she was finished, she rechecked, and hit the send button to Sara. Suddenly Heidi heard Ingrid scream. "Heidi, come quick. These guys are killing me!" Heidi put the wallets back and smiled like

the devil as she rejoined her best friend in the
bedroom. Their mission was now accomplished.

It was almost one in the morning when Sara
received the final good news of the longest day of
her life. It started with Sara running for her life from
men she did not know, found shelter with new
friends who cared about her, and ended with those
same friends uniting with her to help solve the
mystery conspiracy.

She felt so grateful for these kind people who
were strangers to her thirty nine days ago and
thanked her Aunt Kathy for sending them to her.
"Auntie was trying to warn me when she led me out
into the abyss on Monday. She knew something bad
was going to happen to me and she protected me."
Sara fell asleep peacefully, knowing in her heart that
Kathy would always be by her side.

Chad awoke the following morning with a
horrible hangover. He realized that he was naked and
tried to figure out what happened. "I must have
drank too much. Did I have sex with that hooker? She
must have worn me out and left me…. Shit, she must
have left last night." Chad struggled to put his clothes
on and checked his now empty wallet. "God Damn it.
She took all my money. That Bitch!"

Chad ran into the master bedroom to check
all his stuff and sighed with relief. "Everything is still
there and so is Sara's purse." He helped himself to

the rest of her cash. "She won't be needing this anymore." He went into the bathroom to take a cold shower to help sober him up while thinking, "I've only got two days to finish this job and I'm running out of time.... If she won't come to me, I've got to find her somehow."

A 9 AM phone call awoke Wally in a pile of bodies and he went into the kitchen to answer it. Chad was on the other end, barking out orders and Ingrid overheard the conversation as she started to collect her clothes next to Wally. Johnny and Heidi were also wide awake and having one last go around.

Their moaning was so loud that Wally put his conversation with Chad on speaker phone and Ingrid heard, "Get your asses in gear, get rid of those broads, and meet me at the Alhambra Casino at eleven sharp. I'll be waiting at the Dunkin Donuts there." Wally listened as Ingrid started fondling his hair and replied, "We'll meet you at noon; we've got some unfinished business here."

Chad was pissed and told Wally as the horny Dutch girl was touching his chest. "You guys better get your act together. We have got to find that girl today and finish the job. We're running out of time."

Wally countered back. "NO. You're running out of time. I haven't seen a cent of that fifty thousand dollars you got.... We're busy. We'll meet you at noon." Ingrid now had stored all that valuable information in her memory and "finished" Wally for breakfast.

Sara was wide awake and wanted to take an early morning run down the beach, but she couldn't afford to be seen by Chad or his friends. Sara informed Evelyn about last night's "missions" while Marge slept.

Evelyn stated, "The facts are they left your room intact and are still driving around in your van. All this information leads to making the crime scene look like an accident. Chad said you were 'going' for a swim and that statement makes a good case for them drowning you and leaving the van behind as proof to the cops."

Denise called Sara and Evelyn with critical news. "I had my team work on your case as soon as they arrived at work. We've come up with some interesting information. The two men whose IDs you sent late last night are a couple of losers who live in Madison, Ohio. Walter Wotek was recently fired from a winery for stealing money and he's got four DUI's. John Rost is on welfare and has been arrested for many misdemeanors...."

"The other guy is intriguing. Chad Cunningham is currently a private security professional who provides services to the wealthy. He resides in Shaker Heights, Ohio and his business is currently being investigated by the Ohio State

Attorney General, but we haven't found any more information about that."

Sara started putting the pieces together and asked Denise, "He lives near the Cleveland Clinic. Does he have any clients that are doctors?" Denise couldn't answer the question but did say his security license was currently under suspension. "I'll let you know more when I'm able to dig deeper."

Sara thanked Denise and her phone rang again with Heidi now on the other end. "We just left Wally and Johnny and they were so much fun…. Are you sure they're bad boys?"

Sara heard an argument and then Ingrid began to speak. "Don't listen to her, Sara. Heidi's in love for the millionth time. I've got juicy news to tell you…. I overheard the leader tell Wally that they needed to find you and finish the job today. The leader got fifty thousand dollars and our guys are getting screwed…. By the leader, I mean…. Oh yeah, they are all meeting at Dunkin in Alhambra at noon today…. And Heidi's right, those guys were a blast. Thanks for fixing us up with them."

Evelyn was absorbing all the new information and started formulating a plan. "We need to get someone over to Dunkin at noon that Chad doesn't know. Why don't you call Juan and ask him?"

Sara agreed and said she would call Hank and have him "tail" Chad all day. She asked Evelyn to check the Cleveland Clinic's website for any doctors looking for security personnel. "I think somebody from Cleveland Clinic or Mercy wants to shut me up."

Evelyn warned Sara. "Keep your cell phone fully charged and close to you at all times today. They are coming for you and they're going to make it look like an accident…. If we can't figure out who is behind all this by tomorrow, you're going to the police. You have your passport now, and you can fly to New York and stay with me. I'll protect you."

Sara's voice was determined in her reply. "NO. I'm not risking your life. All my friends on this island are trying to protect me and I'm tired of sitting here and hoping for a miracle. I'm going to show myself today and see if they will take the bait…. This all ends in Aruba, one way or another!"

Sara's next call was to Juan and she explained the events of last night to him. She asked if he was up for another "spy mission", but he was unable to help. "Sorry Sara, but I'm working today. I'll give you Maria's cell number…. She might do it."

Her next call was asking a young woman she did not know for a big favor and Maria happily accepted the challenge. "I'd love to do it. Yesterday was so much fun; following those guys around and watching those two blondes seduce them. Do you want me to go to Dunkin and seduce them all?"

Sara curbed Maria's enthusiasm. "No, don't do that; Juan would kill me.... All I want you to do is sit near their table and listen to their conversation and then call me back as soon as you can."

Sara was uneasy and needed to focus. She went through her recovered backpack and found her running shoes and a string bikini among her items. Sara got an idea and then took off down the beach for a much needed run. She knew if she wanted to advertise her presence on Eagle Beach, running half naked was always her "calling card". By the time she was at Divi Phoenix, her mind had channeled out everything around her.

As Sara ran past La Cabana, Toni saw her and sarcastically asked Todd, "Aren't you going to go run after her and make a fool out of yourself again?"

Todd said nothing and leaned his head back, staring at the palm fronds of the palapa. His thoughts of her were so conflicting and seeing her run away was a perfect synopsis of their relationship. Sara didn't see Todd and didn't care; her goal was to make sure the bad guys saw her.

When she made it to Costa Linda, she slowly walked through the resort, waving at her fellow owners and the staff. Joltzy stopped her and asked where she had been and Sara answered him. "I've been busy taking care of my Aunt Kathy's business, but tell everyone that I'll see them for karaoke tonight at nine." Sara left the resort, knowing that Chad was at Alhambra, planning to kill her and she was determined to turn his plan upside down.

Wally and Johnny met Chad for coffee and the leader planned the afternoon. As he was speaking, a young girl sat down at the table next to theirs and was speaking Papiamento on her phone.

Chad was ignorant of her and instructed, "We need to spread out and find Sara today. Wally, you take the van down to Mangel Halto and see if she's down there snorkeling. Johnny, you hang out at Palm Beach and I'll hang around Costa Linda. I've got her plane ticket and credit card in her purse. If she wants to leave on Friday, she's got to come back for them. Understand me. If she gets on that plane Friday, we're not getting paid. She's gotta disappear soon."

Maria continued to play with her phone while recording the conversation. "Man, this is bullshit. We're not going to find her. Me and Johnny just want to get on a plane and get the hell out of here. If that chick goes to the cops, we're all screwed."

Chad was composed in his reply to Wally. "Calm down big boy. She's got nothin' on us and who's even gonna believe her story? Focus…. We need to kill her tonight and make it look like an accident. You've seen these cops. They're more worried about someone spitting on the sidewalk than solving a crime. It's simple: We kill her, get on a plane, get paid, and then we vanish in thin air with a hundred grand each in our pocket."

Johnny argued. "How do we even know this money is legit? You say we got fifty grand up front, but Wally and I haven't seen a dime. Who's the money man behind this?" Chad became very irritated and answered, "That's for me to know ONLY. Focus on today and you'll be rich men on Saturday."

They all left to search for their target and Maria waited a few minutes before casually walking away. When she got into the privacy of her car, Maria called Sara who was running back on the walking path near the road. She stopped running to answer and heard Maria's nervous voice. "Sara. Is that you? I heard their plan. Be careful, they're going to kill you today. I recorded it all on my phone."

Sara regained her breath and asked Maria, "Can you pick me up now? I've got to hear that conversation.... Please, Maria. I'll be waiting at the Butterfly Farm." The two girls met and Maria drove straight to Playa Linda.

Hank soon joined Sara while Marge took the young female spy out for a well-deserved lunch and shopping spree. Sara then contacted both Evelyn and Denise and played the entire recording off of Maria's phone. Evelyn asked Denise, "Is that conversation enough evidence to convict these guys?"

Denise tentatively answered. "If the girl testifies, there is a case, but where do you prosecute? The murder attempt happened in a foreign country. These guys could get lost in the legal paperwork.... I just received some disturbing news about Chad Cunningham. His real name is Douglas Hardly. He was born and raised in Erie, Pennsylvania. Three years in the Army, booted out for insubordination, and a bodyguard for some really bad people.... I quote, 'Douglas Hardly has been investigated for involvement in Pay for Hire Murders in the State of New York', unquote."

Sara broke the eerie silence. "This isn't over by a longshot. Sure, he's the killer, but who wants me dead? I'm not stopping until I find that out." Denise demanded, "Sara. You are in way over your head. This guy is a trained killer and he won't stop until you're dead. GO TO THE POLICE, NOW!"

Sara responded to her demands with logic. "Denise, I respect your opinion and appreciate all your help.... But how would you cope if they arrested this assassin and two years from now, Mandy and I get gunned down by another killer at Cedar Point.... This has got to end NOW and in ARUBA. I don't want anyone else to get hurt because of me. If I die here, then the threat is over for everyone that I care about.

Do you understand me?" Denise became very emotional and mumbled, "I've got to get off the phone. Call me if...." Denise was overwhelmed with grief and quickly left the group.

Evelyn rallied the troops. "There is strength in numbers and you have got a lot of good people surrounding you so let's finish these bastards off tonight. Hank, you go back to Costa Linda and tell everybody you know that Sara is going to be at the beach bar tonight. Sara has already laid down the groundwork earlier today.... Chad or whatever his name is, will find out and scheme to kill her by accident. I would think he would stick with the drowning murder because the police will keep that low key.... Sara, you need to call Luis and Juan for one more favor and it's a dangerous one.... I'm going to sit here at home and try figure out who the real suspects are.... Time is running out so you two need to get going now."

Sara was energized by the pep talk and explained tonight's plan to Maria and Marge after they returned from shopping. Maria volunteered their services. "There is no way I'm missing out on this caper. I'll talk to Juan after work and we'll meet the others when and wherever you want." Sara asked about her offer, "Are you sure Juan will want to do this?"

Maria giggled at Marge and then said, "I'm positive.... Thanks for the fun afternoon and all the great gifts, Marge. I enjoyed shopping at Sextasy Aruba.... Juan is going to be sooo delighted. See you tonight."

After Maria left, Sara sat down with Marge. "You've been so kind to me. We couldn't have done any of this without your help. I promise to pay back everything you spent the last couple of days."

Marge stubbornly disputed, "That's nonsense. This is the first time in years that I have felt useful to others.... My husband Harry and I worked hard our whole lives. We never had a family and Harry penny pinched everything. Always said 'He was saving for the FUTURE'.... About forty-some years ago, Harry started investing our money into a grocery store. I was upset, but he liked to eat 'APPLES' and five years later, we retired and Harry and I lived a very good life together.... Harry always made me feel wanted; just like you do, Sara.... I'm the one that owes you." Sara sat in stunned silence, amazed by Marge's life story.

Sara ran down to Hadicurari to meet Luis before his teaching was over. He was amused when she asked if he needed help bringing in all his equipment and joked, "I've been expecting you for an hour.... I reported off tonight at the restaurant because Anna and I know you are up to something and before you ask, we're both in."

Sara and Luis sat on a wall for a quiet moment of reflection. Sara thanked him for everything he and Anna did for her and Luis joked, "I never realized how boring Aruba really is until you came into my life."

They both laughed and then Luis spoke from his heart. "I also never knew how lonely I was. Anna made a bad choice years ago and I never forgave her. I would parade my women in front of her like a jealous fool. Now, Anna is my woman again, and last night, she was my French Maid. All because of...." Luis became emotional and composed himself. "I taught you how to kitesurf and you taught me how to love again…. What time do you want us there?" Sara tenderly replied, "I'll call" and blew him a kiss, not knowing what else to say.

Her stroll back to Playa Linda was very melancholy. Sara never dreamed in a million years that she would be walking on this white powdered sand and not even appreciating it, grasping that she may be dead tomorrow. She missed her aunt and she regretted how her relationship with Todd never got off the ground, but she had new friends to worry about and prayed that things would go well tonight. "I just gotta find out who's doing this to me."

Marge and Evelyn were chatting away when Sara returned and then Hank called and proudly stated, "He took the bait, Sara. Chad was passing by the bar when Joltzy asked me about you and I yelled back, 'Sara will be at Karaoke tonight. She never misses Karaoke Night' and Chad stopped dead in his tracks and listened to every word I said…. I know he'll be there."

Evelyn overheard Hank's conversation and stated that timing was the key tonight. "Hank, you need to make sure your watch is synchronized with Sara's and Luis's. Sara needs to leave at exactly 11 PM and walk the beach towards Amsterdam Manor. You cannot sit with Sara or interact with her in any way that might scare off these guys. You have to leave her at 10 PM and meet the others at the public beach across from the jet ski booth. Sara will walk to you as the bad guys follow her into our trap…. Hank, it's critical that you understand and can explain these instructions to the others."

Hank listened intently to her plan and then told Evelyn, "I've owned my construction company for thirty years. I know how to give instruction to young kids. Don't worry about me." He assured Sara. "I'll see you tonight."

Evelyn had one more thing to talk about and that was the suspects, but she waited until Marge and Sara were sipping cocktails on the balcony before she started. Sara told Evelyn earlier, "If I'm going to die tonight then I'm watching my last sunset with a drink in my hand."

After the sun went down, Evelyn began her questions. "Robert Presly has to be our main suspect. Your lawsuit filed against the hospital might cost him his career and his family. How well do you know him?"

Sara responded to the question in a strange manner. "Honestly Evelyn, my mind is in a daze when it comes to trying to figure all this out. To answer your question, I don't know Bob very well at all. I've met him a couple of times at dinners, but nothing special. I mean, he's a pervert and he tried to seduce me by offering me a better position at the hospital, but he just doesn't seem like the kind of person that would order a 'hit' on someone."

"Dave. He would be too afraid of being caught to do something like this, but I did destroy his BMW with the engagement ring that his mother bought…. Now, there is the person that would want me dead. His mother always hated me and belittled me in public, acting like I was beneath her; like her son deserved better than me. I can see her paying a lot of money to see me dead…. Actually, I think she is capable of killing me without any help."

Sara sipped on her tasty martini and laughed, "And nobody would kill me for my money. I still owe one hundred and fifty thousand dollars on my student loans, but I am hoping to pay that off soon…. Aunt Kathy's attorney told me that I was her sole beneficiary a couple of days before I left on this trip.... She always thought of me."

Evelyn became very interested in the attorney. "What's his name? Was he the only one who knew about the inheritance? Does he know you're here? Have you spoken with him since you've been in Aruba?"

Sara tried to defend her lawyer. "His name is John Di Albert and he's been a friend of my aunt's for years. He was very nice to me when Auntie passed away and even took on my lawsuit case against Mercy immediately. I think he was the only one who knew about the money and I have talked to him recently about the lawsuit with the hospital."

Evelyn had found her suspect and went after Di Albert's credibility. "Your lawyer knows that you're going to be financially well off and maybe he'll get the money if something happens to you.... I'm going to look into Mr. John Di Albert."

Sara found all the new information very unsettling, but still defended him. "He's a close personal friend of my aunt. I just can't believe that he would hurt me.... Could we please take a break so I can enjoy this cocktail." Evelyn decided to ease the tension and support her friend. "Good Luck tonight, Sara. I'll be here if you need me. Be careful and call me as soon as it's finished."

Marge went back inside as Sara quietly finished her drink. She was too ashamed to tell Evelyn who her number one suspect was and thought of Stacey. "God, I hope it's not my mom. Just when I think she can't get any lower, she always finds a way to surprise me…. I remember the first time she broke my heart at my birthday party when I was five. She was still married to dad and she left my party early to go on a date with another man in front of all my friends. I was so embarrassed and she's been hurting me ever since. If it is Mom, maybe I should just let her kill me and then she'd finally get what she always wanted."

Sara called Luis and Juan to coordinate the meeting at 10 PM and then she put on a nice mini dress and kissed an emotional Marge goodnight. Sara took a taxi to Costa Linda and put on her party face when she approached the Water's Edge Bar and said hello to everyone. As the dinner crowd shuffled out, the noisier bar crowd replaced them and Sara spotted one of the three assailants come in with a baseball cap and sunglasses on. She looked at Hank on the other side of the bar and he acknowledged that he was aware of the adversary.

For the first hour, Sara sipped on a daiquiri and thought of Kathy two years ago when she dragged Sara to the mic and they butchered the song "Baby, One More Time". Hank laughed until his stomach hurt as the girls flirted with the boys and nobody cared what they sounded like.

Her reminiscing abruptly ended as a few guys began flirting with her, which was part of the plan to be noticed. She saw Hank get up and walk toward the DJ and then he quietly snuck out to join her other friends.

Her nerves were at their peak when she heard, "Our next singer is Aunt Kathy's very own Sara Sweeney from Canton Ohio" and Sara put her head on the bar and cheerfully sighed as the Britney Spears classic started. Hank had pranked her just like he always did and she got up with a standing ovation and belted out "Oh Baby Baby" to the delight of crowd.

It was at that moment, Sara became consumed with courage and she thought, "If I die tonight, I'm going to be remembered." She unzipped her top and flirted through the crowd as she continued to sing off-key. She sat on the laps of all the older guys to make their younger counterparts jealous.

Sara started singing to the disguised man and took off his sunglasses and ball cap while serenading him. Wally was having a blast as everyone could now see his delighted face. When Sara finished she dropped the mic and then slowly bent over to pick it up as the bar crowd roared their approval. She yelled into the mic, "That's for you Auntie!"

It was now 11 PM and the guys all begged her to stay, but she had to leave immediately and when Wally started talking on his cell, Sara knew it was "Showtime". She estimated it was a fifteen minute walk to reach her friends and was comforted to know that they were expecting her. Being on time was critical for their plan to succeed.

After five minutes of walking, the beach became pitch black and the only noise she could now hear was the breaking of the waves. Suddenly Sara saw a man approach her from the front and she panicked in her thoughts. "What is going on…. They should be following me." And then she heard, "Sara. Is that you, Sara?" Her heart sank and she shook the man's arms and begged him. "Todd. You need to get out of here. Right Now. Please…. Leave me alone."

Todd refused. "You and I keep playing this hit-or-miss game and I'm tired of doing it. I want to talk to you right now." Sara tried to remove her hands from his strong grip and whispered with frantic anger, "God Damn it Todd. Get out of here before you get hurt…. Oh MY God, Why are you doing this now? Please, I'm begging you, Todd. Get out…." Through the darkness of the night came the thud of a metal object crashing into Todd's skull.

Sara dropped to her knees to try to see if Todd was moving and looked up into the barrel of a handgun. She tried to scream for help, but Johnny grabbed her tightly and Chad knocked her out with his fist.

Wally and Johnny were dragging the unconscious victims into the same sea that Sara loved for the last ten years of her life. The two bodies began to float in and out of the surf when Chad announced tomorrow's headline with a gleam in his eye. "After a lover's quarrel, the man drowns while trying to save the young girl's life…. I like that. I like it a lot…. Let's go boys."

Before they took a step, they could hear screaming and Chad aimed his gun at a charging Luis and fired. Before he got another shot off, Chad was clobbered from the rear and his gun went flying out of his hands. That was the cue for Wally and John to run away, but they were quickly knocked down onto the sand and battered by the much stronger Luis and Juan.

Hank dove into the water to save Sara and swiftly brought her to shore as she coughed the salt water out of her lungs. Everyone could now hear the cussing and thumping of a man possessed. Todd was now conscious and releasing his anger and frustration onto the face and body of a man he didn't even know.

Sara struggled to tell Hank, "He's gonna kill him" and she collapsed in the surf. Hank ran behind Todd, knocked him off of the lifeless body, and yelled, "Calm down Todd. You can't kill him.... We need him alive.... Go help, Sara!"

Todd slowly staggered back towards Sara's body and kneeled down next to her, listening to her heartbeat and trying to examine her bloody nose. She felt his gentle touch and when she opened her eyes she saw his bloodied knuckles and the blood still coming from his head wound. Todd could barely hear Sara whisper, "My Prince Charming has finally come to save me." He stayed next to her, holding her hand for only a short time as they tried to collect themselves.

Luis and Juan were working like madmen. They both knew that a gunshot ringing out on Eagle Beach was like sending a signal flare to the police. Anna grabbed the gun and any other evidence and stashed them into the van. Juan, Luis, and Hank drug the comatose bodies toward the parking lot, tossed them into the van, and then quickly disappeared into the night.

Maria and Anna tended to Sara and Todd's wounds but needed to follow the van. Anna gave Sara Hank's car keys and her backpack and warned Sara, "You don't have time to explain anything to him. Get there as fast as you can.... We can't finish this without you."

Sara stripped naked in front of Todd and put on a tank top, shorts, and running shoes. She no longer felt like Cinderella and was very impatient with Todd. "I'm dropping you off in front of La Cabana and then I need to go.... It wasn't your fault, but you almost got us killed. Those three guys have been trying to kill me since Monday. I've got unfinished business with them and that does not include you. Go get your hands x-rayed. I hope you didn't break them.... This is where you get out."

Before he opened the passenger door, Todd asked to be included into her plan. "Please Sara, I can help. Those guys tried to kill...."

"You've done enough damage tonight.... GET OUT OF THE CAR!" Todd got out of Hank's car dejected and watched Sara speed away while no longer feeling like a man. He decided to get a taxi to the emergency room. His head was throbbing, his knuckles were bloody, and his heart was finally broken.

Sara felt horrible for speaking to Todd that way, but she refused to involve him in all this madness. "I just don't get that guy. He checks all the boxes, but he's too nice?" She knew her nose was broken and hoped Todd didn't need surgery on his hands and realized. "If Todd didn't get to Chad, I might still be floating in the ocean. I shouldn't have made him feel so bad and I hope he understands if I ever get a chance to tell him."

Sara was driving past the bright lights of the Desalination Plant and began to get enraged. "These Bastards tried to kill all of us.... They're going to get what they deserve and I'm going to find out who's behind this craziness.... That asshole had a gun. In Aruba; a gun. How in the hell does that happen?"

She turned off by La Granga and began to take the back roads to Mangel Halto. Sara stayed there overnight many times on this trip and she easily found the others and parked next to her stolen van.

She silently approached her friends and the three perpetrators, who were still unconscious, but now securely tied up. Luis looked for a signal to see if Sara was ready and she nodded yes to start the show. He proceeded to throw a cold bucket of salt water on the three men. They slowly regained their physical functions and then Luis threw another bucket of water on them to help regain their memory. Now, they were moved closer to the edge of the cliff and facing the darkness of the water. Juan forced the prisoners on their knees and Sara began the interrogation.

"I know your real name is Douglas Hardly. You're a long way from Erie, aren't you? You've tried to kill me twice now and for what I do not know, but I can promise that if you don't tell me right now who you're involved with…. I'm going to kill all three of you tonight and your bodies will never be found…. Look out in front of you. This place is sacred and it's called by the ancient natives 'Sharks Cliff'…. This is where the sharks come to eat at night. Legend has been told that when natives committed a violent sin, the villagers would bring them here for punishment and then feed their bodies to the sharks…. You, gentlemen, are bleeding badly and that will quickly summon the sharks…. Tonight, YOU are the feast."

Chad was missing several teeth but was still understandable. "Bravo, Princess…. That was a touching speech. Now, call the cops so I can get out of this lousy country. You ain't doing anything to us." Sara then played the recording of the afternoon conversation from Dunkin and Wally started to panic.

"Tell them what they want to know, Goddamn it. They got us by the balls, Chad…. Just tell them what they want to know!" Chad snapped back, "Shut up! They got nothin' on us. That audio isn't evidence…. Screw them!"

Sara eerily reassured her prey, "Can you hear that noise in the water? They're here and it sounds like they are very hungry." Juan and Luis picked up Johnny and he began screaming, "NO! NO! Please for the love of God, tell them Chad!"

They dragged him to the edge of the cliff as he was fighting for his life along the way. Sara told Johnny. "I'm going to do you a favor.... Cut his ties off before we throw him in. I want to watch him try to outswim the sharks; it's so entertaining." Juan cut his hand ties and they threw Johnny over the cliff and watched as his hysterical screams became silent.

Wally began shouting, "I've got no clue who the guy you're looking for is, but I know he lives in Ohio. He knows the rest. Chad does. Please, I don't know shit! Let me loose on that sonofabitch and I'll beat it out of him.... I'll do it for nothin'."

Sara looked at Chad and he smiled like a Halloween pumpkin and said, "I don't know anything.... Have a nice swim, Waldo." Juan and Luis again dragged the screaming Wally to the edge, cut his ties, and threw him into the darkness of the water. His screams were loud and bloodcurdling.

Sara watched again and when the night became quiet, she admired the sharks' work. "WOW. Did you see that Juan? He never had a chance" and then she slowly walked over to the very uneasy Chad and asked, "How were you going to kill me on Monday?"

Chad answered, "We were gonna throw you in your van and drive to Baby Beach.... I was going to strangle you and throw you in the water. She wanted you to drown."

FORTY NIGHTS IN ARUBA

Sara grabbed his hair and glared into his eyes. "SHE. Who's she?" Chad arrogantly laughed, "I'll tell you, Sweet Thighs, for fifty grand and a one-way plane ticket out of here." Sara yelled a command in Papiamento and Juan began tying ropes to Chad's feet. Sara sarcastically denied his offer. "Sorry, Chad. I don't have fifty grand, but here's your one-way ticket out of here."

Sara took his phone and personal belongings as the men grabbed Chad and began to lift him upside down. Sara revealed the next step to her nemesis. "We're giving you the 'special' tonight.... We're going to lower you head first into the water so that the sharks can feed off of your face.... You'll still be alive to feel their teeth penetrate your brain."

As they began to lower him down, Chad screamed for his life. "SWEENEY! The chick's name is SWEENEY!"

Sara was sick to her stomach when she realized that her mother wanted her dead. "Mom knew I loved to snorkel and she wanted to drown me in the sea," Sara told the men to stop and Chad dangled under the ropes, but still above the water. Sara needed to know one more thing. "How much did Stacey Sweeney pay you to have me killed?"

Chad started weeping and Sara could barely hear him say. "Three hundred thousand altogether. Fifty grand down. Fifty grand when you were officially listed as dead and the rest when she collects her esta...." Sara yelled, "Luis get him up fast…. I think he passed out" and they quickly pulled him back onto the cliff.

Sara stood over Chad, vigorously shaking him to wake up. "When do you get the rest of the money, Chad" and he blurted out, "When she settles with the estate." Again, Sara shook him hard and demanded, "What's her first name, Chad…. What's Sweeney's first name?"

Chad again stammered out, "Megan. Her name Is Megan Sweeney."

Sara was in a state of bizarre disbelief. She turned around and waved her arms madly and two police cars turned their headlights on. That triggered some clapping from the neighbors who were awoken by the screaming voices and the authorities began their investigation.

Chad was immediately read his rights. Anna and Maria handed Wally and John over to three policemen by the ladder going into the water. The assumed "shark bait" were still very much alive and were happy to be back on dry land. Hank handed the shivering women a couple of appreciated towels and helped them out of the chilly water.

Anna cheerfully asked Sara, "Where did you come up with that story about 'Sharks Cliff'…. That was hilarious. I hope nobody heard me laughing down in the water." Maria agreed and added, "I was freezing in the ocean and you guys were taking forever.... Did you see me blowing kisses to you, Juan?"

Luis went over to Constable Henriquez and thanked him for his help. "The handgun he used is in the van.... Thanks for allowing our little production to continue, Sir.... Sara needed to find out who was trying to kill her. We're willing to give our statements and to testify when we are called."

Juan also added that the three Americans stole his father's van on Monday night and tried to use it to kidnap Sara. "We've been tracking these guys for two days and the big guy tried to kill us tonight at Eagle Beach."

While all this commotion was going on, Sara sat speechless on the cliff's edge and watched the stars dance in the sky. Her stepmother was the real criminal and she was too blind to see that coming. "I'm so glad it wasn't Mom, but I never dreamed it would be Megan. She never liked me and I know she didn't want me to be close to my dad, but I never dreamed that she could hate me that much."

Sara recalled the last time they met in April. "Megan was too nice the day of Kathy's funeral and she actually said something to me about Aruba.... She must have known if I was dead, she would inherit all of Aunt Kathy's money.... That's why Auntie led me into the abyss here at Mangel Halto; to open my eyes and I still didn't see it coming."

After she talked to Henriquez, Sara hugged all four of her precious friends and thanked them for their sacrifice. "I'd be floating in that water if it weren't for your help. I hope I can repay all of you someday and that we can grow our friendships together."

Luis was the spokesman for the group. "You sure made this last month a rollercoaster ride for all of us. It's going to be hard to get back to normal after the last two days.... No goodbyes, we'll just say.... See you later, Sara."

Sara was quiet on the ride back to Costa Linda as Hank tried to comfort her. She had dried blood on her face and her body ached all over. "I think my nose is broken. I need to get some ice on it when we get to your place." Hank called Evelyn and Marge about the news when they returned at 4 AM and Sara tried to get a few hours of sleep before they returned to the police department later in the morning.

Sara stared into the mirror, icing down her swollen nose. "That bitch tried to kill me, but I'm still standing, thanks to all my friends." Sara was very grateful to be alive.

DAY FORTY

Hank awoke to Sara writing in her journal, holding a framed picture of Hank and Kathy, taken at Passions just last year. Hank put his hands on her shoulders and admired his picture. "I had that made the week after you sent it to me."

Sara's face was bruised, but her smile shined brightly. "You two were a sexy couple. I can still see her gazing into your eyes that night." Hank picked the frame up and sighed. "We were in love, that's for sure. I remember another sexy couple that night…. Are you going to call him to see if he's okay?"

Sara put her head down and started to write again in her journal. "I don't know…. Maybe when I get back from the police department. I have a lot to do today." Their conversation was cut short by a phone call from Denise and she explained in great length the procedure to arrest her stepmother and how she would help to accomplish that goal. "I have a team of four of my best people collaborating with the police on it as we speak and Megan Sweeney will be served a warrant before your plane lands tomorrow. I promise you that Sara."

Hank was dressed and tapping on his watch so Sara thanked Denise and took off to Playa Linda, to gather her belongings and say goodbye to Marge. "You're a great friend, Marge and I'm so glad we met. Maybe we can get all the girls together this time next year and have some fun."

Marge gently hugged her young comrade, avoiding her swollen nose. "We sure kicked those jerks' asses, didn't we?" Their laughs turned into tears and Sara sighed, Love you.... Gotta go."

As Hank drove down Wilhelmina Straat, Sara's mind began churning and hoping she would not be legally detained. They both entered the Sergeant's office and were explained their rights under Aruban law. Sara spent four hours answering questions. Two constables took her deposition and helped her navigate through the legal procedures.

As the meeting concluded, the Sergeant confirmed the next phase of the case. "You will be kept in the loop and you will need to return to Aruba and testify, but I can assure you that Doug Hardly will be a guest at our prison for many years. Have a safe travel home, Miss Sweeney."

Sara was so relieved when they left the station and Hank merged his car onto L.G. Smith Boulevard going southeast. Hank looked over at her and grinned. "I brought our gear" and Sara's eyes lit up like a Christmas tree. "I don't need a nose to snorkel.... Let's Go!" And off they went, returning to the scene of the crime for their last snorkel of the trip.

As they were walking through the mangroves, Sara heard excited children playing in the water. When she approached them, Sara saw the children admiring a blue parrot fish and she quickly snorkeled towards it. Hank and Sara spent the next two hours snorkeling with their new tour guide. The big blue parrot fish took them to magical underwater places they'd never seen before. At the sunken boat, the parrot fish began to surface and was followed by Sara and Hank.

The big blue parrot fish circled her human friends as they were amazed by a blazing Aruban sun gently fading into the Caribbean Sea. As the sky exhibited its perfect painting, Sara tearfully whimpered, "Looks like Auntie just began a new tradition for us."

Hank and Sara were blissful the whole trip back to Costa Linda and talked about the perfect ending to a horrible week. The resort security informed Sara that she could now return to her room. She kissed Hank on his cheek and then gave him a big hug. "I couldn't have made it through this week without you, Dad. You and I are family…. I gotta go pack. I'll see you tomorrow morning before I leave." Hank remained silent as Sara walked away, thinking to himself, "You raised that kid good, Sweetheart."

After he packed and organized his return information, Hank went to the Water's Edge Bar for a few drinks with his buddies. He noticed a guy sitting alone and asked if he could join him. "I think you and I need to have a long talk, Todd" and Hank began to explain Sara's last four crazy days. Todd had ten stitches in his head and his hands were both bandaged, but he now realized that her pain was far worse.

Todd gratefully listened to the story that he had been denied the previous night and said nothing until Hank finished. "I'm in love with her, Hank, but she's chasing something other than me. Sara's like a 'shooting star' that I just can't seem to catch. She never told me about being here on the island for a month because she didn't want me interfering in her life. I could have got her killed last night because I wanted to propose to her.... I'm just a stupid lovesick guy who never even had a chance."

Hank smiled at his sad friend, produced an engagement ring, and remarked, "You're not the only man on this island that has been turned down by a Sweeney.... After I got divorced, I brought this ring to Aruba and proposed to her Aunt Kathy. She turned me down each time I proposed during our last three years together, but I never gave up. I knew she loved

FORTY NIGHTS IN ARUBA

me so we pretended for the last three years to be 'married' while we were in Aruba. It was the best three weeks of my life and now she's gone, but her spirit is here and her niece is here.... The moral to this sad tale is 'Take whatever you can get from a Sweeney Girl'.... Don't give up Todd."

Todd finally saw the light and asked Hank, "I really need to talk to her soon. Is she going to join you tonight?" Hank looked at him sideways, "Come on Son. You know where she's at?" Todd looked at his watch and panicked. "I gotta go…. Thanks for the advice, Hank…. See you next year!"

Todd sprinted down the beach and hung a right at the public parking lot, then quickly crossed the street. After racing the final two blocks, he arrived at Chalet Suisse twenty minutes until closing and quickly asked the bartender for a drink. Todd saw Sara sitting alone and staring at the wall.

Sara was lost in the thoughts of her aunt and how special this island was to them both. "It's been a crazy Forty Nights in Aruba. If you had told me this would've all happened, I would have laughed at you, Auntie…. I could write a book about this and nobody would believe it!"

Suddenly a raspberry cosmopolitan appeared in front of her face from a bandaged presenter and Sara giggled, "I hope you don't drop my drink with that broken hand."

Todd sat down across from her and gazed into her eyes. "Is it okay if I join you for a toast to the end of your trip?" Sara looked at all the empty cocktail glasses in front of her and slurred, "I've done that a few times already.... Would you like some of Aunt Kathy's chocolate mousse or maybe, you desire my 'Hot' Framboise Kisses?"

Todd could tell by her response that Sara was deservedly drunk and knew that this was not a good time for a heart to heart talk so he settled, "You look beautiful tonight" and she laughed, "That hole in your head must have blinded you. I'm a mess.... I'm really sorry you got hurt last night.... I got myself into trouble with a guy. I always get myself into trouble with men. I've probably slept with every guy in Aruba but you.... Why is that Todd? Do you not find me attractive?"

Todd asked Joaquin for the check and some coffee for the lady as Sara continued her drunken banter. "I came to Aruba to tell you 'I love you'.... Well, I said it, so I can go home happy now.... I wish you would have screwed me ten years ago so I would have something to compare you with all the other guys."

Todd paid the bill and said, "Sara, let's get you home" and escorted her to Costa Linda. She playfully did a striptease in front of him and jumped into the pool as some late night guests looked on. Todd shook his head, took off his shirt, and jumped into the pool to make sure she didn't drown.

Sara sighed, "Make Love to me" and Todd removed her from the water and covered her naked body with his shirt. He then carried Sara and her belongings up to her room as she kept kissing him on his neck.

Todd put her down once he was inside her suite and Sara took his shirt off and begged him to make love to her. "Let's do this NOW. I'm tired of waiting for you!" Todd led her into the bedroom while she groped every part of his body and she lay on her bed waiting for him. "Please. Todd.... I want you inside me so bad."

Todd joined her on the bed and lifted the bedsheets over her naked body. Sara became irate and started cussing her Prince Charming. "What in the hell is wrong with you? Are you gay Todd? I always knew you were gay."

Before Sara passed out, she felt his swollen fingers softly stroking her face and heard his whisper. "Oh, Sara My Love. Why do you keep dangling this carrot in front of me? I've loved you since the first day I walked with you on Eagle Beach.... You're the only woman I ever see in my dreams.... Why won't you love me?" Todd kissed Cinderella goodnight and said, "I hope to see you next year" and quietly walked out her bedroom door.

OHIO BOUND

Her alcohol abuse caused Sara to oversleep and her last day in Aruba flew by rapidly. Javier assembled her luggage and held them until she was ready to leave. Sara took one last stroll around her "second" home and then found Hank eating breakfast. "Hey Dad, are you ready to roll?"

Hank rolled his eyes while devouring his omelet and uttered between his bites. "This is the only thing I hate about Aruba…. Leaving it." Sara noted, "I've got an early afternoon flight so I want to get to the airport around three hours early. Ricardo knows about the van being impounded so I'm going to take a taxi to the airport."

Hank quickly finished his breakfast and requested a favor from Sara. "How about a farewell walk on the beach with this old man?" Sara took his hand and said, "I'd love to" and they began their stroll towards Bucuti Resort.

Hank reminded Sara, "This was always my saddest time with your aunt and I would ask her to marry me before she left me for another year." Hank pulled out a box and handed it to Sara. "I used to give Kathy this ring. She'd gaze at it, admire it on her finger, and then she'd just give it back."

Hank stopped in the sand and revealed, "I want you to have this ring. Whether she took it or not, this is Kathy's ring and I would like to pass it down to her lovely child. It represents my.... Our love for Kathy."

Sara put the ring on her finger and embraced Hank tightly. "Yes. I would be honored to own her ring. This is the best present I've ever gotten.... You're too kind to me Hank, I love you."

Sara and Hank walked hand in hand on their way back to Costa Linda and she promised to come visit him in Michigan. They passed an older couple on the way to the lobby who congratulated Sara. Hank awkwardly stated, "We're not engaged, she's like a daughter to me." The old lady looked at her husband and smirked, "That's the girl who was skinny dipping in the pool last night, Don."

Hank was laughing at the woman's comments. "You must have been having fun last night.... Was that the second marriage proposal you've had recently?" Sara was puzzled. "What do you mean 'second' proposal?" Hank tried to explain. I talked to Todd last night. Didn't he meet you at Chalet Suisse? He wanted to.... WOW. We better get going.... The airport is going to be a zoo. Have a safe flight, Sara... Call me when you get home. Love ya." Hank quickly exited for his car before his "foot" went farther into his mouth.

Sara was thinking about Hank's last comment on the taxi ride, but once inside the terminal, she became focused on the fast paced "waiting" to get through all the gates and lines. Sara looked at all the sad faces and listened to their "greatest week ever" stories and thought, "My God. I've been in Aruba for SIX weeks.... I wonder if they want to hear any of my stories?"

Sara barely made it to her gate and started to vaguely remember last night. She sent Todd a text filled with question marks and he quickly resent one with hearts and smiley faces and then typed, "See you next year!"

The tanned crowd began to pile into the airplane and when Sara saw Hooiberg from the air, she knew her forty nights in Aruba had come to an end.

BACK TO REALITY

Every visitor to the island paradise of Aruba needs time to adjust to the reality of their normal life. They spend the first week boasting to their friends and families and then they settle into their daily grind. Each person takes their fond memories and future adventures and stores them in a treasure box for next year.

Todd Powell was no different than all the others who came and went before him. He recovered from his hand and head injuries and after a month of office confinement, he was allowed to return to his surgery duties. Todd was very active in catching up with his backlogged schedule and after another month of nonstop work, he finally exhaled.

One afternoon after his last operation was completed, Todd was overwhelmed when he entered through his office door. He saw a beautiful woman wearing an engagement ring and admiring his framed picture of him and a young girl he met ten years ago. Todd said halfheartedly, "So someone finally found a way into your heart. Congratulations…. What are you doing here, Sara?"

Sara, still looking at the picture, sighed, "We were so young back then…. What? You don't give hugs to old friends" and she came over and kissed him on the cheek. "Do you have a few minutes to chat?"

Todd shut the door and sat at his desk. "I would love to chat with you, Sara…. So, why are you in my office in Buffalo, New York on this beautiful day? Have you run out of brokenhearted friends from Aruba?"

Sara asked, "May I sit down, Doctor Powell, and I will explain myself and at the end of our conversation, I have a favor to ask of you." Todd leaned back in his chair and smirked, "I can't wait to hear this one…. How have you been, Sara? I haven't heard from you for over two months."

Sara's perky attitude dissolved and she told him. "Honestly, Todd, the last two months have been very difficult for me. I've been dealing with lawyers every day and the stress is wearing me down. Between my lawsuit against the hospital, Aunt Kathy's estate, and the criminal proceedings against my stepmother, I see attorneys in my sleep. My ex and my mother are now engaged and Stacey had the nerve to ask me to help plan her wedding."

Todd apologized for his sarcastic attitude and Sara continued, "I love my Aunt Kathy's home and my fondest memories growing up were in that house, but I've worn out my welcome in Canton and probably in Ohio too…. So, I've decided to start all over again and make new memories. I heard Buffalo

General Hospital has an outstanding pediatric program so I'm here today for a job interview."

Todd became very intrigued and offered his help. "I'm friends with a lot of people in upper management. I'll talk to them on your behalf if you would like that. BGH is a great hospital and they're always looking for young professionals. I think you'd be a great fit here."

Sara thanked Todd for his offer. "I completed my interview process today and was offered a nice position, but I haven't accepted it yet until I talked to you first. I left you out of the loop because I knew you would try to help and I wanted to be accepted on my own merits…. How do you feel about me working near you in the real world?"

Todd put up a good front. "That's the favor you wanted. I won't be a problem for you Sara. I think it would be nice to see you once in a while and maybe hang out with you and your fiancée. What does he do for a living?"

Sara was very short in her answer. "He's a doctor…. So, you wouldn't have a problem seeing me and him together in this hospital…. Did you know that I recently spent forty nights in Aruba and the only night I clearly remember being with you, we almost died. I talk to Hank every day and I know about your conversation with him that last night and

I need to know what happened at Chalet Suisse before I can take this job."

Todd put his hand on his chin and began to restore his thoughts of that night. "For starters, you were a very cute drunk and I mean 'very'. You pretty much told me that you screwed every guy in Aruba but me and you said, 'I love you', but you didn't really mean it…. I tried to get you safely back to your room, but you jumped into the pool naked. I went in and got you out and took you to your room. I tucked you in bed and read you a bedtime story until you fell asleep…. That's the last time I saw that big swollen nose of yours. Is that the favor you asked of me? Your conscience is pure, Sara…. We didn't do anything."

Sara pulled her chair closer to Todd and was not amused by his answer. "And why is that, Doctor Powell? Ever since we met on Eagle Beach, you have been a perfect gentleman to me, but I seem to like bad boys, not nice guys like you. You had so many chances to take me, Todd, but you chose not to…. Was it out of chivalry or was it because deep down, you were too afraid to be with a girl like me? Hank told me that you were going to propose to me, but I never heard a word come out of your mouth about marriage…. Is it fate that keeps us apart or is it our unwillingness to commit to each other?"

Todd tried to explain his feelings, but Sara put her finger on his lips and continued. "I'm sorry, but you've had plenty of chances to say this.... I had a girl crush on you ten years ago and was hurt deeply when you pretended not to remember me the day you introduced me to your fiancée. I knew you were the man for me when you saved my Aunt Kathy's life in the water that night, but you refused to act on my emotions.... Always the gentleman."

Todd lifted her left hand and sadly asked, "If you still feel that way, why are you wearing this rock on your finger?"

Sara shyly smiled and asked him to hear her out. "Don't you remember this ring? Hank showed it to you that night. It's my Aunt Kathy's engagement ring that she never accepted. Hank gave it to me on our last morning together.... Todd, this ring is my most cherished possession. It will remain on my finger until the man of my dreams asks me for my hand in marriage. Then I will give it to him and watch him slide it gently back on my finger.... I hope that man is you."

Sara kissed Todd softly on the lips and whispered, "The favor I ask of you is 'Patience'.... I need our love to grow outside of Aruba. I need us to hold each other in good times and bad. I come with a lot of 'baggage' and I desire to know the real you. I want us to start dating like high school kids and make out in the backseat of your car. I want to make you dinner on Friday night and I want to fight with you when we disagree…. And I desperately want to moan your name when you are deep inside me…. I want it all, Todd."

Todd lifted her up off of the chair and pulled her close to him. "To finally be with you, Sara, is my dream come true. All I ever wanted was a 'chance' with you. To wake up every morning lying next to you, knowing that I would make love to you at the end of that same day…. I want it all too, Sara. I'm willing to start whenever you desire."

Sara kissed him and whispered into his ear. "Todd, My Love. I have only one more request and it's way off in our future…. If I ever give birth to your daughter, her legal name has to be Katherine Sweeney Powell. That's the only thing I ask from you."

Todd caressed her shoulders softly. "I'd like that and I understand what your Aunt Kathy means to you; I really do get it. I can imagine holding little Kathy in my arms and reading to her about Cinderella and Prince Charming…. I hope we'll experience all those feelings someday."

Sara began to giggle, "We need to practice a lot to make that perfect little girl…. Let's go get a hotel room right now…. Please Todd, I can't wait any longer." Todd immediately cleared everything off his desk while Sara quickly took off her clothes and then undressed her now ready and willing lover. She surrendered herself into Todd's waiting arms and began to explore his naked body for the very first time.

Todd lay Sara down on the makeshift bed and she felt his soft touch throughout her trembling body. She looked at him with her blue eyes and tenderly ran her fingers through his hair. Her gentle words were music to his ears. "I Love You, Todd…. Make love to me."

They started making passionate love and Sara became romantically lost on island time. The desk was a palapa and the floor felt like the soft sand of Eagle Beach. Each thrust felt like she was floating on the gentle ocean waves and then she sensed the freedom of riding the surf as Todd increased his rhythm. Their moans sounded like seagulls as they filled the morning sky and Sara felt the explosion of the Aruban sunset inside her soul. Todd collapsed caressing her naked body as Sara envisioned them sunning themselves at Costa Linda. Her tender hands held him inside her as Sara closed her eyes and thought of that big blue parrot fish shining down on her new love affair. Her thoughts of gratitude were pure…………………………….

"Thanks Auntie!"

ABOUT THE AUTHOR

Bea Ann Argh is a pseudonym for the author of Forty Nights in Aruba. She has a true love for the island and its wonderful people. "I have been treated so kindly in all of my trips to Aruba and I always try to be respectful of the island and its culture. We, as tourists, need to understand that we should be honored to share this magical place with our hosts and keep it as pristine as possible. Before our vacations end, we need to do our part in keeping the reefs, beaches, and water as clean as it was when we came. We all owe that to this special place that we have all come to love."

Made in the USA
Monee, IL
06 January 2025